A Sportsman's Sketches, Vol 1 of 2

by Ivan Sergeevich Turgenev

Translated from the Russian By Constance Garnett

Copyright © 10/23/2015
Jefferson Publication

ISBN-13: 978-1518756122

Printed in the United States of America

Table of Contents

I

HOR AND KALINITCH

Anyone who has chanced to pass from the Bolhovsky district into the Zhizdrinsky district, must have been impressed by the striking difference between the race of people in the province of Orel and the population of the province of Kaluga. The peasant of Orel is not tall, is bent in figure, sullen and suspicious in his looks; he lives in wretched little hovels of aspen-wood, labours as a serf in the fields, and engages in no kind of trading, is miserably fed, and wears slippers of bast: the rent-paying peasant of Kaluga lives in roomy cottages of pine-wood; he is tall, bold, and cheerful in his looks, neat and clean of countenance; he carries on a trade in butter and tar, and on holidays he wears boots. The village of the Orel province (we are speaking now of the eastern part of the province) is usually situated in the midst of ploughed fields, near a water-course which has been converted into a filthy pool. Except for a few of the ever- accommodating willows, and two or three gaunt birch-trees, you do not see a tree for a mile round; hut is huddled up against hut, their roofs covered with rotting thatch.... The villages of Kaluga, on the contrary, are generally surrounded by forest; the huts stand more freely, are more upright, and have boarded roofs; the gates fasten closely, the hedge is not broken down nor trailing about; there are no gaps to invite the visits of the passing pig.... And things are much better in the Kaluga province for the sportsman. In the Orel province the last of the woods and copses will have disappeared five years hence, and there is no trace of moorland left; in Kaluga, on the contrary, the moors extend over tens, the forest over hundreds of miles, and a splendid bird, the grouse, is still extant there; there are abundance of the friendly larger snipe, and the loud-clapping partridge cheers and startles the sportsman and his dog by its abrupt upward flight.

On a visit to the Zhizdrinsky district in search of sport, I met in the fields a petty proprietor of the Kaluga province called Polutikin, and made his acquaintance. He was an enthusiastic sportsman; it follows, therefore, that he was an excellent fellow. He was liable, indeed, to a few weaknesses; he used, for instance, to pay his addresses to every unmarried heiress in the province, and when he had been refused her hand and house, broken-hearted he confided his sorrows to all his friends and acquaintances, and continued to shower offerings of sour peaches and other raw produce from his garden upon the young lady's relatives; he was fond of repeating one and the same anecdote, which, in spite of Mr. Polutikin's appreciation of its merits, had certainly never amused anyone; he admired the works of Akim Nahimov and the novel *Pinna*; he stammered; he called his dog Astronomer; instead of 'however' said 'howsomever'; and had established in his household a French system of cookery, the secret of which consisted, according to his cook's interpretation, in a complete transformation of the natural taste of each dish; in this *artiste's* hands meat assumed the flavour of fish, fish of mushrooms, macaroni of gunpowder; to make up for this, not a single carrot went into the soup without taking the shape of a rhombus or a trapeze. But, with the exception of these few and insignificant failings, Mr. Polutikin was, as has been said already, an excellent fellow.

On the first day of my acquaintance with Mr. Polutikin, he invited me to stay the night at his house.

'It will be five miles farther to my house,' he added; 'it's a long way to walk; let us first go to Hor's.' (The reader must excuse my omitting his stammer.)

'Who is Hor?'

'A peasant of mine. He is quite close by here.'

We went in that direction. In a well-cultivated clearing in the middle of the forest rose Hor's solitary homestead. It consisted of several pine-wood buildings, enclosed by plank fences; a porch ran along the front of the principal building, supported on slender posts. We went in. We were met by a young lad of twenty, tall and good-looking.

'Ah, Fedya! is Hor at home?' Mr. Polutikin asked him.

'No. Hor has gone into town,' answered the lad, smiling and showing a row of snow-white teeth. 'You would like the little cart brought out?'

'Yes, my boy, the little cart. And bring us some kvas.'

We went into the cottage. Not a single cheap glaring print was pasted up on the clean boards of the walls; in the corner, before the heavy, holy picture in its silver setting, a lamp was burning; the table of linden-wood had been lately planed and scrubbed; between the joists and in the cracks of the window-frames there were no lively Prussian beetles running about, nor gloomy cockroaches in hiding. The young lad soon reappeared with a great white pitcher filled with excellent kvas, a huge hunch of wheaten bread, and a dozen salted cucumbers in a wooden bowl. He put all these provisions on the table, and then, leaning with his back against the door, began to gaze with a smiling face at us. We had not had time to finish eating our lunch when the cart was already rattling before the doorstep. We went out. A curly-headed, rosy-cheeked boy of fifteen was sitting in the cart as driver, and with difficulty holding in the well-fed piebald horse. Round the cart stood six young giants, very like one another, and Fedya.

'All of these Hor's sons!' said Polutikin.

'These are all Horkies' (*i.e.* wild cats), put in Fedya, who had come after us on to the step; 'but that's not all of them: Potap is in the wood, and Sidor has gone with old Hor to the town. Look out, Vasya,' he went on, turning to the coachman; 'drive like the wind; you are driving the master. Only mind what you're about over the ruts, and easy a little; don't tip the cart over, and upset the master's stomach!'

The other Horkies smiled at Fedya's sally. 'Lift Astronomer in!' Mr. Polutikin called majestically. Fedya, not without amusement, lifted the dog, who wore a forced smile, into the air, and laid her at the bottom of the cart. Vasya let the horse go. We rolled away. 'And here is my counting-house,' said Mr. Polutikin suddenly to me, pointing to a little low-pitched house. 'Shall we go in?' 'By all means.' 'It is no longer used,' he observed, going in; 'still, it is worth looking at.' The counting-house consisted of two empty rooms. The caretaker, a one- eyed old man, ran out of the yard. 'Good day, Minyaitch,' said Mr. Polutikin; 'bring us some water.' The one-eyed old man disappeared, and at once returned with a bottle of water and two glasses. 'Taste it,' Polutikin said to me; 'it is splendid spring water.' We drank off a glass each, while the old man bowed low. 'Come, now, I think we can go on,' said my new Friend. 'In that counting-house I sold the merchant Alliluev four acres of forest-land for a good price.' We took our seats in the cart, and in half-an-hour we had reached the court of the manor- house.

'Tell me, please,' I asked Polutikin at supper; 'why does Hor live apart from your other peasants?'

'Well, this is why; he is a clever peasant. Twenty-five years ago his cottage was burnt down; so he came up to my late father and said: "Allow me, Nikolai Kouzmitch," says he, "to settle in your forest, on the bog. I will pay you a good rent." "But what do you want to settle on the bog for?" "Oh, I want to; only, your honour, Nikolai Kouzmitch, be so good as not to claim any labour from me, but fix a rent as you think best." "Fifty roubles a year!" "Very well." "But I'll have no arrears, mind!" "Of course, no arrears"; and so he settled on the bog. Since then they have called him Hor' (*i.e.* wild cat).

'Well, and has he grown rich?' I inquired.

'Yes, he has grown rich. Now he pays me a round hundred for rent, and I shall raise it again, I dare say. I have said to him more than once, "Buy your freedom, Hor; come, buy your freedom." ... But he declares, the rogue, that he can't; has no money, he says.... As though that were likely....'

The next day, directly after our morning tea, we started out hunting again. As we were driving through the village, Mr. Polutikin ordered the coachman to stop at a low-pitched cottage and called loudly, 'Kalinitch!' 'Coming, your honour, coming' sounded a voice from the yard; 'I am tying on my shoes.' We went on at a walk; outside the village a man of about forty over-took us. He was tall and thin, with a small and erect head. It was Kalinitch. His good-humoured; swarthy face, somewhat pitted with small-pox, pleased me from the first glance. Kalinitch (as I learnt afterwards) went hunting every day with his master, carried his bag, and sometimes also his gun, noted where game was to be found, fetched water, built shanties, and gathered strawberries, and ran behind the droshky; Mr. Polutikin could not stir a step without him. Kalinitch was a man of the merriest and gentlest disposition; he was constantly singing to himself in a low voice, and looking carelessly about him. He spoke a little through his nose, with a laughing twinkle in his light blue eyes, and he had a habit of plucking at his scanty, wedge-shaped beard with his hand. He walked not rapidly, but with long strides, leaning lightly on a long thin staff. He addressed me more than once during the day, and he waited on me without, obsequiousness, but he looked after his master as if he were a child. When the unbearable heat drove us at mid-day to seek shelter, he took us to his beehouse in the very heart of the forest. There Kalinitch opened the little hut for us, which was hung round with bunches of dry scented herbs. He made us comfortable on some dry hay, and then put a kind of bag of network over his head, took a knife, a little pot, and a smouldering stick, and went to the hive to cut us out some honey-comb. We had a draught of spring water after the warm transparent honey, and then dropped asleep to the sound of the monotonous humming of the bees and the rustling chatter of the leaves. A slight gust of wind awakened me.... I opened my eyes and saw Kalinitch: he was sitting on the threshold of the half-opened door, carving a spoon with his knife. I gazed a long time admiring his face, as sweet and clear as an evening sky. Mr. Polutikin too woke up. We did not get up at once. After our long walk and our deep sleep it was pleasant to lie without moving in the hay; we felt weary and languid in body, our faces were in a slight glow of warmth, our eyes were closed in delicious laziness. At last we got up, and set off on our wanderings again till evening. At supper I began again to talk of Hor and Kalinitch. 'Kalinitch is a good peasant,' Mr. Polutikin told me; 'he is a willing and useful peasant; he can't farm his land properly; I am always taking him away from it. He goes out hunting every day with me.... You can judge for yourself how his farming must fare.'

I agreed with him, and we went to bed.

The next day Mr. Polutikin was obliged to go to town about some business with his neighbour Pitchukoff. This neighbour Pitchukoff had ploughed over some land of Polutikin's, and had flogged a peasant woman of his on this same piece of land. I went out hunting alone, and before evening I turned into Hor's house. On the threshold of the cottage I was met by an old man—bald, short, broad-shouldered, and stout—Hor himself. I looked with curiosity at the man. The cut of his face recalled Socrates; there was the same high, knobby forehead, the same little eyes, the same snub nose. We went into the cottage together. The same Fedya brought me some milk and black bread. Hor sat down on a bench, and, quietly stroking his curly beard, entered into conversation with me. He seemed to know his own value; he spoke and moved slowly; from time to time a chuckle came from between his long moustaches.

We discussed the sowing, the crops, the peasant's life.... He always seemed to agree with me; only afterwards I had a sense of awkwardness and felt I was talking foolishly.... In this way our conversation was rather curious. Hor, doubtless through caution, expressed himself very obscurely at times.... Here is a specimen of our talk.

"Tell me, Hor," I said to him, "why don't you buy your freedom from your master?"

"And what would I buy my freedom for? Now I know my master, and I know my rent.... We have a good master."

'It's always better to be free,' I remarked. Hor gave me a dubious look.

'Surely,' he said.

'Well, then, why don't you buy your freedom?' Hor shook his head.

'What would you have me buy it with, your honour?'

'Oh, come, now, old man!'

'If Hor were thrown among free men,' he continued in an undertone, as though to himself, 'everyone without a beard would be a better man than Hor.'

'Then shave your beard.'

'What is a beard? a beard is grass: one can cut it.'

'Well, then?'

'But Hor will be a merchant straight away; and merchants have a fine life, and they have beards.'

'Why, do you do a little trading too?' I asked him.

'We trade a little in a little butter and a little tar.... Would your honour like the cart put to?'

'You're a close man and keep a tight rein on your tongue,' I thought to myself. 'No,' I said aloud, 'I don't want the cart; I shall want to be near your homestead to-morrow, and if you will let me, I will stay the night in your hay-barn.'

'You are very welcome. But will you be comfortable in the barn? I will tell the women to lay a sheet and put you a pillow.... Hey, girls!' he cried, getting up from his place; 'here, girls!... And you, Fedya, go with them. Women, you know, are foolish folk.'

A quarter of an hour later Fedya conducted me with a lantern to the barn. I threw myself down on the fragrant hay; my dog curled himself up at my feet; Fedya wished me good-night; the door creaked and slammed to. For rather a long time I could not get to sleep. A cow came up to the door, and breathed heavily twice; the dog growled at her with dignity; a pig passed by, grunting pensively; a horse somewhere near began to munch the hay and snort.... At last I fell asleep.

At sunrise Fedya awakened me. This brisk, lively young man pleased me; and, from what I could see, he was old Hor's favourite too. They used to banter one another in a very friendly way. The old man came to meet me. Whether because I had spent the night under his roof, or for some other reason, Hor certainly treated me far more cordially than the day before.

'The samovar is ready,' he told me with a smile; 'let us come and have tea.'

We took our seats at the table. A robust-looking peasant woman, one of his daughters-in-law, brought in a jug of milk. All his sons came one after another into the cottage.

'What a fine set of fellows you have!' I remarked to the old man.

'Yes,' he said, breaking off a tiny piece of sugar with his teeth; 'me and my old woman have nothing to complain of, seemingly.'

'And do they all live with you?'

'Yes; they choose to, themselves, and so they live here.'

'And are they all married?'

'Here's one not married, the scamp!' he answered, pointing to Fedya, who was leaning as before against the door. 'Vaska, he's still too young; he can wait.'

'And why should I get married?' retorted Fedya; 'I'm very well off as I am. What do I want a wife for? To squabble with, eh?'

'Now then, you ... ah, I know you! you wear a silver ring.... You'd always be after the girls up at the manor house.... "Have done, do, for shame!"' the old man went on, mimicking the servant girls. 'Ah, I know you, you white-handed rascal!'

'But what's the good of a peasant woman?'

'A peasant woman—is a labourer,' said Hor seriously; 'she is the peasant's servant.'

'And what do I want with a labourer?'

'I dare say; you'd like to play with the fire and let others burn their fingers: we know the sort of chap you are.'

'Well, marry me, then. Well, why don't you answer?'

'There, that's enough, that's enough, giddy pate! You see we're disturbing the gentleman. I'll marry you, depend on it.... And you, your honour, don't be vexed with him; you see, he's only a baby; he's not had time to get much sense.'

Fedya shook his head.

'Is Hor at home?' sounded a well-known voice; and Kalinitch came into the cottage with a bunch of wild strawberries in his hands, which he had gathered for his friend Hor. The old man gave him a warm welcome. I looked with surprise at Kalinitch. I confess I had not expected such a delicate attention on the part of a peasant.

That day I started out to hunt four hours later than usual, and the following three days I spent at Hor's. My new friends interested me. I don't know how I had gained their confidence, but they began to talk to me without constraint. The two friends were not at all alike. Hor was a positive, practical man, with a head for management, a rationalist; Kalinitch, on the other hand, belonged to the order of idealists and dreamers, of romantic and enthusiastic spirits. Hor had a grasp of actuality—that is to say, he looked ahead, was saving a little money, kept on good terms with his master and the other authorities; Kalinitch wore shoes of bast, and lived from hand to mouth. Hor had reared a large family, who were obedient and united; Kalinitch had once had a wife, whom he had been afraid of, and he had had no children. Hor took a very critical view of Mr. Polutikin; Kalinitch revered his master. Hor loved Kalinitch, and took protecting care of him; Kalinitch loved and respected Hor. Hor spoke little, chuckled, and thought for himself; Kalinitch expressed himself with warmth, though he had not the flow of fine language of a smart factory hand. But Kalinitch was endowed with powers which even Hor recognised; he could charm away haemorrhages, fits, madness, and worms; his bees always did well; he had a light hand. Hor asked him before me to introduce a newly bought horse to his stable, and with scrupulous gravity Kalinitch carried out the old sceptic's request. Kalinitch was in closer contact with nature; Hor with men and society. Kalinitch had no liking for argument, and believed in everything blindly; Hor had reached even an ironical point of view of life. He had seen and experienced much, and I learnt a good deal from him. For instance, from his account I learnt that every year before mowing-time a small, peculiar-looking cart makes its appearance in the villages. In this cart sits a man in a long coat, who sells scythes. He charges one rouble twenty-five copecks—a rouble and a half in notes—for ready money; four roubles if he gives credit. All the peasants, of course, take the scythes from him on credit. In two or three weeks he reappears and asks for the money. As the peasant has only just cut his oats, he is able to pay him; he goes with the merchant to the tavern, and there the debt is settled. Some landowners conceived the idea of buying the scythes themselves for ready money and letting the peasants have them on credit for the same price; but the peasants seemed dissatisfied, even dejected; they had deprived them of the pleasure of tapping the scythe and listening to the ring of the metal, turning it over and over in their hands, and telling the scoundrelly city-trader twenty times over, 'Eh, my friend, you won't take me in with your scythe!' The same tricks are played over the sale of sickles, only with this difference, that the women have a hand in the business then, and they sometimes drive the trader himself to the necessity—for their good, of course—of beating them. But the women suffer most ill-treatment through the following circumstances. Contractors for the supply of stuff for paper factories employ for the purchase of rags a special class of men, who in some districts are called eagles. Such an 'eagle' receives two hundred roubles in bank- notes from the merchant, and starts off in search of his prey. But, unlike the noble bird from whom he has derived his name, he does not swoop down openly and boldly upon it; quite the contrary; the 'eagle' has recourse to deceit and cunning. He leaves his cart somewhere in a thicket near the village, and goes himself to the back-yards and back-doors, like someone casually passing, or simply a tramp. The women scent out his proximity and steal out to meet him. The bargain is hurriedly concluded. For a few copper half-pence a woman gives the 'eagle' not only every useless rag she has, but often even her husband's shirt and her own petticoat. Of late the women have thought it profitable to steal even from themselves, and to sell hemp in the same way—a great extension and improvement of the business for the 'eagles'! To meet this, however, the peasants have grown more cunning in their turn, and on the slightest suspicion, on the most distant rumors of the approach of an 'eagle,' they have prompt and sharp recourse to corrective and preventive measures. And, after all, wasn't it disgraceful? To sell the hemp was the men's business—and they certainly do sell it—not in the town (they would have to drag it there themselves), but to traders who come for it, who, for want of scales, reckon forty handfuls to the pood—and you know what a Russian's hand is and what it can hold, especially when he 'tries his best'! As I had had no experience and was not 'country-bred' (as they say in Orel) I heard plenty of such descriptions. But Hor was not always the narrator; he questioned me too about many things. He learned that I had been in foreign parts, and his curiosity was aroused.... Kalinitch was not behind him in curiosity; but he was more attracted by descriptions of nature, of mountains and waterfalls, extraordinary buildings and great towns; Hor was interested in questions of government and administration. He went through everything in order. 'Well, is that with them as it is with us, or different?... Come, tell us, your honour, how is it?' 'Ah, Lord, thy will be done!' Kalinitch would exclaim while I told my story; Hor did not speak, but frowned with his bushy eyebrows, only observing at times, 'That wouldn't do for us; still, it's a good thing—it's right.' All his inquiries, I cannot recount, and it is unnecessary; but from our conversations I carried away one conviction, which my readers will certainly not anticipate ... the conviction that Peter the Great was pre-eminently a Russian—Russian, above all, in his reforms. The Russian is so convinced of his own strength and powers that he is not afraid of putting himself to severe strain; he takes little interest in his past, and looks boldly forward. What is good he likes, what is sensible he will have, and where it comes from he does not care. His vigorous sense is fond of ridiculing the thin theorising of the German; but, in Hor's words, 'The Germans are curious folk,' and he was ready to learn from them a little. Thanks to his exceptional position, his practical independence, Hor told me a great deal which you could not screw or—as the peasants say—grind with a grindstone, out of any other man. He did, in fact, understand his position. Talking with Hor, I for the first time listened to the simple, wise discourse of the Russian peasant. His acquirements were, in his own opinion, wide enough; but he could not read, though Kalinitch could. 'That ne'er-do-weel has school-learning,' observed Hor, 'and his bees never die in the winter.' 'But haven't you had your children taught to read?' Hor was silent a minute. 'Fedya can read.' 'And the others?' 'The others can't.' 'And why?' The old man made no answer, and changed the subject. However, sensible as he was, he had many prejudices and crotchets. He despised women, for instance, from the depths of his soul, and in his merry moments he amused himself by jesting at their expense. His wife was a cross old woman who lay all day long on the stove, incessantly grumbling and scolding; her sons paid no attention to her, but she kept her daughters-in-law in the fear of God. Very significantly the mother-in-law sings in the Russian ballad: 'What a son art thou to me! What a head of a household! Thou dost not beat thy wife; thou dost not beat thy young wife....' I once attempted to intercede for the daughters-in-law, and tried to rouse Hor's sympathy; but he met me with the tranquil rejoinder, 'Why did I want to trouble about such ... trifles; let the women fight it out. ... If anything separates them, it only makes it worse ... and it's not worth dirtying one's hands over.' Sometimes the spiteful old woman got down from the stove and called the yard dog out of the hay, crying, 'Here, here, doggie'; and then beat it on its thin back with the poker, or she would stand in the porch and 'snarl,' as Hor expressed it, at everyone that passed. She stood in awe of her husband though, and would return, at his command, to her place on the stove. It was specially curious to hear Hor and Kalinitch dispute whenever Mr. Polutikin was touched upon.

'There, Hor, do let him alone,' Kalinitch would say. 'But why doesn't he order some boots for you?' Hor retorted. 'Eh? boots!... what do I want with boots? I am a peasant.' 'Well, so am I a peasant, but look!' And Hor lifted up his leg and showed Kalinitch a boot which looked as if it had been cut out of a mammoth's hide. 'As if you were like one of us!' replied Kalinitch. 'Well, at least he might pay for your bast shoes; you go out hunting with him; you must use a pair a day.' 'He does give me something for bast shoes.' 'Yes, he gave you two coppers last year.'

Kalinitch turned away in vexation, but Hor went off into a chuckle, during which his little eyes completely disappeared.

Kalinitch sang rather sweetly and played a little on the balalaëca. Hor was never weary of listening to him: all at once he would let his head drop on one side and begin to chime in, in a lugubrious voice. He was particularly fond of the song, 'Ah, my fate, my fate!' Fedya never lost an opportunity of making fun of his father, saying, 'What are you so mournful about, old man?' But Hor leaned his cheek on his hand, covered his eyes, and continued to mourn over his fate.... Yet at other times there could not be a more active man; he was always busy over something—mending the cart, patching up the fence, looking after the harness. He did not insist on a very high degree of cleanliness, however; and, in answer to some remark of mine, said once, 'A cottage ought to smell as if it were lived in.'

'Look,' I answered, 'how clean it is in Kalinitch's beehouse.'

'The bees would not live there else, your honour,' he said with a sigh.

'Tell me,' he asked me another time, 'have you an estate of your own?' 'Yes.' 'Far from here?' 'A hundred miles.' 'Do you live on your land, your honour?' 'Yes.'

'But you like your gun best, I dare say?'

'Yes, I must confess I do.' 'And you do well, your honour; shoot grouse to your heart's content, and change your bailiff pretty often.'

On the fourth day Mr. Polutikin sent for me in the evening. I was sorry to part from the old man. I took my seat with Kalinitch in the trap. 'Well, good-bye, Hor—good luck to you,' I said; 'good-bye, Fedya.'

'Good-bye, your honour, good-bye; don't forget us.' We started; there was the first red glow of sunset. 'It will be a fine day to-morrow,' I remarked looking at the clear sky. 'No, it will rain,' Kalinitch replied; 'the ducks yonder are splashing, and the scent of the grass is strong.' We drove into the copse. Kalinitch began singing in an undertone as he was jolted up and down on the driver's seat, and he kept gazing and gazing at the sunset.

The next day I left the hospitable roof of Mr. Polutikin.

II

YERMOLAÏ AND THE MILLER'S WIFE

One evening I went with the huntsman Yermolaï 'stand-shooting.' ... But perhaps all my readers may not know what 'stand-shooting' is. I will tell you.

A quarter of an hour before sunset in spring-time you go out into the woods with your gun, but without your dog. You seek out a spot for yourself on the outskirts of the forest, take a look round, examine your caps, and glance at your companion. A quarter of an hour passes; the sun has set, but it is still light in the forest; the sky is clear and transparent; the birds are chattering and twittering; the young grass shines with the brilliance of emerald.... You wait. Gradually the recesses of the forest grow dark; the blood-red glow of the evening sky creeps slowly on to the roots and the trunks of the trees, and keeps rising higher and higher, passes from the lower, still almost leafless branches, to the motionless, slumbering tree-tops.... And now even the topmost branches are darkened; the purple sky fades to dark-blue. The forest fragrance grows stronger;

there is a scent of warmth and damp earth; the fluttering breeze dies away at your side. The birds go to sleep—not all at once—but after their kinds; first the finches are hushed, a few minutes later the warblers, and after them the yellow buntings. In the forest it grows darker and darker. The trees melt together into great masses of blackness; in the dark-blue sky the first stars come timidly out. All the birds are asleep. Only the redstarts and the nuthatches are still chirping drowsily.... And now they too are still. The last echoing call of the pee-wit rings over our heads; the oriole's melancholy cry sounds somewhere in the distance; then the nightingale's first note. Your heart is weary with suspense, when suddenly—but only sportsmen can understand me—suddenly in the deep hush there is a peculiar croaking and whirring sound, the measured sweep of swift wings is heard, and the snipe, gracefully bending its long beak, sails smoothly down behind a dark bush to meet your shot.

That is the meaning of 'stand-shooting.' And so I had gone out stand- shooting with Yermolaï; but excuse me, reader: I must first introduce you to Yermolaï.

Picture to yourself a tall gaunt man of forty-five, with a long thin nose, a narrow forehead, little grey eyes, a bristling head of hair, and thick sarcastic lips. This man wore, winter and summer alike, a yellow nankin coat of German cut, but with a sash round the waist; he wore blue pantaloons and a cap of astrakhan, presented to him in a merry hour by a spendthrift landowner. Two bags were fastened on to his sash, one in front, skilfully tied into two halves, for powder and for shot; the other behind for game: wadding Yermolaï used to produce out of his peculiar, seemingly inexhaustible cap. With the money he gained by the game he sold, he might easily have bought himself a cartridge-box and powder-flask; but he never once even contemplated such a purchase, and continued to load his gun after his old fashion, exciting the admiration of all beholders by the skill with which he avoided the risks of spilling or mixing his powder and shot. His gun was a single- barrelled flint-lock, endowed, moreover, with a villainous habit of 'kicking.' It was due to this that Yermolaï's right cheek was permanently swollen to a larger size than the left. How he ever succeeded in hitting anything with this gun, it would take a shrewd man to discover—but he did. He had too a setter-dog, by name Valetka, a most extraordinary creature. Yermolaï never fed him. 'Me feed a dog!' he reasoned; 'why, a dog's a clever beast; he finds a living for himself.' And certainly, though Valetka's extreme thinness was a shock even to an indifferent observer, he still lived and had a long life; and in spite of his pitiable position he was not even once lost, and never showed an inclination to desert his master. Once indeed, in his youth, he had absented himself for two days, on courting bent, but this folly was soon over with him. Valetka's most noticeable peculiarity was his impenetrable indifference to everything in the world.... If it were not a dog I was speaking of, I should have called him 'disillusioned.' He usually sat with his cropped tail curled up under him, scowling and twitching at times, and he never smiled. (It is well known that dogs can smile, and smile very sweetly.) He was exceedingly ugly; and the idle house-serfs never lost an opportunity of jeering cruelly at his appearance; but all these jeers, and even blows, Valetka bore with astonishing indifference. He was a source of special delight to the cooks, who would all leave their work at once and give him chase with shouts and abuse, whenever, through a weakness not confined to dogs, he thrust his hungry nose through the half-open door of the kitchen, tempting with its warmth and appetising smells. He distinguished himself by untiring energy in the chase, and had a good scent; but if he chanced to overtake a slightly wounded hare, he devoured it with relish to the last bone, somewhere in the cool shade under the green bushes, at a respectful distance from Yermolaï, who was abusing him in every known and unknown dialect. Yermolaï belonged to one of my neighbours, a landowner of the old style. Landowners of the old style don't care for game, and prefer the domestic fowl. Only on extraordinary occasions,

11

such as birthdays, namedays, and elections, the cooks of the old-fashioned landowners set to work to prepare some long-beaked birds, and, falling into the state of frenzy peculiar to Russians when they don't quite know what to do, they concoct such marvellous sauces for them that the guests examine the proffered dishes curiously and attentively, but rarely make up their minds to try them. Yermolaï was under orders to provide his master's kitchen with two brace of grouse and partridges once a month. But he might live where and how he pleased. They had given him up as a man of no use for work of any kind— 'bone lazy,' as the expression is among us in Orel. Powder and shot, of course, they did not provide him, following precisely the same principle in virtue of which he did not feed his dog. Yermolaï was a very strange kind of man; heedless as a bird, rather fond of talking, awkward and vacant-looking; he was excessively fond of drink, and never could sit still long; in walking he shambled along, and rolled from side to side; and yet he got over fifty miles in the day with his rolling, shambling gait. He exposed himself to the most varied adventures: spent the night in the marshes, in trees, on roofs, or under bridges; more than once he had got shut up in lofts, cellars, or barns; he sometimes lost his gun, his dog, his most indispensable garments; got long and severe thrashings; but he always returned home, after a little while, in his clothes, and with his gun and his dog. One could not call him a cheerful man, though one almost always found him in an even frame of mind; he was looked on generally as an eccentric. Yermolaï liked a little chat with a good companion, especially over a glass, but he would not stop long; he would get up and go. 'But where the devil are you going? It's dark out of doors.' 'To Tchaplino.' 'But what's taking you to Tchaplino, ten miles away?' 'I am going to stay the night at Sophron's there.' 'But stay the night here.' 'No, I can't.' And Yermolaï, with his Valetka, would go off into the dark night, through woods and water-courses, and the peasant Sophron very likely did not let him into his place, and even, I am afraid, gave him a blow to teach him 'not to disturb honest folks.' But none could compare with Yermolaï in skill in deep-water fishing in spring-time, in catching crayfish with his hands, in tracking game by scent, in snaring quails, in training hawks, in capturing the nightingales who had the greatest variety of notes. ... One thing he could not do, train a dog; he had not patience enough. He had a wife too. He went to see her once a week. She lived in a wretched, tumble-down little hut, and led a hand-to-mouth existence, never knowing overnight whether she would have food to eat on the morrow; and in every way her lot was a pitiful one. Yermolaï, who seemed such a careless and easy-going fellow, treated his wife with cruel harshness; in his own house he assumed a stern, and menacing manner; and his poor wife did everything she could to please him, trembled when he looked at her, and spent her last farthing to buy him vodka; and when he stretched himself majestically on the stove and fell into an heroic sleep, she obsequiously covered him with a sheepskin. I happened myself more than once to catch an involuntary look in him of a kind of savage ferocity; I did not like the expression of his face when he finished off a wounded bird with his teeth. But Yermolaï never remained more than a day at home, and away from home he was once more the same 'Yermolka' (i.e. the shooting-cap), as he was called for a hundred miles round, and as he sometimes called himself. The lowest house-serf was conscious of being superior to this vagabond —and perhaps this was precisely why they treated him with friendliness; the peasants at first amused themselves by chasing him and driving him like a hare over the open country, but afterwards they left him in God's hands, and when once they recognised him as 'queer,' they no longer tormented him, and even gave him bread and entered into talk with him.... This was the man I took as my huntsman, and with him I went stand-shooting to a great birch-wood on the banks of the Ista.

Many Russian rivers, like the Volga, have one bank rugged and precipitous, the other bounded by level meadows; and so it is with the Ista. This small river winds extremely capriciously, coils like a snake, and does not keep a straight course for half-a-mile together; in some places, from the top of a sharp declivity, one can see the river for ten miles, with its dykes, its pools and mills, and the gardens on its banks, shut in with willows and thick flower-gardens. There are fish in the Ista in endless numbers, especially roaches (the peasants take them in hot weather from under the bushes with their hands); little sand-pipers flutter whistling along the stony banks, which are streaked with cold clear streams; wild ducks dive in the middle of the pools, and look round warily; in the coves under the overhanging cliffs herons stand out in the shade.... We stood in ambush nearly an hour, killed two brace of wood snipe, and, as we wanted to try our luck again at sunrise (stand-shooting can be done as well in the early morning), we resolved to spend the night at the nearest mill. We came out of the wood, and went down the slope. The dark-blue waters of the river ran below; the air was thick with the mists of night. We knocked at the gate. The dogs began barking in the yard.

'Who is there?' asked a hoarse and sleepy voice.

'We are sportsmen; let us stay the night.' There was no reply. 'We will pay.'

'I will go and tell the master—Sh! Curse the dogs! Go to the devil with you!'

We listened as the workman went into the cottage; he soon came back to the gate. 'No,' he said; 'the master tells me not to let you in.'

'Why not?'

'He is afraid; you are sportsmen; you might set the mill on fire; you've firearms with you, to be sure.'

'But what nonsense!'

'We had our mill on fire like that last year; some fish-dealers stayed the night, and they managed to set it on fire somehow.'

'But, my good friend, we can't sleep in the open air!'

'That's your business.' He went away, his boots clacking as he walked.

Yermolaï promised him various unpleasant things in the future. 'Let us go to the village,' he brought out at last, with a sigh. But it was two miles to the village.

'Let us stay the night here,' I said, 'in the open air—the night is warm; the miller will let us have some straw if we pay for it.'

Yermolaï agreed without discussion. We began again to knock.

'Well, what do you want?' the workman's voice was heard again; 'I've told you we can't.'

We explained to him what we wanted. He went to consult the master of the house, and returned with him. The little side gate creaked. The miller appeared, a tall, fat-faced man with a bull-neck, round-bellied and corpulent. He agreed to my proposal. A hundred paces from the mill there was a little outhouse open to the air on all sides. They carried straw and hay there for us; the workman set a samovar down on the grass near the river, and, squatting on his heels, began to blow vigorously into the pipe of it. The embers glowed, and threw a bright light on his young face. The miller ran to wake his wife, and suggested at last that I myself should sleep in the cottage; but I preferred to remain in the open air. The miller's wife brought us milk, eggs, potatoes and bread. Soon the samovar boiled, and we began drinking tea. A mist had risen from the river; there was no wind; from all round came the cry of the corn-crake, and faint sounds from the mill-wheels of drops that dripped from the paddles and of water gurgling through the bars of the lock. We built a small fire on the ground. While Yermolaï was baking the potatoes in the embers, I had time to fall into a doze. I was waked by a discreetly-subdued whispering near me. I lifted my head; before the fire, on a tub turned upside down, the miller's wife sat talking to my huntsman. By her dress, her movements, and her manner of speaking, I had already recognised that she had been in domestic service, and was neither peasant nor city-bred; but now for the first time I got a clear view of her features. She looked about thirty; her thin, pale face still showed the traces of remarkable beauty; what particularly charmed me was her eyes, large and mournful in expression. She was leaning her elbows on her knees, and had her face in her hands. Yermolaï was sitting with his back to me, and thrusting sticks into the fire.

'They've the cattle-plague again at Zheltonhiny,' the miller's wife was saying; 'father Ivan's two cows are dead—Lord have mercy on them!'

'And how are your pigs doing?' asked Yermolaï, after a brief pause.

'They're alive.'

'You ought to make me a present of a sucking pig.'

The miller's wife was silent for a while, then she sighed.

'Who is it you're with?' she asked.

'A gentleman from Kostomarovo.'

Yermolaï threw a few pine twigs on the fire; they all caught fire at once, and a thick white smoke came puffing into his face.

'Why didn't your husband let us into the cottage?'

'He's afraid.'

'Afraid! the fat old tub! Arina Timofyevna, my darling, bring me a little glass of spirits.'

The miller's wife rose and vanished into the darkness. Yermolaï began to sing in an undertone—

'When I went to see my sweetheart,
I wore out all my shoes.'

Arina returned with a small flask and a glass. Yermolaï got up, crossed himself, and drank it off at a draught. 'Good!' was his comment.

The miller's wife sat down again on the tub.

'Well, Arina Timofyevna, are you still ill?'

'Yes.'

'What is it?'

'My cough troubles me at night.'

'The gentleman's asleep, it seems,' observed Yermolaï after a short silence. 'Don't go to a doctor, Arina; it will be worse if you do.'

'Well, I am not going.'

'But come and pay me a visit.'

Arina hung down her head dejectedly.

'I will drive my wife out for the occasion,' continued Yermolaï 'Upon my word, I will.'

'You had better wake the gentleman, Yermolaï Petrovitch; you see, the potatoes are done.'

'Oh, let him snore,' observed my faithful servant indifferently; 'he's tired with walking, so he sleeps sound.'

I turned over in the hay. Yermolaï got up and came to me. 'The potatoes are ready; will you come and eat them?'

I came out of the outhouse; the miller's wife got up from the tub and was going away. I addressed her.

'Have you kept this mill long?'

'It's two years since I came on Trinity day.'

'And where does your husband come from?'

Arina had not caught my question.

'Where's your husband from?' repeated Yermolaï, raising his voice.

'From Byelev. He's a Byelev townsman.'

'And are you too from Byelev?'

'No, I'm a serf; I was a serf.'

'Whose?'

'Zvyerkoff was my master. Now I am free.'

'What Zvyerkoff?'

'Alexandr Selitch.'

'Weren't you his wife's lady's maid?'

'How did you know? Yes.'

I looked at Arina with redoubled curiosity and sympathy.

'I know your master,' I continued.

'Do you?' she replied in a low voice, and her head drooped.

I must tell the reader why I looked with such sympathy at Arina. During my stay at Petersburg I had become by chance acquainted with Mr. Zvyerkoff. He had a rather influential position, and was reputed a man of sense and education. He had a wife, fat, sentimental, lachrymose and spiteful—a vulgar and disagreeable creature; he had too a son, the very type of the young swell of to-day, pampered and stupid. The exterior of Mr. Zvyerkoff himself did not prepossess one in his favour; his little mouse-like eyes peeped slyly out of a broad, almost square, face; he had a large, prominent nose, with distended nostrils; his close-cropped grey hair stood up like a brush above his scowling brow; his thin lips were for ever twitching and smiling mawkishly. Mr. Zvyerkoff's favourite position was standing with his legs wide apart and his fat hands in his trouser pockets. Once I happened somehow to be driving alone with Mr. Zvyerkoff in a coach out of town. We fell into conversation. As a man of experience and of judgment, Mr. Zvyerkoff began to try to set me in 'the path of truth.'

'Allow me to observe to you,' he drawled at last; 'all you young people criticise and form judgments on everything at random; you have little knowledge of your own country; Russia, young gentlemen, is an unknown land to you; that's where it is!... You are for ever reading German. For instance, now you say this and that and the other about anything; for instance, about the house-serfs.... Very fine; I don't dispute it's all very fine; but you don't know them; you don't know the kind of people they are.' (Mr. Zvyerkoff blew his nose loudly and took a pinch of snuff.) 'Allow me to tell you as an illustration one little anecdote; it may perhaps interest you.' (Mr. Zvyerkoff cleared his throat.) 'You know, doubtless, what my wife is; it would be difficult, I should imagine, to find a more kind-hearted woman, you will agree. For her waiting-maids, existence is simply a perfect paradise, and no mistake about it.... But my wife has made it a rule never to keep married lady's maids. Certainly it would not do; children come—and one thing and the other— and how is a lady's maid to look after her mistress as she ought, to fit in with her ways; she is no longer able to do it; her mind is in other things. One must look at things through human nature. Well, we were driving once through our village, it must be—let me be correct—yes, fifteen years ago. We saw, at the bailiff's, a young girl, his daughter, very pretty indeed; something even—you know—something attractive in her manners. And my wife said to me: "Koko"—you understand, of course, that is her pet name for me— "let us take this girl to Petersburg; I like her, Koko...." I said, "Let us take her, by all means." The bailiff, of course, was at our feet; he could not have expected such good fortune, you can imagine.... Well, the girl of course cried violently. Of course, it was hard for her at first; the parental home ... in fact ... there was nothing surprising in that. However, she soon got used to us: at first we put her in the maidservants' room; they trained her, of course. And what do you think? The girl made wonderful progress; my wife became simply devoted to her, promoted her at last above the rest to wait on herself ... observe.... And one must do her the justice to say, my wife had never such a maid, absolutely never; attentive, modest, and obedient—simply all that could be desired. But my wife, I must confess, spoilt her too much; she dressed her well, fed her from our own table, gave her tea to drink, and so on, as you can imagine! So she waited on my wife like this for ten years. Suddenly, one fine morning, picture to yourself, Arina—her name was Arina—rushes unannounced into my study, and flops down at my feet. That's a thing, I tell you plainly, I can't endure. No human being ought ever to lose sight of their personal dignity. Am I not right? What do you say? "Your honour, Alexandr Selitch, I beseech a favour of you." "What favour?" "Let me be married." I must confess I was taken aback. "But you know, you stupid, your mistress has no other lady's maid?" "I will wait on mistress as before." "Nonsense! nonsense! your mistress can't endure married lady's maids." "Malanya could take my place." "Pray don't argue." "I obey your will." I must confess it was quite a shock, I assure you, I am like that; nothing wounds me so— nothing, I venture to say, wounds me so deeply as ingratitude. I need not tell you—you know what my wife is; an angel upon earth, goodness inexhaustible. One would fancy even the worst of men would be ashamed to hurt her. Well, I got rid of Arina. I thought, perhaps, she would come to her senses; I was unwilling, do you know, to believe in wicked, black ingratitude in anyone. What do you think? Within six months she thought fit to come to me again with the same request. I felt revolted. But imagine my amazement when, some time later, my wife comes to me in tears, so agitated that I felt positively alarmed. "What has happened?" "Arina.... You understand ... I am ashamed to tell it." ... "Impossible! ... Who is the man?" "Petrushka, the footman." My indignation broke out then. I am like that. I don't like half measures! Petrushka was not to blame. We might flog him, but in my opinion he was not to blame. Arina.... Well, well, well! what more's to be said? I gave orders, of course, that her hair should be cut off, she should be dressed in sackcloth, and sent into the country. My wife was deprived of an excellent lady's maid; but there was no help for it: immorality cannot be tolerated in a household in any case. Better to cut off the infected member at once. There, there! now you can judge the thing for yourself—you know that my wife is ... yes, yes, yes! indeed!... an angel! She had grown attached to Arina, and Arina knew it, and had the face to ... Eh? no, tell me ... eh? And what's the use of talking about it. Any way, there was no help for it. I, indeed—I, in particular, felt hurt, felt wounded for a long time by the ingratitude of this girl. Whatever you say—it's no good to look for feeling, for heart, in these people! You may feed the wolf as you will; he has always a hankering for the woods. Education, by all means! But I only wanted to give you an example....'

And Mr. Zvyerkoff, without finishing his sentence, turned away his head, and, wrapping himself more closely into his cloak, manfully repressed his involuntary emotion.

The reader now probably understands why I looked with sympathetic interest at Arina.

'Have you long been married to the miller?' I asked her at last.

'Two years.'

'How was it? Did your master allow it?'

'They bought my freedom.'

'Who?'

'Savely Alexyevitch.'

'Who is that?'

'My husband.' (Yermolaï smiled to himself.) 'Has my master perhaps spoken to you of me?' added Arina, after a brief silence.

I did not know what reply to make to her question.

'Arina!' cried the miller from a distance. She got up and walked away.

'Is her husband a good fellow?' I asked Yermolaï.

'So-so.'

'Have they any children?'

'There was one, but it died.'

'How was it? Did the miller take a liking to her? Did he give much to buy her freedom?'

'I don't know. She can read and write; in their business it's of use. I suppose he liked her.'

'And have you known her long?'

'Yes. I used to go to her master's. Their house isn't far from here.'

'And do you know the footman Petrushka?'

'Piotr Vassilyevitch? Of course, I knew him.'

'Where is he now?'

'He was sent for a soldier.'

We were silent for a while.

'She doesn't seem well?' I asked Yermolaï at last.

'I should think not! To-morrow, I say, we shall have good sport. A little sleep now would do us no harm.'

A flock of wild ducks swept whizzing over our heads, and we heard them drop down into the river not far from us. It was now quite dark, and it began to be cold; in the thicket sounded the melodious notes of a nightingale. We buried ourselves in the hay and fell asleep.

III

RASPBERRY SPRING

At the beginning of August the heat often becomes insupportable. At that season, from twelve to three o'clock, the most determined and ardent sportsman is not able to hunt, and the most devoted dog begins to 'clean his master's spurs,' that is, to follow at his heels, his eyes painfully blinking, and his tongue hanging out to an exaggerated length; and in response to his master's reproaches he humbly wags his tail and shows his confusion in his face; but he does not run forward. I happened to be out hunting on exactly such a day. I had long been fighting against the temptation to lie down somewhere in the shade, at least for a moment; for a long time my indefatigable dog went on running about in the bushes, though he clearly did not himself expect much good from his feverish activity. The stifling heat compelled me at last to begin to think of husbanding our energies and strength. I managed to reach the little river Ista, which is already known to my indulgent readers, descended the steep bank, and walked along the damp, yellow sand in the direction of the spring, known to the whole neighbourhood as Raspberry Spring. This spring gushes out of a cleft in the bank, which widens out by degrees into a small but deep creek, and, twenty paces beyond it, falls with a merry babbling sound into the river; the short velvety grass is green about the source: the sun's rays scarcely ever reach its cold, silvery water. I came as far as the spring; a cup of birch-wood lay on the grass, left by a passing peasant for the public benefit. I quenched my thirst, lay down in the shade, and looked round. In the cave, which had been formed by the flowing of the stream into the river, and hence marked for ever with the trace of ripples, two old men were sitting with their backs to me. One, a rather stout and tall man in a neat dark-green coat and lined cap, was fishing; the other was thin and little; he wore a patched fustian coat and no cap; he held a little pot full of worms on his knees, and sometimes lifted his hand up to his grizzled little head, as though he wanted to protect it from the sun. I looked at him more attentively, and recognised in him Styopushka of Shumihino. I must ask the reader's leave to present this man to him.

A few miles from my place there is a large village called Shumihino, with a stone church, erected in the name of St. Kosmo and St. Damian. Facing this church there had once stood a large and stately manor-house, surrounded by various outhouses, offices, workshops, stables and coach-houses, baths and temporary kitchens, wings for visitors and for bailiffs, conservatories, swings for the people, and other more or less useful edifices. A family of rich landowners lived in this manor-house, and all went well with them, till suddenly one morning all this prosperity was burnt to ashes. The owners removed to another home; the place was deserted. The blackened site of the immense house was transformed into a kitchen-garden, cumbered up in parts by piles of bricks, the remains of the old foundations. A little hut had been hurriedly put together out of the beams that had escaped the fire; it was roofed with timber bought ten years before for the construction of a pavilion in the Gothic style; and the gardener, Mitrofan, with his wife Axinya and their seven children, was installed in it. Mitrofan received orders to send greens and garden-stuff for the master's table, a hundred and fifty miles away; Axinya was put in charge of a Tyrolese cow, which had been bought for a high price in Moscow, but had not given a drop of milk since its acquisition; a crested smoke-coloured drake too had been left in her hands, the solitary 'seignorial' bird; for the children, in consideration of their tender age, no special duties had been provided, a fact, however, which had not hindered them from growing up utterly lazy. It happened to me on two occasions to stay the night at this gardener's, and when I passed by I used to get cucumbers from him, which, for some unknown reason, were even in summer peculiar for their size, their poor, watery flavour, and their thick yellow skin. It was there I first saw Styopushka. Except Mitrofan and his family, and the old deaf churchwarden Gerasim, kept out of charity in a little room at the one-eyed soldier's widow's, not one man among the house-serfs had remained at Shumihino; for Styopushka, whom I intend to introduce to the reader, could not be classified under the special order of house-serfs, and hardly under the genus 'man' at all.

Every man has some kind of position in society, and at least some ties of some sort; every house-serf receives, if not wages, at least some so-called 'ration.' Styopushka had absolutely no means of subsistence of any kind; had no relationship to anyone; no one knew of his existence. This man had not even a past; there was no story told of him; he had probably never been enrolled on a census-revision. There were vague rumours that he had once belonged to someone as a valet; but who he was, where he came from, who was his father, and how he had come to be one of the Shumihino people; in what way he had come by the fustian coat he had worn from immemorial times; where he lived and what he lived on—on all these questions no one had the least idea; and, to tell the truth, no one took any interest in the subject. Grandfather Trofimitch, who knew all the pedigrees of all the house-serfs in the direct line to the fourth generation, had once indeed been known to say that he remembered that Styopushka was related to a Turkish woman whom the late master, the brigadier Alexy Romanitch had been pleased to bring home from a campaign in the baggage waggon. Even on holidays, days of general money-giving and of feasting on buckwheat dumplings and vodka, after the old Russian fashion—even on such days Styopushka did not put in an appearance at the trestle-tables nor at the barrels; he did not make his bow nor kiss the master's hand, nor toss off to the master's health and under the master's eye a glass filled by the fat hands of the bailiff. Some kind soul who passed by him might share an unfinished bit of dumpling with the poor beggar, perhaps. At Easter

18

they said 'Christ is risen!' to him; but he did not pull up his greasy sleeve, and bring out of the depths of his pocket a coloured egg, to offer it, panting and blinking, to his young masters or to the mistress herself. He lived in summer in a little shed behind the chicken-house, and in winter in the ante-room of the bathhouse; in the bitter frosts he spent the night in the hayloft. The house-serfs had grown used to seeing him; sometimes they gave him a kick, but no one ever addressed a remark to him; as for him, he seems never to have opened his lips from the time of his birth. After the conflagration, this forsaken creature sought a refuge at the gardener Mitrofan's. The gardener left him alone; he did not say 'Live with me,' but he did not drive him away. And Styopushka did not live at the gardener's; his abode was the garden. He moved and walked about quite noiselessly; he sneezed and coughed behind his hand, not without apprehension; he was for ever busy and going stealthily to and fro like an ant; and all to get food— simply food to eat. And indeed, if he had not toiled from morning till night for his living, our poor friend would certainly have died of hunger. It's a sad lot not to know in the morning what you will find to eat before night! Sometimes Styopushka sits under the hedge and gnaws a radish or sucks a carrot, or shreds up some dirty cabbage-stalks; or he drags a bucket of water along, for some object or other, groaning as he goes; or he lights a fire under a small pot, and throws in some little black scraps which he takes from out of the bosom of his coat; or he is hammering in his little wooden den—driving in a nail, putting up a shelf for bread. And all this he does silently, as though on the sly: before you can look round, he's in hiding again. Sometimes he suddenly disappears for a couple of days; but of course no one notices his absence.... Then, lo and behold! he is there again, somewhere under the hedge, stealthily kindling a fire of sticks under a kettle. He had a small face, yellowish eyes, hair coming down to his eyebrows, a sharp nose, large transparent ears, like a bat's, and a beard that looked as if it were a fortnight's growth, and never grew more nor less. This, then, was Styopushka, whom I met on the bank of the Ista in company with another old man.

I went up to him, wished him good-day, and sat down beside him. Styopushka's companion too I recognised as an acquaintance; he was a freed serf of Count Piotr Ilitch's, one Mihal Savelitch, nicknamed Tuman (*i.e.* fog). He lived with a consumptive Bolhovsky man, who kept an inn, where I had several times stayed. Young officials and other persons of leisure travelling on the Orel highroad (merchants, buried in their striped rugs, have other things to do) may still see at no great distance from the large village of Troitska, and almost on the highroad, an immense two-storied wooden house, completely deserted, with its roof falling in and its windows closely stuffed up. At mid-day in bright, sunny weather nothing can be imagined more melancholy than this ruin. Here there once lived Count Piotr Ilitch, a rich grandee of the olden time, renowned for his hospitality. At one time the whole province used to meet at his house, to dance and make merry to their heart's content to the deafening sound of a home-trained orchestra, and the popping of rockets and Roman candles; and doubtless more than one aged lady sighs as she drives by the deserted palace of the boyar and recalls the old days and her vanished youth. The count long continued to give balls, and to walk about with an affable smile among the crowd of fawning guests; but his property, unluckily, was not enough to last his whole life. When he was entirely ruined, he set off to Petersburg to try for a post for himself, and died in a room at a hotel, without having gained anything by his efforts. Tuman had been a steward of his, and had received his freedom already in the count's lifetime. He was a man of about seventy, with a regular and pleasant face. He was almost continually smiling, as only men of the time of Catherine ever do smile—a smile at once stately and indulgent; in speaking, he slowly opened and closed his lips, winked genially with his eyes, and spoke slightly through his nose. He blew his nose and took snuff too in a leisurely fashion, as though he were doing something serious.

'Well, Mihal Savelitch,' I began, 'have you caught any fish?'

'Here, if you will deign to look in the basket: I have caught two perch and five roaches.... Show them, Styopka.'

Styopushka stretched out the basket to me.

'How are you, Styopka?' I asked him.

'Oh—oh—not—not—not so badly, your honour,' answered Stepan, stammering as though he had a heavy weight on his tongue.

'And is Mitrofan well?'

'Well—yes, yes—your honour.'

The poor fellow turned away.

'But there are not many bites,' remarked Tuman; 'it's so fearfully hot; the fish are all tired out under the bushes; they're asleep. Put on a worm, Styopka.' (Styopushka took out a worm, laid it on his open hand, struck it two or three times, put it on the hook, spat on it, and gave it to Tuman.) 'Thanks, Styopka.... And you, your honour,' he continued, turning to me, 'are pleased to be out hunting?'

'As you see.'

'Ah—and is your dog there English or German?'

The old man liked to show off on occasion, as though he would say, 'I, too, have lived in the world!'

'I don't know what breed it is, but it's a good dog.'

'Ah! and do you go out with the hounds too?'

'Yes, I have two leashes of hounds.'

Tuman smiled and shook his head.

'That's just it; one man is devoted to dogs, and another doesn't want them for anything. According to my simple notions, I fancy dogs should be kept rather for appearance' sake ... and all should be in style too; horses too should be in style, and huntsmen in style, as they ought to be, and all. The late count—God's grace be with him!—was never, I must own, much of a hunter; but he kept dogs, and twice a year he was pleased to go out with them. The huntsmen assembled in the courtyard, in red caftans trimmed with galloon, and blew their horns; his excellency would be pleased to come out, and his excellency's horse would be led up; his excellency would mount, and the chief huntsman puts his feet in the stirrups, takes his hat off, and puts the reins in his hat to offer them to his excellency. His excellency is pleased to click his whip like this, and the huntsmen give a shout, and off they go out of the gate away. A huntsman rides behind the count, and holds in a silken leash two of the master's favourite dogs, and looks after them well, you may fancy.... And he, too, this huntsman, sits up high, on a Cossack saddle: such a red-cheeked fellow he was, and rolled his eyes like this.... And there were guests too, you may be sure, on such occasions, and entertainment, and ceremonies observed.... Ah, he's got away, the Asiatic!' He interrupted himself suddenly, drawing in his line.

'They say the count used to live pretty freely in his day?' I asked.

The old man spat on the worm and lowered the line in again.

'He was a great gentleman, as is well-known. At times the persons of the first rank, one may say, at Petersburg, used to visit him. With coloured ribbons on their breasts they used to sit down to table and eat. Well, he knew how to entertain them. He called me sometimes. "Tuman," says he, "I want by to-morrow some live sturgeon; see there are some, do you hear?" "Yes, your excellency." Embroidered coats, wigs, canes, perfumes, *eau de Cologne* of the best sort, snuff-boxes, huge pictures: he would order them all from Paris itself! When he gave a banquet, God Almighty, Lord of my being! there were fireworks, and carriages driving up! They even fired off the cannon. The orchestra alone consisted of forty men. He kept a German as conductor of the band, but the German gave himself dreadful airs; he wanted to eat at the same table as the masters; so his excellency gave orders to get rid of him! "My musicians," says he, "can do their work even without a conductor." Of course he was master. Then they would fall to dancing, and dance till morning, especially at the écossaise-matrador. ... Ah— ah—there's one caught!' (The old man drew a small perch out of the water.) 'Here you are, Styopka! The master was all a master should be,' continued the old man, dropping his line in again, 'and he had a kind heart too. He would give you a blow at times, and before you could look round, he'd forgotten it already. There was only one thing: he kept mistresses. Ugh, those mistresses! God forgive them! They were the ruin of him too; and yet, you know, he took them most generally from a low station. You would fancy they would not want much? Not a bit— they must have everything of the most expensive in all Europe! One may say, "Why shouldn't he live as he likes; it's the master's business" ... but there was no need to ruin himself. There was one especially; Akulina was her name. She is dead now; God rest her soul! the daughter of the watchman at Sitoia; and such a vixen! She would slap the count's face sometimes. She simply bewitched him. My nephew she sent for a soldier; he spilt some chocolate on a new dress of hers ... and he wasn't the only one she served so. Ah, well, those were good times, though!' added the old man with a deep sigh. His head drooped forward and he was silent.

'Your master, I see, was severe, then?' I began after a brief silence.

'That was the fashion then, your honour,' he replied, shaking his head.

'That sort of thing is not done now?' I observed, not taking my eyes off him.

He gave me a look askance.

'Now, surely it's better,' he muttered, and let out his line further.

We were sitting in the shade; but even in the shade it was stifling. The sultry atmosphere was faint and heavy; one lifted one's burning face uneasily, seeking a breath of wind; but there was no wind. The sun beat down from blue and darkening skies; right opposite us, on the other bank, was a yellow field of oats, overgrown here and there with wormwood; not one ear of the oats quivered. A little lower down a peasant's horse stood in the river up to its knees, and slowly shook its wet tail; from time to time, under an overhanging bush, a large fish shot up, bringing bubbles to the surface, and gently sank down to the bottom, leaving a slight ripple behind it. The grasshoppers chirped in the scorched grass; the quail's cry sounded languid and reluctant; hawks sailed smoothly over the meadows, often resting in the same spot, rapidly fluttering their wings and opening their tails into a fan. We sat motionless, overpowered with the heat. Suddenly there was a sound behind us in the creek; someone came down to the spring. I looked round, and saw a peasant of about fifty, covered with dust, in a smock, and wearing bast slippers; he carried a wickerwork pannier and a cloak on his shoulders. He went down to the spring, drank thirstily, and got up.

'Ah, Vlass!' cried Tuman, staring at him; 'good health to you, friend! Where has God sent you from?'

'Good health to you, Mihal Savelitch!' said the peasant, coming nearer to us; 'from a long way off.'

'Where have you been?' Tuman asked him.

'I have been to Moscow, to my master.'

'What for?'

'I went to ask him a favour.'

'What about?'

'Oh, to lessen my rent, or to let me work it out in labour, or to put me on another piece of land, or something…. My son is dead—so I can't manage it now alone.'

'Your son is dead?'

'He is dead. My son,' added the peasant, after a pause, 'lived in Moscow as a cabman; he paid, I must confess, rent for me.'

'Then are you now paying rent?'

'Yes, we pay rent.'

'What did your master say?'

'What did the master say! He drove me away! Says he, "How dare you come straight to me; there is a bailiff for such things. You ought first," says he, "to apply to the bailiff … and where am I to put you on other land? You first," says he, "bring the debt you owe." He was angry altogether.'

'What then—did you come back?'

'I came back. I wanted to find out if my son had not left any goods of his own, but I couldn't get a straight answer. I say to his employer, "I am Philip's father"; and he says, "What do I know about that? And your son," says he, "left nothing; he was even in debt to me." So I came away.'

The peasant related all this with a smile, as though he were speaking of someone else; but tears were starting into his small, screwed-up eyes, and his lips were quivering.

'Well, are you going home then now?'

'Where can I go? Of course I'm going home. My wife, I suppose, is pretty well starved by now.'

'You should—then,' Styopushka said suddenly. He grew confused, was silent, and began to rummage in the worm-pot.

'And shall you go to the bailiff?' continued Tuman, looking with some amazement at Styopka.

'What should I go to him for?—I'm in arrears as it is. My son was ill for a year before his death; he could not pay even his own rent. But it can't hurt me; they can get nothing from me…. Yes, my friend, you can be as cunning as you please—I'm cleaned out!' (The peasant began to laugh.) 'Kintlyan Semenitch'll have to be clever if—'

Vlass laughed again.

'Oh! things are in a sad way, brother Vlass,' Tuman ejaculated deliberately.

'Sad! No!' (Vlass's voice broke.) 'How hot it is!' he went on, wiping his face with his sleeve.

'Who is your master?' I asked him.

'Count Valerian Petrovitch.'

'The son of Piotr Ilitch?'

'The son of Piotr Ilitch,' replied Tuman. 'Piotr Ilitch gave him Vlass's village in his lifetime.'

'Is he well?'

'He is well, thank God!' replied Vlass. 'He has grown so red, and his face looks as though it were padded.'

'You see, your honour,' continued Tuman, turning to me, 'it would be very well near Moscow, but it's a different matter to pay rent here.'

'And what is the rent for you altogether?'

'Ninety-five roubles,' muttered Vlass.

'There, you see; and it's the least bit of land; all there is is the master's forest.'

'And that, they say, they have sold,' observed the peasant.

'There, you see. Styopka, give me a worm. Why, Styopka, are you asleep —eh?'

Styopushka started. The peasant sat down by us. We sank into silence again. On the other bank someone was singing a song—but such a mournful one. Our poor Vlass grew deeply dejected.

Half-an-hour later we parted.

IV

THE DISTRICT DOCTOR

One day in autumn on my way back from a remote part of the country I caught cold and fell ill. Fortunately the fever attacked me in the district town at the inn; I sent for the doctor. In half-an-hour the district doctor appeared, a thin, dark-haired man of middle height. He prescribed me the usual sudorific, ordered a mustard-plaster to be put on, very deftly slid a five-rouble note up his sleeve, coughing drily and looking away as he did so, and then was getting up to go home, but somehow fell into talk and remained. I was exhausted with feverishness; I foresaw a sleepless night, and was glad of a little chat with a pleasant companion. Tea was served. My doctor began to converse freely. He was a sensible fellow, and expressed himself with vigour and some humour. Queer things happen in the world: you may live a long while with some people, and be on friendly terms with them, and never once speak openly with them from your soul; with others you have scarcely time to get acquainted, and all at once you are pouring out to him—or he to you—all your secrets, as though you were at confession. I don't know how I gained the confidence of my new friend—any way, with nothing to lead up to it, he told me a rather curious incident; and here I will report his tale for the information of the indulgent reader. I will try to tell it in the doctor's own words.

'You don't happen to know,' he began in a weak and quavering voice (the common result of the use of unmixed Berezov snuff); 'you don't happen to know the judge here, Mylov, Pavel Lukitch?... You don't know him?... Well, it's all the same.' (He cleared his throat and rubbed his eyes.) 'Well, you see, the thing happened, to tell you exactly without mistake, in Lent, at the very time of the thaws. I was sitting at his house—our judge's, you know—playing preference. Our judge is a good fellow, and fond of playing preference. Suddenly' (the doctor made frequent use of this word, suddenly) 'they tell me, "There's a servant asking for you." I say, "What does he want?" They say, "He has brought a note—it must be from a patient." "Give me the note," I say. So it is from a patient—well and good—you understand—it's our bread and butter. ... But this is how it was: a lady, a widow, writes to me; she says, "My daughter is dying. Come, for God's sake!" she says; "and the horses have been sent for you." ... Well, that's all right. But she was twenty miles from the town, and it was midnight out of doors, and the roads in such a state, my word! And as she was poor herself, one could not expect more than two silver roubles, and even that problematic; and perhaps it might only be a matter of a roll of linen and a sack of oatmeal in payment. However, duty, you know, before everything: a fellow-creature may be dying. I hand over my cards at once to Kalliopin, the member of the provincial commission, and return home. I look; a wretched little trap was standing at the steps, with peasant's horses, fat—too fat—and their coat as shaggy as felt; and the coachman sitting with his cap off out of respect. Well, I think to myself, "It's clear, my friend, these patients aren't rolling in riches." ... You smile; but I tell you, a poor man like me has to take everything into consideration.... If the coachman sits like a prince, and doesn't touch his cap, and even sneers at you behind his beard, and flicks his whip— then you may bet on six roubles. But this case, I saw, had a very different air. However, I think there's no help for it; duty before everything. I snatch up the most necessary drugs, and set off. Will you believe it? I only just managed to get there at all. The road was infernal: streams, snow, watercourses, and the dyke had suddenly burst there—that was the worst of it! However, I arrived at last. It was a little thatched house. There was a light in the windows; that meant they expected me. I was met by an old lady, very venerable, in a cap. "Save her!" she says; "she is dying." I say, "Pray don't distress yourself—Where is the invalid?" "Come this way." I see a clean little room, a lamp in the corner; on the bed a girl of twenty, unconscious. She was in a burning heat, and breathing heavily—it was fever. There were two other girls, her sisters, scared and in tears. "Yesterday," they tell me, "she was perfectly well and had a good appetite; this morning she complained of her head, and this evening, suddenly, you see, like this." I say again: "Pray don't be uneasy." It's a doctor's duty, you know—and I went up to her and bled her, told them to put on a mustard-plaster, and prescribed a mixture. Meantime I looked at her; I looked at her, you know—there, by God! I had never seen such a face!—she was a beauty, in a word! I felt quite shaken with pity. Such lovely features; such eyes!... But, thank God! she became easier; she fell into a perspiration, seemed to come to her senses, looked round, smiled, and passed her hand over her face.... Her sisters bent over her. They ask, "How are you?" "All right," she says, and turns away. I looked at her; she had fallen asleep. "Well," I say, "now the patient should be left alone." So we all went out on tiptoe; only a maid remained, in case she was wanted. In the parlour there was a samovar standing on the table, and a bottle of rum; in our profession one can't get on without it. They gave me tea; asked me to stop the night. ... I consented: where could I go, indeed, at that time of night? The old lady kept groaning. "What is it?" I say; "she will live; don't worry yourself; you had better take a little rest yourself; it is about two o'clock." "But will you send to wake me if anything happens?" "Yes, yes." The old lady went away, and the girls too went to their own room; they made up a bed for me in the parlour. Well, I went to bed—but I could not get to sleep, for a wonder! for in reality I was very tired. I could not get my patient out of my head. At last I could not put up with it any longer; I got up suddenly; I think to myself, "I will go and see how the patient is getting on." Her bedroom was next to the parlour. Well, I got up, and gently opened the door—how my heart beat! I looked in: the servant was asleep, her mouth wide open, and even snoring, the wretch! but the patient lay with her face towards me, and her arms flung wide apart, poor girl! I went up to her ... when suddenly she opened her eyes and stared at me! "Who is it? who is it?" I was in confusion. "Don't be alarmed, madam," I say; "I am the doctor; I have come to see how you feel." "You the doctor?" "Yes, the doctor; your mother sent for me from the town; we have bled you, madam; now pray go to sleep, and in a day or two, please God! we will set you on your feet again." "Ah, yes, yes, doctor, don't let me die.... please, please." "Why do you talk like that? God bless you!" She is in a fever again, I think to myself; I felt her pulse; yes, she was feverish. She looked at me, and then took me by the hand. "I will tell you why I don't want to die; I will tell you.... Now we are alone; and only, please don't you ... not to anyone ... Listen...." I bent down; she moved her lips quite to my ear; she touched my cheek with her hair—I confess my head went round—and began to whisper.... I could make out nothing of it.... Ah, she was delirious!... She whispered and whispered, but so quickly, and as if it were not in Russian; at last she finished, and shivering dropped her head on the pillow, and threatened me with her finger: "Remember, doctor, to no one." I calmed her somehow, gave her something to drink, waked the servant, and went away.'

At this point the doctor again took snuff with exasperated energy, and for a moment seemed stupefied by its effects.

'However,' he continued, 'the next day, contrary to my expectations, the patient was no better. I thought and thought, and suddenly decided to remain there, even though my other patients were expecting me.... And you know one can't afford to disregard that;

one's practice suffers if one does. But, in the first place, the patient was really in danger; and secondly, to tell the truth, I felt strongly drawn to her. Besides, I liked the whole family. Though they were really badly off, they were singularly, I may say, cultivated people.... Their father had been a learned man, an author; he died, of course, in poverty, but he had managed before he died to give his children an excellent education; he left a lot of books too. Either because I looked after the invalid very carefully, or for some other reason; any way, I can venture to say all the household loved me as if I were one of the family.... Meantime the roads were in a worse state than ever; all communications, so to say, were cut off completely; even medicine could with difficulty be got from the town.... The sick girl was not getting better. ... Day after day, and day after day ... but ... here....' (The doctor made a brief pause.) 'I declare I don't know how to tell you.' ... (He again took snuff, coughed, and swallowed a little tea.) 'I will tell you without beating about the bush. My patient ... how should I say?... Well, she had fallen in love with me ... or, no, it was not that she was in love ... however ... really, how should one say?' (The doctor looked down and grew red.) 'No,' he went on quickly, 'in love, indeed! A man should not over-estimate himself. She was an educated girl, clever and well- read, and I had even forgotten my Latin, one may say, completely. As to appearance' (the doctor looked himself over with a smile) 'I am nothing to boast of there either. But God Almighty did not make me a fool; I don't take black for white; I know a thing or two; I could see very clearly, for instance, that Alexandra Andreevna—that was her name—did not feel love for me, but had a friendly, so to say, inclination—a respect or something for me. Though she herself perhaps mistook this sentiment, any way this was her attitude; you may form your own judgment of it. But,' added the doctor, who had brought out all these disconnected sentences without taking breath, and with obvious embarrassment, 'I seem to be wandering rather—you won't understand anything like this.... There, with your leave, I will relate it all in order.'

He drank off a glass of tea, and began in a calmer voice.

'Well, then. My patient kept getting worse and worse. You are not a doctor, my good sir; you cannot understand what passes in a poor fellow's heart, especially at first, when he begins to suspect that the disease is getting the upper hand of him. What becomes of his belief in himself? You suddenly grow so timid; it's indescribable. You fancy then that you have forgotten everything you knew, and that the patient has no faith in you, and that other people begin to notice how distracted you are, and tell you the symptoms with reluctance; that they are looking at you suspiciously, whispering.... Ah! it's horrid! There must be a remedy, you think, for this disease, if one could find it. Isn't this it? You try— no, that's not it! You don't allow the medicine the necessary time to do good.... You clutch at one thing, then at another. Sometimes you take up a book of medical prescriptions—here it is, you think! Sometimes, by Jove, you pick one out by chance, thinking to leave it to fate.... But meantime a fellow-creature's dying, and another doctor would have saved him. "We must have a consultation," you say; "I will not take the responsibility on myself." And what a fool you look at such times! Well, in time you learn to bear it; it's nothing to you. A man has died—but it's not your fault; you treated him by the rules. But what's still more torture to you is to see blind faith in you, and to feel yourself that you are not able to be of use. Well, it was just this blind faith that the whole of Alexandra Andreevna's family had in me; they had forgotten to think that their daughter was in danger. I, too, on my side assure them that it's nothing, but meantime my heart sinks into my boots. To add to our troubles, the roads were in such a state that the coachman was gone for whole days together to get medicine. And I never left the patient's room; I could not tear myself away; I tell her amusing stories, you know, and play cards with her. I watch by her side at night. The old mother thanks me with tears in her eyes; but I think to myself, "I don't deserve your gratitude." I frankly confess to

25

you—there is no object in concealing it now—I was in love with my patient. And
Alexandra Andreevna had grown fond of me; she would not sometimes let anyone be in
her room but me. She began to talk to me, to ask me questions; where I had studied, how
I lived, who are my people, whom I go to see. I feel that she ought not to talk; but to
forbid her to—to forbid her resolutely, you know—I could not. Sometimes I held my
head in my hands, and asked myself, "What are you doing, villain?" ... And she would
take my hand and hold it, give me a long, long look, and turn away, sigh, and say, "How
good you are!" Her hands were so feverish, her eyes so large and languid.... "Yes," she
says, "you are a good, kind man; you are not like our neighbours.... No, you are not like
that. ... Why did I not know you till now!" "Alexandra Andreevna, calm yourself," I
say.... "I feel, believe me, I don't know how I have gained ... but there, calm yourself....
All will be right; you will be well again." And meanwhile I must tell you,' continued the
doctor, bending forward and raising his eyebrows, 'that they associated very little with the
neighbours, because the smaller people were not on their level, and pride hindered them
from being friendly with the rich. I tell you, they were an exceptionally cultivated family;
so you know it was gratifying for me. She would only take her medicine from my hands
... she would lift herself up, poor girl, with my aid, take it, and gaze at me.... My heart
felt as if it were bursting. And meanwhile she was growing worse and worse, worse and
worse, all the time; she will die, I think to myself; she must die. Believe me, I would
sooner have gone to the grave myself; and here were her mother and sisters watching me,
looking into my eyes ... and their faith in me was wearing away. "Well? how is she?"
"Oh, all right, all right!" All right, indeed! My mind was failing me. Well, I was sitting
one night alone again by my patient. The maid was sitting there too, and snoring away in
full swing; I can't find fault with the poor girl, though; she was worn out too. Alexandra
Andreevna had felt very unwell all the evening; she was very feverish. Until midnight she
kept tossing about; at last she seemed to fall asleep; at least, she lay still without stirring.
The lamp was burning in the corner before the holy image. I sat there, you know, with my
head bent; I even dozed a little. Suddenly it seemed as though someone touched me in the
side; I turned round.... Good God! Alexandra Andreevna was gazing with intent eyes at
me ... her lips parted, her cheeks seemed burning. "What is it?" "Doctor, shall I die?"
"Merciful Heavens!" "No, doctor, no; please don't tell me I shall live ... don't say so.... If
you knew.... Listen! for God's sake don't conceal my real position," and her breath came
so fast. "If I can know for certain that I must die ... then I will tell you all—all!"
"Alexandra Andreevna, I beg!" "Listen; I have not been asleep at all ... I have been
looking at you a long while.... For God's sake! ... I believe in you; you are a good man,
an honest man; I entreat you by all that is sacred in the world—tell me the truth! If you
knew how important it is for me.... Doctor, for God's sake tell me.... Am I in danger?"
"What can I tell you, Alexandra Andreevna, pray?" "For God's sake, I beseech you!" "I
can't disguise from you," I say, "Alexandra Andreevna; you are certainly in danger; but
God is merciful." "I shall die, I shall die." And it seemed as though she were pleased; her
face grew so bright; I was alarmed. "Don't be afraid, don't be afraid! I am not frightened
of death at all." She suddenly sat up and leaned on her elbow. "Now ... yes, now I can
tell you that I thank you with my whole heart ... that you are kind and good—that I love
you!" I stare at her, like one possessed; it was terrible for me, you know. "Do you hear, I
love you!" "Alexandra Andreevna, how have I deserved—" "No, no, you don't—you
don't understand me." ... And suddenly she stretched out her arms, and taking my head in
her hands, she kissed it.... Believe me, I almost screamed aloud.... I threw myself on my
knees, and buried my head in the pillow. She did not speak; her fingers trembled in my
hair; I listen; she is weeping. I began to soothe her, to assure her.... I really don't know
what I did say to her. "You will wake up the girl," I say to her; "Alexandra Andreevna, I
thank you ... believe me ... calm yourself." "Enough, enough!" she persisted; "never
mind all of them; let them wake, then; let them come in—it does not matter; I am dying,

you see.... And what do you fear? why are you afraid? Lift up your head.... Or, perhaps, you don't love me; perhaps I am wrong.... In that case, forgive me." "Alexandra Andreevna, what are you saying!... I love you, Alexandra Andreevna." She looked straight into my eyes, and opened her arms wide. "Then take me in your arms." I tell you frankly, I don't know how it was I did not go mad that night. I feel that my patient is killing herself; I see that she is not fully herself; I understand, too, that if she did not consider herself on the point of death, she would never have thought of me; and, indeed, say what you will, it's hard to die at twenty without having known love; this was what was torturing her; this was why, in despair, she caught at me—do you understand now? But she held me in her arms, and would not let me go. "Have pity on me, Alexandra Andreevna, and have pity on yourself," I say. "Why," she says; "what is there to think of? You know I must die." ... This she repeated incessantly.... "If I knew that I should return to life, and be a proper young lady again, I should be ashamed ... of course, ashamed ... but why now?" "But who has said you will die?" "Oh, no, leave off! you will not deceive me; you don't know how to lie—look at your face." ... "You shall live, Alexandra Andreevna; I will cure you; we will ask your mother's blessing ... we will be united—we will be happy." "No, no, I have your word; I must die ... you have promised me ... you have told me." ... It was cruel for me—cruel for many reasons. And see what trifling things can do sometimes; it seems nothing at all, but it's painful. It occurred to her to ask me, what is my name; not my surname, but my first name. I must needs be so unlucky as to be called Trifon. Yes, indeed; Trifon Ivanitch. Every one in the house called me doctor. However, there's no help for it. I say, "Trifon, madam." She frowned, shook her head, and muttered something in French—ah, something unpleasant, of course!—and then she laughed— disagreeably too. Well, I spent the whole night with her in this way. Before morning I went away, feeling as though I were mad. When I went again into her room it was daytime, after morning tea. Good God! I could scarcely recognise her; people are laid in their grave looking better than that. I swear to you, on my honour, I don't understand—I absolutely don't understand—now, how I lived through that experience. Three days and nights my patient still lingered on. And what nights! What things she said to me! And on the last night—only imagine to yourself—I was sitting near her, and kept praying to God for one thing only: "Take her," I said, "quickly, and me with her." Suddenly the old mother comes unexpectedly into the room. I had already the evening before told her—the mother—there was little hope, and it would be well to send for a priest. When the sick girl saw her mother she said: "It's very well you have come; look at us, we love one another—we have given each other our word." "What does she say, doctor? what does she say?" I turned livid. "She is wandering," I say; "the fever." But she: "Hush, hush; you told me something quite different just now, and have taken my ring. Why do you pretend? My mother is good—she will forgive —she will understand— and I am dying.... I have no need to tell lies; give me your hand." I jumped up and ran out of the room. The old lady, of course, guessed how it was.

'I will not, however, weary you any longer, and to me too, of course, it's painful to recall all this. My patient passed away the next day. God rest her soul!' the doctor added, speaking quickly and with a sigh. 'Before her death she asked her family to go out and leave me alone with her.'

'"Forgive me," she said; "I am perhaps to blame towards you ... my illness ... but believe me, I have loved no one more than you ... do not forget me ... keep my ring."'

The doctor turned away; I took his hand.

'Ah!' he said, 'let us talk of something else, or would you care to play preference for a small stake? It is not for people like me to give way to exalted emotions. There's only one thing for me to think of; how to keep the children from crying and the wife from scolding. Since then, you know, I have had time to enter into lawful wed-lock, as they

27

say.... Oh ... I took a merchant's daughter—seven thousand for her dowry. Her name's Akulina; it goes well with Trifon. She is an ill- tempered woman, I must tell you, but luckily she's asleep all day.... Well, shall it be preference?'

We sat down to preference for halfpenny points. Trifon Ivanitch won two roubles and a half from me, and went home late, well pleased with his success.

V

MY NEIGHBOUR RADILOV

For the autumn, woodcocks often take refuge in old gardens of lime- trees. There are a good many such gardens among us, in the province of Orel. Our forefathers, when they selected a place for habitation, invariably marked out two acres of good ground for a fruit-garden, with avenues of lime-trees. Within the last fifty, or seventy years at most, these mansions—'noblemen's nests,' as they call them—have gradually disappeared off the face of the earth; the houses are falling to pieces, or have been sold for the building materials; the stone outhouses have become piles of rubbish; the apple-trees are dead and turned into firewood, the hedges and fences are pulled up. Only the lime-trees grow in all their glory as before, and with ploughed fields all round them, tell a tale to this light-hearted generation of 'our fathers and brothers who have lived before us.'

A magnificent tree is such an old lime-tree.... Even the merciless axe of the Russian peasant spares it. Its leaves are small, its powerful limbs spread wide in all directions; there is perpetual shade under them.

Once, as I was wandering about the fields after partridges with Yermolaï, I saw some way off a deserted garden, and turned into it. I had hardly crossed its borders when a snipe rose up out of a bush with a clatter. I fired my gun, and at the same instant, a few paces from me, I heard a shriek; the frightened face of a young girl peeped out for a second from behind the trees, and instantly disappeared. Yermolaï ran up to me: 'Why are you shooting here? there is a landowner living here.'

Before I had time to answer him, before my dog had had time to bring me, with dignified importance, the bird I had shot, swift footsteps were heard, and a tall man with moustaches came out of the thicket and stopped, with an air of displeasure, before me. I made my apologies as best I could, gave him my name, and offered him the bird that had been killed on his domains.

'Very well,' he said to me with a smile; 'I will take your game, but only on one condition: that you will stay and dine with us.'

I must confess I was not greatly delighted at his proposition, but it was impossible to refuse.

'I am a landowner here, and your neighbour, Radilov; perhaps you have heard of me?' continued my new acquaintance; 'to-day is Sunday, and we shall be sure to have a decent dinner, otherwise I would not have invited you.'

I made such a reply as one does make in such circumstances, and turned to follow him. A little path that had lately been cleared soon led us out of the grove of lime-trees; we came into the kitchen-garden. Between the old apple-trees and gooseberry bushes were rows of curly whitish-green cabbages; the hop twined its tendrils round high poles; there were thick ranks of brown twigs tangled over with dried peas; large flat pumpkins seemed rolling on the ground; cucumbers showed yellow under their dusty angular leaves; tall nettles were waving along the hedge; in two or three places grew clumps of tartar honeysuckle, elder, and wild rose—the remnants of former flower-beds. Near a small fish-pond, full of reddish and slimy water, we saw the well, surrounded by puddles. Ducks were busily splashing and waddling about these puddles; a dog blinking and twitching in every limb was gnawing a bone in the meadow, where a piebald cow was lazily chewing the grass, from time to time flicking its tail over its lean back. The little path turned to one side; from behind thick willows and birches we caught sight of a little grey old house, with a boarded roof and a winding flight of steps. Radilov stopped short.

'But,' he said, with a good-humoured and direct look in my face,' on second thoughts ... perhaps you don't care to come and see me, after all.... In that case—'

I did not allow him to finish, but assured him that, on the contrary, it would be a great pleasure to me to dine with him.

'Well, you know best.'

We went into the house. A young man in a long coat of stout blue cloth met us on the steps. Radilov at once told him to bring Yermolaï some vodka; my huntsman made a respectful bow to the back of the munificent host. From the hall, which was decorated with various parti-coloured pictures and check curtains, we went into a small room—Radilov's study. I took off my hunting accoutrements, and put my gun in a corner; the young man in the long-skirted coat busily brushed me down.

'Well, now, let us go into the drawing-room.' said Radilov cordially.
'I will make you acquainted with my mother.'

I walked after him. In the drawing-room, in the sofa in the centre of the room, was sitting an old lady of medium height, in a cinnamon- coloured dress and a white cap, with a thinnish, kind old face, and a timid, mournful expression.

'Here, mother, let me introduce to you our neighbour....'

The old lady got up and made me a bow, not letting go out of her withered hands a fat worsted reticule that looked like a sack.

'Have you been long in our neighbourhood?' she asked, in a weak and gentle voice, blinking her eyes.

'No, not long.'

'Do you intend to remain here long?'

'Till the winter, I think.'

The old lady said no more.

'And here,' interposed Radilov, indicating to me a tall and thin man, whom I had not noticed on entering the drawing-room, 'is Fyodor Miheitch. ... Come, Fedya, give the visitor a specimen of your art. Why have you hidden yourself away in that corner?'

Fyodor Miheitch got up at once from his chair, fetched a wretched little fiddle from the window, took the bow—not by the end, as is usual, but by the middle—put the fiddle to his chest, shut his eyes, and fell to dancing, singing a song, and scraping on the strings. He looked about seventy; a thin nankin overcoat flapped pathetically about his dry and bony limbs. He danced, at times skipping boldly, and then dropping his little bald head with his scraggy neck stretched out as if he were dying, stamping his feet on the ground, and sometimes bending his knees with obvious difficulty. A voice cracked with age came from his toothless mouth.

Radilov must have guessed from the expression of my face that Fedya's 'art' did not give me much pleasure.

'Very good, old man, that's enough,' he said. 'You can go and refresh yourself.'

Fyodor Miheitch at once laid down the fiddle on the window-sill, bowed first to me as the guest, then to the old lady, then to Radilov, and went away.

'He too was a landowner,' my new friend continued, 'and a rich one too, but he ruined himself—so he lives now with me.... But in his day he was considered the most dashing fellow in the province; he eloped with two married ladies; he used to keep singers, and sang himself, and danced like a master.... But won't you take some vodka? dinner is just ready.'

A young girl, the same that I had caught a glimpse of in the garden, came into the room.

'And here is Olga!' observed Radilov, slightly turning his head; 'let me present you.... Well, let us go into dinner.'

We went in and sat down to the table. While we were coming out of the drawing-room and taking our seats, Fyodor Miheitch, whose eyes were bright and his nose rather red after his 'refreshment,' sang 'Raise the cry of Victory.' They laid a separate cover for him in a corner on a little table without a table-napkin. The poor old man could not boast of very nice habits, and so they always kept him at some distance from society. He crossed himself, sighed, and began to eat like a shark. The dinner was in reality not bad, and in honour of Sunday was accompanied, of course, with shaking jelly and Spanish puffs of pastry. At the table Radilov, who had served ten years in an infantry regiment and had been in Turkey, fell to telling anecdotes; I listened to him with attention, and secretly watched Olga. She was not very pretty; but the tranquil and resolute expression of her face, her broad, white brow, her thick hair, and especially her brown eyes—not large, but clear, sensible and lively—would have made an impression on anyone in my place. She seemed to be following every word Radilov uttered—not so much sympathy as passionate attention was expressed on her face. Radilov in years might have been her father; he called her by her Christian name, but I guessed at once that she was not his daughter. In the course of conversation he referred to his deceased wife—'her sister,' he added, indicating Olga. She blushed quickly and dropped her eyes. Radilov paused a moment and then changed the subject. The old lady did not utter a word during the whole of dinner; she ate scarcely anything herself, and did not press me to partake. Her features had an air of timorous and hopeless expectation, that melancholy of old age which it pierces one's heart to look upon. At the end of dinner Fyodor Miheitch was beginning to 'celebrate' the hosts and guests, but Radilov looked at me and asked him to be quiet; the old man passed his hand over his lips, began to blink, bowed, and sat down again, but only on the very edge of his chair. After dinner I returned with Radilov to his study.

In people who are constantly and intensely preoccupied with one idea, or one emotion, there is something in common, a kind of external resemblance in manner, however different may be their qualities, their abilities, their position in society, and their education. The more I watched Radilov, the more I felt that he belonged to the class of such people. He talked of husbandry, of the crops, of the war, of the gossip of the district and the approaching elections; he talked without constraint, and even with interest; but suddenly he would sigh and drop into a chair, and pass his hand over his face, like a man wearied out by a tedious task. His whole nature—a good and warm-hearted one too—seemed saturated through, steeped in some one feeling. I was amazed by the fact that I could not discover in him either a passion for eating, nor for wine, nor for sport, nor for Kursk nightingales, nor for epileptic pigeons, nor for Russian literature, nor for trotting-hacks, nor for Hungarian coats, nor for cards, nor billiards, nor for dances, nor trips to the provincial town or the capital, nor for paper- factories and beet-sugar refineries, nor for painted pavilions, nor for tea, nor for trace-horses trained to hold their heads askew, nor even for fat coachmen belted under their very armpits—those magnificent coachmen whose eyes, for some mysterious reason, seem rolling and starting out of their heads at every movement.... 'What sort of landowner is this, then?' I thought. At the same time he did not in the least pose as a gloomy man discontented with his destiny; on the contrary, he seemed full of indiscrimating good-will, cordial and even offensive readiness to become intimate with every one he came across. In reality you felt at the same time that he could not be friends, nor be really intimate with anyone, and that he could not be so, not because in general he was independent of other people, but because his whole being was for a time turned inwards upon himself. Looking at Radilov, I could never imagine him happy either now or at any time. He, too, was not handsome; but in his eyes, his smile, his whole being, there was a something, mysterious and extremely attractive—yes, mysterious is just what it was. So that you felt you would like to know him better, to get to love him. Of course, at times the landowner and the man of the steppes peeped out in him; but all the same he was a capital fellow.

We were beginning to talk about the new marshal of the district, when suddenly we heard Olga's voice at the door: 'Tea is ready.' We went into the drawing-room. Fyodor Miheitch was sitting as before in his corner between the little window and the door, his legs curled up under him. Radilov's mother was knitting a stocking. From the opened windows came a breath of autumn freshness and the scent of apples. Olga was busy pouring out tea. I looked at her now with more attention than at dinner. Like provincial girls as a rule, she spoke very little, but at any rate I did not notice in her any of their anxiety to say something fine, together with their painful consciousness of stupidity and helplessness; she did not sigh as though from the burden of unutterable emotions, nor cast up her eyes, nor smile vaguely and dreamily. Her look expressed tranquil self-possession, like a man who is taking breath after great happiness or great excitement. Her carriage and her movements were resolute and free. I liked her very much.

I fell again into conversation with Radilov. I don't recollect what brought us to the familiar observation that often the most insignificant things produce more effect on people than the most important.

'Yes,' Radilov agreed, 'I have experienced that in my own case. I, as you know, have been married. It was not for long—three years; my wife died in child-birth. I thought that I should not survive her; I was fearfully miserable, broken down, but I could not weep—I wandered about like one possessed. They decked her out, as they always do, and laid her on a table—in this very room. The priest came, the deacons came, began to sing, to pray, and to burn incense; I bowed to the ground, and hardly shed a tear. My heart seemed turned to stone—and my head too—I was heavy all over. So passed my first day. Would you believe it? I even slept in the night. The next morning I went in to look at my wife: it was summer-time, the sunshine fell upon her from head to foot, and it was so bright. Suddenly I saw ...' (here Radilov gave an involuntary shudder) 'what do you think? One of her eyes was not quite shut, and on this eye a fly was moving.... I fell down in a heap, and when I came to myself, I began to weep and weep ... I could not stop myself....'

Radilov was silent. I looked at him, then at Olga.... I can never forget the expression of her face. The old lady had laid the stocking down on her knees, and taken a handkerchief out of her reticule; she was stealthily wiping away her tears. Fyodor Miheitch suddenly got up, seized his fiddle, and in a wild and hoarse voice began to sing a song. He wanted doubtless to restore our spirits; but we all shuddered at his first note, and Radilov asked him to be quiet.

'Still what is past, is past,' he continued; 'we cannot recall the past, and in the end ... all is for the best in this world below, as I think Voltaire said,' he added hurriedly.

'Yes,' I replied, 'of course. Besides, every trouble can be endured, and there is no position so terrible that there is no escape from it.'

'Do you think so?' said Radilov. 'Well, perhaps you are right. I recollect I lay once in the hospital in Turkey half dead; I had typhus fever. Well, our quarters were nothing to boast of—of course, in time of war—and we had to thank God for what we had! Suddenly they bring in more sick—where are they to put them? The doctor goes here and there— there is no room left. So he comes up to me and asks the attendant, "Is he alive?" He answers, "He was alive this morning." The doctor bends down, listens; I am breathing. The good man could not help saying, "Well, what an absurd constitution; the man's dying; he's certain to die, and he keeps hanging on, lingering, taking up space for nothing, and keeping out others." Well, I thought to myself, "So you are in a bad way, Mihal Mihalitch...." And, after all, I got well, and am alive till now, as you may see for yourself. You are right, to be sure.'

'In any case I am right,' I replied; 'even if you had died, you would just the same have escaped from your horrible position.'

'Of course, of course,' he added, with a violent blow of his fist on the table. 'One has only to come to a decision.... What is the use of being in a horrible position?... What is the good of delaying, lingering.'

Olga rose quickly and went out into the garden.

'Well, Fedya, a dance!' cried Radilov.

Fedya jumped up and walked about the room with that artificial and peculiar motion which is affected by the man who plays the part of a goat with a tame bear. He sang meanwhile, 'While at our Gates....'

The rattle of a racing droshky sounded in the drive, and in a few minutes a tall, broad-shouldered and stoutly made man, the peasant proprietor, Ovsyanikov, came into the room.

But Ovsyanikov is such a remarkable and original personage that, with the reader's permission, we will put off speaking about him till the next sketch. And now I will only add for myself that the next day I started off hunting at earliest dawn with Yermolaï, and returned home after the day's sport was over ... that a week later I went again to Radilov's, but did not find him or Olga at home, and within a fortnight I learned that he had suddenly disappeared, left his mother, and gone away somewhere with his sister-in-law. The whole province was excited, and talked about this event, and I only then completely understood the expression of Olga's face while Radilov was telling us his story. It was breathing, not with sympathetic suffering only: it was burning with jealousy.

Before leaving the country I called on old Madame Radilov. I found her in the drawing-room; she was playing cards with Fyodor Miheitch.

'Have you news of your son?' I asked her at last.

The old lady began to weep. I made no more inquiries about Radilov.

VI

THE PEASANT PROPRIETOR OVSYANIKOV

Picture to yourselves, gentle readers, a stout, tall man of seventy, with a face reminding one somewhat of the face of Kriloff, clear and intelligent eyes under overhanging brows, dignified in bearing, slow in speech, and deliberate in movement: there you have Ovsyanikov. He wore an ample blue overcoat with long sleeves, buttoned all the way up, a lilac silk-handkerchief round his neck, brightly polished boots with tassels, and altogether resembled in appearance a well-to-do merchant. His hands were handsome, soft, and white; he often fumbled with the buttons of his coat as he talked. With his dignity and his composure, his good sense and his indolence, his uprightness and his obstinacy, Ovsyanikov reminded me of the Russian boyars of the times before Peter the Great.... The national holiday dress would have suited him well. He was one of the last men left of the old time. All his neighbours had a great respect for him, and considered it an honour to be acquainted with him. His fellow peasant-proprietors almost worshipped him, and took off their hats to him from a distance: they were proud of him. Generally speaking, in these days, it is difficult to tell a peasant- proprietor from a peasant; his husbandry is almost worse than the peasant's; his calves are wretchedly small; his horses are only half alive; his harness is made of rope. Ovsyanikov was an exception to the general rule, though he did not pass for a wealthy man. He lived alone with his wife in a clean and comfortable little house, kept a few servants, whom he dressed in the Russian style and called his 'workmen.' They were employed also in ploughing his land. He did not attempt to pass for a nobleman, did not affect to be a landowner; never, as they say, forgot himself; he did not take a seat at the first invitation to do so, and he never failed to rise from his seat on the entrance of a new guest, but with such dignity, with such stately courtesy, that the guest involuntarily made him a more deferential bow. Ovsyanikov adhered to the antique usages, not from superstition (he was naturally rather independent in mind), but from habit. He did not, for instance, like carriages with springs, because he did not find them comfortable, and preferred to drive in a racing droshky, or in a pretty little trap with leather cushions, and he always drove his good bay himself (he kept none but bay horses). His coachman, a young, rosy- cheeked fellow, his hair cut round like a basin, in a dark blue coat with a strap round the waist, sat respectfully beside him. Ovsyanikov always had a nap after dinner and visited the bath-house on Saturdays; he read none but religious books and used gravely to fix his round silver spectacles on his nose when he did so; he got up, and went to bed early. He shaved his beard, however, and wore his hair in the German style. He always received visitors cordially and affably, but he did not bow down to the ground, nor fuss over them and press them to partake of every kind of dried and salted delicacy. 'Wife!' he would say deliberately, not getting up from his seat, but only turning his head a little in her direction, 'bring the gentleman a little of something to eat.' He regarded it as a sin to sell wheat: it was the gift of God. In the year '40, at the time of the general famine and terrible scarcity, he shared all his store with the surrounding landowners and peasants; the following year they gratefully repaid their debt to him in kind. The neighbours often had recourse to Ovsyanikov as arbitrator and mediator between them, and they almost always acquiesced in his decision, and listened to his advice. Thanks to his intervention, many had conclusively settled their boundaries.... But after two or three tussles with lady-landowners, he announced that he declined all mediation between persons of the feminine gender. He could not bear the flurry and excitement, the chatter of women and the 'fuss.' Once his house had somehow got on fire. A workman ran to him in headlong haste shrieking, 'Fire, fire!' 'Well, what are you screaming about?' said Ovsyanikov tranquilly, 'give me my cap and my stick.' He liked to break in his horses himself. Once a spirited horse he was training bolted with him down a hillside and over a precipice. 'Come, there, there, you young colt, you'll kill yourself!' said Ovsyanikov soothingly to him, and an instant later he flew over the precipice together with the racing droshky, the boy who was sitting behind, and the horse. Fortunately, the bottom of the ravine was covered with heaps of sand. No one was injured; only the horse sprained a leg. 'Well, you see,' continued Ovsyanikov in a calm voice as he got up from the ground, 'I told you so.' He had found a wife to match him. Tatyana Ilyinitchna Ovsyanikov was a tall woman, dignified and taciturn, always dressed in a cinnamon-coloured silk dress. She had a cold air, though none complained of her severity, but, on the contrary, many poor creatures called her their little mother and benefactress. Her regular features, her large dark eyes, and her delicately cut lips, bore witness even now to her once celebrated beauty. Ovsyanikov had no children.

I made his acquaintance, as the reader is already aware, at Radilov's, and two days later I went to see him. I found him at home. He was reading the lives of the Saints. A grey cat was purring on his shoulder. He received me, according to his habit, with stately cordiality. We fell into conversation.

'But tell me the truth, Luka Petrovitch,' I said to him, among other things; 'weren't things better of old, in your time?'

'In some ways, certainly, things were better, I should say,' replied Ovsyanikov; 'we lived more easily; there was a greater abundance of everything. ... All the same, things are better now, and they will be better still for your children, please God.'

'I had expected you, Luka Petrovitch, to praise the old times.'

'No, I have no special reason to praise old times. Here, for instance, though you are a landowner now, and just as much a landowner as your grandfather was, you have not the same power—and, indeed, you are not yourself the same kind of man. Even now, some noblemen oppress us; but, of course, it is impossible to help that altogether. Where there are mills grinding there will be flour. No; I don't see now what I have experienced myself in my youth.'

'What, for instance?'

'Well, for instance, I will tell you about your grandfather. He was an overbearing man; he oppressed us poorer folks. You know, perhaps— indeed, you surely know your own estates—that bit of land that runs from Tchepligin to Malinina—you have it under oats now.... Well, you know, it is ours—it is all ours. Your grandfather took it away from us; he rode by on his horse, pointed to it with his hand, and said, "It's my property," and took possession of it. My father (God rest his soul!) was a just man; he was a hot-tempered man, too; he would not put up with it—indeed, who does like to lose his property?—and he laid a petition before the court. But he was alone: the others did not appear —they were afraid. So they reported to your grandfather that "Piotr Ovsyanikov is making a complaint against you that you were pleased to take away his land." Your grandfather at once sent his huntsman Baush with a detachment of men.... Well, they seized my father, and carried him to your estate. I was a little boy at that time; I ran after him barefoot. What happened? They brought him to your house, and flogged him right under your windows. And your grandfather stands on the balcony and looks on; and your grandmother sits at the window and looks on too. My father cries out, "Gracious lady, Marya Vasilyevna, intercede for me! have mercy on me!" But her only answer was to keep getting up to have a look at him. So they exacted a promise from my father to give up the land, and bade him be thankful they let him go alive. So it has remained with you. Go and ask your peasants—what do they call the land, indeed? It's called "The Cudgelled Land," because it was gained by the cudgel. So you see from that, we poor folks can't bewail the old order very much.'

I did not know what answer to make Ovsyanikov, and I had not the courage to look him in the face.

'We had another neighbour who settled amongst us in those days, Komov, Stepan Niktopolionitch. He used to worry my father out of his life; when it wasn't one thing, it was another. He was a drunken fellow, and fond of treating others; and when he was drunk he would say in French, "*Say bon*," and "Take away the holy images!" He would go to all the neighbours to ask them to come to him. His horses stood always in readiness, and if you wouldn't go he would come after you himself at once!... And he was such a strange fellow! In his sober times he was not a liar; but when he was drunk he would begin to relate how he had three houses in Petersburg—one red, with one chimney; another yellow, with two chimneys; and a third blue, with no chimneys; and three sons (though he had never even been married), one in the infantry, another in the cavalry, and the third was his own master.... And he would say that in each house lived one of his sons; that admirals visited the eldest, and generals the second, and the third only Englishmen! Then he would get up and say, "To the health of my eldest son; he is the most dutiful!" and he would begin to weep. Woe to anyone who refused to drink the toast! "I will shoot him!" he would say; "and I won't let him be buried!" ... Then he would jump up and scream, "Dance, God's people, for your pleasure and my diversion!" Well, then, you must dance; if you had to die for it, you must dance. He thoroughly worried his serf-girls to death. Sometimes all night long till morning they would be singing in chorus, and the one who made the most noise would have a prize. If they began to be tired, he would lay his head down in his hands, and begins moaning: "Ah, poor forsaken orphan that I am! They abandon me, poor little dove!" And the stable-boys would wake the girls up at once. He took a liking to my father; what was he to do? He almost drove my father into his grave, and would actually have driven him into it, but (thank Heaven!) he died himself; in one of his drunken fits he fell off the pigeon-house. … There, that's what our sweet little neighbours were like!'

'How the times have changed!' I observed.

'Yes, yes,' Ovsyanikov assented. 'And there is this to be said—in the old days the nobility lived more sumptuously. I'm not speaking of the real grandees now. I used to see them in Moscow. They say such people are scarce nowadays.'

'Have you been in Moscow?'

'I used to stay there long, very long ago. I am now in my seventy-third year; and I went to Moscow when I was sixteen.'

Ovsyanikov sighed.

'Whom did you see there?'

'I saw a great many grandees—and every one saw them; they kept open house for the wonder and admiration of all! Only no one came up to Count Alexey Grigoryevitch Orlov-Tchesmensky. I often saw Alexey Grigoryevitch; my uncle was a steward in his service. The count was pleased to live in Shabolovka, near the Kaluga Gate. He was a grand gentleman! Such stateliness, such gracious condescension you can't imagine! and it's impossible to describe it. His figure alone was worth something, and his strength, and the look in his eyes! Till you knew him, you did not dare come near him—you were afraid, overawed indeed; but directly you came near him he was like sunshine warming you up and making you quite cheerful. He allowed every man access to him in person, and he was devoted to every kind of sport. He drove himself in races and out-stripped every one, and he would never get in front at the start, so as not to offend his adversary; he would not cut it short, but would pass him at the finish; and he was so pleasant—he would soothe his adversary, praising his horse. He kept tumbler-pigeons of a first-rate kind. He would come out into the court, sit down in an arm-chair, and order them to let loose the pigeons; and his men would stand all round on the roofs with guns to keep off the hawks. A large silver basin of water used to be placed at the count's feet, and he looked at the pigeons reflected in the water. Beggars and poor people were fed in hundreds at his expense; and what a lot of money he used to give away!… When he got angry, it was like a clap of thunder. Everyone was in a great fright, but there was nothing to weep over; look round a minute after, and he was all smiles again! When he gave a banquet he made all Moscow drunk!—and see what a clever man he was! you know he beat the Turk. He was fond of wrestling too; strong men used to come from Tula, from Harkoff, from Tamboff, and from everywhere to him. If he threw any one he would pay him a reward; but if any one threw him, he perfectly loaded him with presents, and kissed him on the lips…. And once, during my stay at Moscow, he arranged a hunting party such as had never been in Russia before; he sent invitations to all the sportsmen in the whole empire, and fixed a day for it, and gave them three months' notice. They brought with them dogs and grooms: well, it was an army of people—a regular army!

'First they had a banquet in the usual way, and then they set off into the open country. The people flocked there in thousands! And what do you think?… Your father's dog outran them all.'

'Wasn't that Milovidka?' I inquired.

'Milovidka, Milovidka!… So the count began to ask him, "Give me your dog," says he; "take what you like for her." "No, count," he said, "I am not a tradesman; I don't sell anything for filthy lucre; for your sake I am ready to part with my wife even, but not with Milovidka…. I would give myself into bondage first." And Alexey Grigoryevitch praised him for it. "I like you for it," he said. Your grandfather took her back in the coach with him, and when Milovidka died, he buried her in the garden with music at the burial—yes, a funeral for a dog—and put a stone with an inscription on it over the dog.'

'Then Alexey Grigoryevitch did not oppress anyone,' I observed.

'Yes, it is always like that; those who can only just keep themselves afloat are the ones to drag others under.'

'And what sort of a man was this Baush?' I asked after a short silence.

'Why, how comes it you have heard about Milovidka, and not about Baush? He was your grandfather's chief huntsman and whipper-in. Your grandfather was as fond of him as of Milovidka. He was a desperate fellow, and whatever order your grandfather gave him, he would carry it out in a minute—he'd have run on to a sword at his bidding.... And when he hallooed ... it was something like a tally-ho in the forest. And then he would suddenly turn nasty, get off his horse, and lie down on the ground ... and directly the dogs ceased to hear his voice, it was all over! They would give up the hottest scent, and wouldn't go on for anything. Ay, ay, your grandfather did get angry! "Damn me, if I don't hang the scoundrel! I'll turn him inside out, the antichrist! I'll stuff his heels down his gullet, the cut-throat!" And it ended by his going up to find out what he wanted; why he wouldn't halloo to the hounds? Usually, on such occasions, Baush asked for some vodka, drank it up, got on his horse, and began to halloo as lustily as ever again.'

'You seem to be fond of hunting too, Luka Petrovitch?'

'I should have been—certainly, not now; now my time is over—but in my young days.... But you know it was not an easy matter in my position. It's not suitable for people like us to go trailing after noblemen. Certainly you may find in our class some drinking, good-for-nothing fellow who associates with the gentry—but it's a queer sort of enjoyment.... He only brings shame on himself. They mount him on a wretched stumbling nag, keep knocking his hat off on to the ground and cut at him with a whip, pretending to whip the horse, and he must laugh at everything, and be a laughing-stock for the others. No, I tell you, the lower your station, the more reserved must be your behaviour, or else you disgrace yourself directly.'

'Yes,' continued Ovsyanikov with a sigh, 'there's many a gallon of water has flowed down to the sea since I have been living in the world; times are different now. Especially I see a great change in the nobility. The smaller landowners have all either become officials, or at any rate do not stop here; as for the larger owners, there's no making them out. I have had experience of them—the larger landowners— in cases of settling boundaries. And I must tell you; it does my heart good to see them: they are courteous and affable. Only this is what astonishes me; they have studied all the sciences, they speak so fluently that your heart is melted, but they don't understand the actual business in hand; they don't even perceive what's their own interest; some bailiff, a bondservant, drives them just where he pleases, as though they were in a yoke. There's Korolyov—Alexandr Vladimirovitch—for instance; you know him, perhaps—isn't he every inch a nobleman? He is handsome, rich, has studied at the 'versities, and travelled, I think, abroad; he speaks simply and easily, and shakes hands with us all. You know him?... Well, listen then. Last week we assembled at Beryozovka at the summons of the mediator, Nikifor Ilitch. And the mediator, Nikifor Ilitch, says to us: "Gentlemen, we must settle the boundaries; it's disgraceful; our district is behind all the others; we must get to work." Well, so we got to work. There followed discussions, disputes, as usual; our attorney began to make objections. But the first to make an uproar was Porfiry Ovtchinnikov.... And what had the fellow to make an uproar about?... He hasn't an acre of ground; he is acting as representative of his brother. He bawls: "No, you shall not impose on me! no, you shan't drive me to that! give the plans here! give me the surveyor's plans, the Judas's plans here!" "But what is your claim, then?" "Oh, you think I'm a fool!

Indeed! do you suppose I am going to lay bare my claim to you offhand? No, let me have the plans here—that's what I want!" And he himself is banging his fist on the plans all the time. Then he mortally offended Marfa Dmitrievna. She shrieks out, "How dare you asperse my reputation?" "Your reputation," says he; "I shouldn't like my chestnut mare to have your reputation." They poured him out some Madeira at last, and so quieted him; then others begin to make a row. Alexandr Vladimirovitch Korolyov, the dear fellow, sat in a corner sucking the knob of his cane, and only shook his head. I felt ashamed; I could hardly sit it out. "What must he be thinking of us?" I said to myself. When, behold! Alexandr Vladimirovitch has got up, and shows signs of wanting to speak. The mediator exerts himself, says, "Gentlemen, gentlemen, Alexandr Vladimirovitch wishes to speak." And I must do them this credit; they were all silent at once. And so Alexandr Vladimirovitch began and said "that we seemed to have forgotten what we had come together for; that, indeed, the fixing of boundaries was indisputably advantageous for owners of land, but actually what was its object? To make things easier for the peasant, so that he could work and pay his dues more conveniently; that now the peasant hardly knows his own land, and often goes to work five miles away; and one can't expect too much of him." Then Alexandr Vladimirovitch said "that it was disgraceful in a landowner not to interest himself in the well-being of his peasants; that in the end, if you look at it rightly, their interests and our interests are inseparable; if they are well-off we are well-off, and if they do badly we do badly, and that, consequently, it was injudicious and wrong to disagree over trifles" … and so on—and so on…. There, how he did speak! He seemed to go right to your heart…. All the gentry hung their heads; I myself, faith, it nearly brought me to tears. To tell the truth, you would not find sayings like that in the old books even…. But what was the end of it? He himself would not give up four acres of peat marsh, and wasn't willing to sell it. He said, "I am going to drain that marsh for my people, and set up a cloth-factory on it, with all the latest improvements. I have already," he said, "fixed on that place; I have thought out my plans on the subject." And if only that had been the truth, it would be all very well; but the simple fact is, Alexandr Vladimirovitch's neighbour, Anton Karasikov, had refused to buy over Korolyov's bailiff for a hundred roubles. And so we separated without having done anything. But Alexandr Vladimirovitch considers to this day that he is right, and still talks of the cloth-factory; but he does not start draining the marsh.'

'And how does he manage in his estate?'

'He is always introducing new ways. The peasants don't speak well of him—but it's useless to listen to them. Alexandr Vladimirovitch is doing right.'

'How's that, Luka Petrovitch? I thought you kept to the old ways.'

'I—that's another thing. You see I am not a nobleman or a landowner. What sort of management is mine?… Besides, I don't know how to do things differently. I try to act according to justice and the law, and leave the rest in God's hands! Young gentlemen don't like the old method; I think they are right…. It's the time to take in ideas. Only this is the pity of it; the young are too theoretical. They treat the peasant like a doll; they turn him this way and that way; twist him about and throw him away. And their bailiff, a serf, or some overseer from the German natives, gets the peasant under his thumb again. Now, if any one of the young gentlemen would set us an example, would show us, "See, this is how you ought to manage!" … What will be the end of it? Can it be that I shall die without seeing the new methods?… What is the proverb?—the old is dead, but the young is not born!'

I did not know what reply to make to Ovsyanikov. He looked round, drew himself nearer to me, and went on in an undertone:

'Have you heard talk of Vassily Nikolaitch Lubozvonov?'

'No, I haven't.'

'Explain to me, please, what sort of strange creature he is. I can't make anything of it. His peasants have described him, but I can't make any sense of their tales. He is a young man, you know; it's not long since he received his heritage from his mother. Well, he arrived at his estate. The peasants were all collected to stare at their master. Vassily Nikolaitch came out to them. The peasants looked at him— strange to relate! the master wore plush pantaloons like a coachman, and he had on boots with trimming at the top; he wore a red shirt and a coachman's long coat too; he had let his beard grow, and had such a strange hat and such a strange face—could he be drunk? No, he wasn't drunk, and yet he didn't seem quite right. "Good health to you, lads!" he says; "God keep you!" The peasants bow to the ground, but without speaking; they began to feel frightened, you know. And he too seemed timid. He began to make a speech to them: "I am a Russian," he says, "and you are Russians; I like everything Russian…. Russia," says he, "is my heart, and my blood too is Russian"…. Then he suddenly gives the order: "Come, lads, sing a Russian national song!" The peasants' legs shook under them with fright; they were utterly stupefied. One bold spirit did begin to sing, but he sat down at once on the ground and hid himself behind the others…. And what is so surprising is this: we have had landowners like that, dare-devil gentlemen, regular rakes, of course: they dressed pretty much like coachmen, and danced themselves and played on the guitar, and sang and drank with their house-serfs and feasted with the peasants; but this Vassily Nikolaitch is like a girl; he is always reading books or writing, or else declaiming poetry aloud—he never addresses any one; he is shy, walks by himself in his garden; seems either bored or sad. The old bailiff at first was in a thorough scare; before Vassily Nikolaitch's arrival he was afraid to go near the peasants' houses; he bowed to all of them— one could see the cat knew whose butter he had eaten! And the peasants were full of hope; they thought, 'Fiddlesticks, my friend!—now they'll make you answer for it, my dear; they'll lead you a dance now, you robber!' … But instead of this it has turned out—how shall I explain it to you?—God Almighty could not account for how things have turned out! Vassily Nikolaitch summoned him to his presence and says, blushing himself and breathing quick, you know: "Be upright in my service; don't oppress any one—do you hear?" And since that day he has never asked to see him in person again! He lives on his own property like a stranger. Well, the bailiff's been enjoying himself, and the peasants don't dare to go to Vassily Nikolaitch; they are afraid. And do you see what's a matter for wonder again; the master even bows to them and looks graciously at them; but he seems to turn their stomachs with fright! 'What do you say to such a strange state of things, your honour? Either I have grown stupid in my old age, or something…. I can't understand it.'

I said to Ovsyanikov that Mr. Lubozvonov must certainly be ill.

'Ill, indeed! He's as broad as he's long, and a face like this—God bless him!—and bearded, though he is so young…. Well, God knows!' And Ovsyanikov gave a deep sigh.

'Come, putting the nobles aside,' I began, 'what have you to tell me about the peasant proprietors, Luka Petrovitch?'

'No, you must let me off that,' he said hurriedly. 'Truly…. I could tell you … but what's the use!' (with a wave of his hand). 'We had better have some tea…. We are common peasants and nothing more; but when we come to think of it, what else could we be?'

He ceased talking. Tea was served. Tatyana Ilyinitchna rose from her place and sat down rather nearer to us. In the course of the evening she several times went noiselessly out and as quietly returned. Silence reigned in the room. Ovsyanikov drank cup after cup with gravity and deliberation.

'Mitya has been to see us to-day,' said Tatyana Ilyinitchna in a low voice.

Ovsyanikov frowned.

'What does he want?'

'He came to ask forgiveness.'

Ovsyanikov shook his head.

'Come, tell me,' he went on, turning to me, 'what is one to do with relations? And to abandon them altogether is impossible.... Here God has bestowed on me a nephew. He's a fellow with brains—a smart fellow —I don't dispute that; he has had a good education, but I don't expect much good to come of him. He went into a government office; threw up his position—didn't get on fast enough, if you please.... Does he suppose he's a noble? And even noblemen don't come to be generals all at once. So now he is living without an occupation.... And that, even, would not be such a great matter—except that he has taken to litigation! He gets up petitions for the peasants, writes memorials; he instructs the village delegates, drags the surveyors over the coals, frequents drinking houses, is seen in taverns with city tradesmen and inn-keepers. He's bound to come to ruin before long. The constables and police-captains have threatened him more than once already. But he luckily knows how to turn it off—he makes them laugh; but they will boil his kettle for him some day.... But, there, isn't he sitting in your little room?' he added, turning to his wife; 'I know you, you see; you're so soft-hearted—you will always take his part.'

Tatyana Ilyinitchna dropped her eyes, smiled, and blushed.

'Well, I see it is so,' continued Ovsyanikov. 'Fie! you spoil the boy! Well, tell him to come in.... So be it, then; for the sake of our good guest I will forgive the silly fellow.... Come, tell him, tell him.'

Tatyana Ilyinitchna went to the door, and cried 'Mitya!'

Mitya, a young man of twenty-eight, tall, well-made, and curly-headed, came into the room, and seeing me, stopped short in the doorway. His costume was in the German style, but the unnatural size of the puffs on his shoulders was enough alone to prove convincingly that the tailor who had cut it was a Russian of the Russians.

'Well, come in, come in,' began the old man; 'why are you bashful? You must thank your aunt—you're forgiven.... Here, your honour, I commend him to you,' he continued, pointing to Mitya; 'he's my own nephew, but I don't get on with him at all. The end of the world is coming!' (We bowed to one another.) 'Well, tell me what is this you have got mixed up in? What is the complaint they are making against you? Explain it to us.'

Mitya obviously did not care to explain matters and justify himself before me.

'Later on, uncle,' he muttered.

'No, not later—now,' pursued the old man.... 'You are ashamed, I see, before this gentleman; all the better—it's only what you deserve. Speak, speak; we are listening.'

'I have nothing to be ashamed of,' began Mitya spiritedly, with a toss of his head. 'Be so good as to judge for yourself, uncle. Some peasant proprietors of Reshetilovo came to me, and said, "Defend us, brother." "What is the matter?"' "This is it: our grain stores were in perfect order—in fact, they could not be better; all at once a government inspector came to us with orders to inspect the granaries. He inspected them, and said, 'Your granaries are in disorder—serious neglect; it's my duty to report it to the authorities.' 'But what does the neglect consist in?' 'That's my business,' he says.... We met together, and decided to tip the official in the usual way; but old Prohoritch prevented us. He said, 'No; that's only giving him a taste for more. Come; after all, haven't we the courts of justice?' We obeyed the old man, and the official got in a rage, and made a complaint, and wrote a report. So now we are called up to answer to his charges." "But are your granaries actually in order?" I asked. "God knows they are in order; and the legal quantity of corn is in them." "Well, then," say I, "you have nothing to fear"; and I drew up a document for them.... And it is not yet known in whose favour it is decided.... And as to the complaints they have made to you about me over that affair—it's very easy to understand that—every man's shirt is nearest to his own skin.

'Everyone's, indeed—but not yours seemingly,' said the old man in an undertone. 'But what plots have you been hatching with the Shutolomovsky peasants?'

'How do you know anything of it?'

'Never mind; I do know of it.'

'And there, too, I am right—judge for yourself again. A neighbouring landowner, Bezpandin, has ploughed over four acres of the Shutolomovsky peasants' land. "The land's mine," he says. The Shutolomovsky people are on the rent-system; their landowner has gone abroad—who is to stand up for them? Tell me yourself? But the land is theirs beyond dispute; they've been bound to it for ages and ages. So they came to me, and said, "Write us a petition." So I wrote one. And Bezpandin heard of it, and began to threaten me. "I'll break every bone in that Mitya's body, and knock his head off his shoulders...." We shall see how he will knock it off; it's still on, so far.'

'Come, don't boast; it's in a bad way, your head,' said the old man. 'You are a mad fellow altogether!'

'Why, uncle, what did you tell me yourself?'

'I know, I know what you will say,' Ovsyanikov interrupted him; 'of course a man ought to live uprightly, and he is bound to succour his neighbour. Sometimes one must not spare oneself.... But do you always behave in that way? Don't they take you to the tavern, eh? Don't they treat you; bow to you, eh? "Dmitri Alexyitch," they say, "help us, and we will prove our gratitude to you." And they slip a silver rouble or note into your hand. Eh? doesn't that happen? Tell me, doesn't that happen?'

'I am certainly to blame in that,' answered Mitya, rather confused; 'but I take nothing from the poor, and I don't act against my conscience.'

'You don't take from them now; but when you are badly off yourself, then you will. You don't act against your conscience—fie on you! Of course, they are all saints whom you defend!... Have you forgotten Borka Perohodov? Who was it looked after him? Who took him under his protection—eh?'

'Perohodov suffered through his own fault, certainly.'

'He appropriated the public moneys.... That was all!'

'But, consider, uncle: his poverty, his family.'

'Poverty, poverty.... He's a drunkard, a quarrelsome fellow; that's what it is!'

'He took to drink through trouble,' said Mitya, dropping his voice.

'Through trouble, indeed! Well, you might have helped him, if your heart was so warm to him, but there was no need for you to sit in taverns with the drunken fellow yourself. Though he did speak so finely ... a prodigy, to be sure!'

'He was a very good fellow.'

'Every one is good with you.... But did you send him?' ... pursued Ovsyanikov, turning to his wife; 'come; you know?'

Tatyana Ilyinitchna nodded.

'Where have you been lately?' the old man began again.

'I have been in the town.'

'You have been doing nothing but playing billiards, I wager, and drinking tea, and running to and fro about the government offices, drawing up petitions in little back rooms, flaunting about with merchants' sons? That's it, of course?... Tell us!'

'Perhaps that is about it,' said Mitya with a smile.... 'Ah! I had almost forgotten—Funtikov, Anton Parfenitch asks you to dine with him next Sunday.'

'I shan't go to see that old tub. He gives you costly fish and puts rancid butter on it. God bless him!'

'And I met Fedosya Mihalovna.'

'What Fedosya is that?'

'She belongs to Garpentchenko, the landowner, who bought Mikulino by auction. Fedosya is from Mikulino. She lived in Moscow as a dress- maker, paying her service in money, and she paid her service-money accurately—a hundred and eighty two-roubles and a half a year.... And she knows her business; she got good orders in Moscow. But now Garpentchenko has written for her back, and he retains her here, but does not provide any duties for her. She would be prepared to buy her freedom, and has spoken to the master, but he will not give any decisive answer. You, uncle, are acquainted with Garpentchenko ... so couldn't you just say a word to him?... And Fedosya would give a good price for her freedom.'

'Not with your money I hope? Hey? Well, well, all right; I will speak to him, I will speak to him. But I don't know,' continued the old man with a troubled face; 'this Garpentchenko, God forgive him! is a shark; he buys up debts, lends money at interest, purchases estates at auctions.... And who brought him into our parts? Ugh, I can't bear these new-comers! One won't get an answer out of him very quickly.... However, we shall see.'

'Try to manage it, uncle.'

'Very well, I will see to it. Only you take care; take care of yourself! There, there, don't defend yourself.... God bless you! God bless you!... Only take care for the future, or else, Mitya, upon my word, it will go ill with you.... Upon my word, you will come to grief.... I can't always screen you ... and I myself am not a man of influence. There, go now, and God be with you!'

Mitya went away. Tatyana Ilyinitchna went out after him.

'Give him some tea, you soft-hearted creature,' cried Ovsyanikov after her. 'He's not a stupid fellow,' he continued, 'and he's a good heart, but I feel afraid for him.... But pardon me for having so long kept you occupied with such details.'

The door from the hall opened. A short grizzled little man came in, in a velvet coat.

'Ah, Frantz Ivanitch!' cried Ovsyanikov, 'good day to you. Is God merciful to you?'

Allow me, gentle reader, to introduce to you this gentleman.

Frantz Ivanitch Lejeune, my neighbour, and a landowner of Orel, had arrived at the respectable position of a Russian nobleman in a not quite ordinary way. He was born in Orleans of French parents, and had gone with Napoleon, on the invasion of Russia, in the capacity of a drummer. At first all went smoothly, and our Frenchman arrived in Moscow with his head held high. But on the return journey poor Monsieur Lejeune, half-frozen and without his drum, fell into the hands of some peasants of Smolensk. The peasants shut him up for the night in an empty cloth factory, and the next morning brought him to an ice-hole near the dyke, and began to beg the drummer *'de la Grrrrande Armée'* to oblige them; in other words, to swim under the ice. Monsieur Lejeune could not agree to their proposition, and in his turn began to try to persuade the Smolensk peasants, in the dialect of France, to let him go to Orleans. 'There, messieurs,' he said, *'my mother is living, une tendre mère'* But the peasants, doubtless through their ignorance of the geographical position of Orleans, continued to offer him a journey under water along the course of the meandering river Gniloterka, and had already begun to encourage him with slight blows on the vertebrae of the neck and back, when suddenly, to the indescribable delight of Lejeune, the sound of bells was heard, and there came along the dyke a huge sledge with a striped rug over its excessively high dickey, harnessed with three roan horses. In the sledge sat a stout and red- faced landowner in a wolfskin pelisse.

'What is it you are doing there?' he asked the peasants.

'We are drowning a Frenchman, your honour.'

'Ah!' replied the landowner indifferently, and he turned away.

'Monsieur! Monsieur!' shrieked the poor fellow.

'Ah, ah!' observed the wolfskin pelisse reproachfully, 'you came with twenty nations into Russia, burnt Moscow, tore down, you damned heathen! the cross from Ivan the Great, and now—mossoo, mossoo, indeed! now you turn tail! You are paying the penalty of your sins!... Go on, Filka!'

The horses were starting.

'Stop, though!' added the landowner. 'Eh? you mossoo, do you know anything of music?'

'*Sauvez-moi, sauvez-moi, mon bon monsieur!*' repeated Lejeune.

'There, see what a wretched people they are! Not one of them knows Russian! Muzeek, muzeek, savey muzeek voo? savey? Well, speak, do! Compreny? savey muzeek voo? on the piano, savey zhooey?'

Lejeune comprehended at last what the landowner meant, and persistently nodded his head.

'*Oui, monsieur, oui, oui, je suis musicien; je joue tous les instruments possibles! Oui, monsieur.... Sauvez-moi, monsieur!*'

'Well, thank your lucky star!' replied the landowner. 'Lads, let him go: here's a twenty-copeck piece for vodka.'

'Thank you, your honour, thank you. Take him, your honour.'

They sat Lejeune in the sledge. He was gasping with delight, weeping, shivering, bowing, thanking the landowner, the coachman, the peasants. He had nothing on but a green jacket with pink ribbons, and it was freezing very hard. The landowner looked at his blue and benumbed shoulders in silence, wrapped the unlucky fellow in his own pelisse, and took him home. The household ran out. They soon thawed the Frenchman, fed him, and clothed him. The landowner conducted him to his daughters.

'Here, children!' he said to them, 'a teacher is found for you. You were always entreating me to have you taught music and the French jargon; here you have a Frenchman, and he plays on the piano.... Come, mossoo,' he went on, pointing to a wretched little instrument he had bought five years before of a Jew, whose special line was eau de Cologne, 'give us an example of your art; zhooey!'

Lejeune, with a sinking heart, sat down on the music-stool; he had never touched a piano in his life.

'Zhooey, zhooey!' repeated the landowner.

In desperation, the unhappy man beat on the keys as though on a drum, and played at hazard. 'I quite expected,' he used to tell afterwards, 'that my deliverer would seize me by the collar, and throw me out of the house.' But, to the utmost amazement of the unwilling improvisor, the landowner, after waiting a little, patted him good-humouredly on the shoulder.

'Good, good,' he said; 'I see your attainments; go now, and rest yourself.'

Within a fortnight Lejeune had gone from this landowner's to stay with another, a rich and cultivated man. He gained his friendship by his bright and gentle disposition, was married to a ward of his, went into a government office, rose to the nobility, married his daughter to Lobizanyev, a landowner of Orel, and a retired dragoon and poet, and settled himself on an estate in Orel.

It was this same Lejeune, or rather, as he is called now, Frantz Ivanitch, who, when I was there, came in to see Ovsyanikov, with whom he was on friendly terms....

But perhaps the reader is already weary of sitting with me at the Ovsyanikovs', and so I will become eloquently silent.

VII

LGOV

'Let us go to Lgov,' Yermolaï, whom the reader knows already, said to me one day; 'there we can shoot ducks to our heart's content.'

Although wild duck offers no special attraction for a genuine sportsman, still, through lack of other game at the time (it was the beginning of September; snipe were not on the wing yet, and I was tired of running across the fields after partridges), I listened to my huntsman's suggestion, and we went to Lgov.

Lgov is a large village of the steppes, with a very old stone church with a single cupola, and two mills on the swampy little river Rossota. Five miles from Lgov, this river becomes a wide swampy pond, overgrown at the edges, and in places also in the centre, with thick reeds. Here, in the creeks or rather pools between the reeds, live and breed a countless multitude of ducks of all possible kinds—quackers, half- quackers, pintails, teals, divers, etc. Small flocks are for ever flitting about and swimming on the water, and at a gunshot, they rise in such clouds that the sportsman involuntarily clutches his hat with one hand and utters a prolonged Pshaw! I walked with Yermolaï along beside the pond; but, in the first place, the duck is a wary bird, and is not to be met quite close to the bank; and secondly, even when some straggling and inexperienced teal exposed itself to our shots and lost its life, our dogs were not able to get it out of the thick reeds; in spite of their most devoted efforts they could neither swim nor tread on the bottom, and only cut their precious noses on the sharp reeds for nothing.

'No,' was Yermolaï's comment at last, 'it won't do; we must get a boat.... Let us go back to Lgov.'

We went back. We had only gone a few paces when a rather wretched- looking setter-dog ran out from behind a bushy willow to meet us, and behind him appeared a man of middle height, in a blue and much-worn greatcoat, a yellow waistcoat, and pantaloons of a nondescript grey colour, hastily tucked into high boots full of holes, with a red handkerchief round his neck, and a single-barrelled gun on his shoulder. While our dogs, with the ordinary Chinese ceremonies peculiar to their species, were sniffing at their new acquaintance, who was obviously ill at ease, held his tail between his legs, dropped his ears back, and kept turning round and round showing his teeth—the stranger approached us, and bowed with extreme civility. He appeared to be about twenty-five; his long dark hair, perfectly saturated with kvas, stood up in stiff tufts, his small brown eyes twinkled genially; his face was bound up in a black handkerchief, as though for toothache; his countenance was all smiles and amiability.

'Allow me to introduce myself,' he began in a soft and insinuating voice; 'I am a sportsman of these parts—Vladimir.... Having heard of your presence, and having learnt that you proposed to visit the shores of our pond, I resolved, if it were not displeasing to you, to offer you my services.'

The sportsman, Vladimir, uttered those words for all the world like a young provincial actor in the *rôle* of leading lover. I agreed to his proposition, and before we had reached Lgov I had succeeded in learning his whole history. He was a freed house-serf; in his tender youth had been taught music, then served as valet, could read and write, had read—so much I could discover—some few trashy books, and existed now, as many do exist in Russia, without a farthing of ready money; without any regular occupation; fed by manna from heaven, or something hardly less precarious. He expressed himself with extraordinary elegance, and obviously plumed himself on his manners; he must have been devoted to the fair sex too, and in all probability popular with them: Russian girls love fine talking. Among other things, he gave me to understand that he sometimes visited the neighbouring landowners, and went to stay with friends in the town, where he played preference, and that he was acquainted with people in the metropolis. His smile was masterly and exceedingly varied; what specially suited him was a modest, contained smile which played on his lips as he listened to any other man's conversation. He was attentive to you; he agreed with you completely, but still he did not lose sight of his own dignity, and seemed to wish to give you to understand that he could, if occasion arose, express convictions of his own. Yermolaï, not being very refined, and quite devoid of 'subtlety,' began to address him with coarse familiarity. The fine irony with which Vladimir used 'Sir' in his reply was worth seeing.

'Why is your face tied up?' I inquired; 'have you toothache?'

'No,' he answered; 'it was a most disastrous consequence of carelessness. I had a friend, a good fellow, but not a bit of a sportsman, as sometimes occurs. Well, one day he said to me, "My dear friend, take me out shooting; I am curious to learn what this diversion consists in." I did not like, of course, to refuse a comrade; I got him a gun and took him out shooting. Well, we shot a little in the ordinary way; at last we thought we would rest I sat down under a tree; but he began instead to play with his gun, pointing it at me meantime. I asked him to leave off, but in his inexperience he did not attend to my words, the gun went off, and I lost half my chin, and the first finger of my right hand.'

We reached Lgov. Vladimir and Yermolaï had both decided that we could not shoot without a boat.

'Sutchok (*i.e.* the twig) has a punt,' observed Vladimir, 'but I don't know where he has hidden it. We must go to him.'

'To whom?' I asked.

'The man lives here; Sutchok is his nickname.'

Vladimir went with Yermolaï to Sutchok's. I told them I would wait for them at the church. While I was looking at the tombstones in the churchyard, I stumbled upon a blackened, four-cornered urn with the following inscription, on one side in French: 'Ci-git Théophile-Henri, Vicomte de Blangy'; on the next; 'Under this stone is laid the body of a French subject, Count Blangy; born 1737, died 1799, in the 62nd year of his age': on the third, 'Peace to his ashes': and on the fourth:—

'Under this stone there lies from France an emigrant.
Of high descent was he, and also of talent.
A wife and kindred murdered he bewailed,
And left his land by tyrants cruel assailed;
The friendly shores of Russia he attained,
And hospitable shelter here he gained;
Children he taught; their parents' cares allayed:
Here, by God's will, in peace he has been laid.'

The approach of Yermolaï with Vladimir and the man with the strange nickname, Sutchok, broke in on my meditations.

Barelegged, ragged and dishevelled, Sutchok looked like a discharged stray house-serf of sixty years old.

'Have you a boat?' I asked him.

'I have a boat,' he answered in a hoarse, cracked voice; 'but it's a very poor one.'

'How so?'

'Its boards are split apart, and the rivets have come off the cracks.'

'That's no great disaster!' interposed Yermolaï; 'we can stuff them up with tow.'

'Of course you can,' Sutchok assented.

'And who are you?'

'I am the fisherman of the manor.'

'How is it, when you're a fisherman, your boat is in such bad condition?'

'There are no fish in our river.'

'Fish don't like slimy marshes,' observed my huntsman, with the air of an authority.

'Come,' I said to Yermolaï, 'go and get some tow, and make the boat right for us as soon as you can.'

Yermolaï went off.

'Well, in this way we may very likely go to the bottom,' I said to Vladimir. 'God is merciful,' he answered. 'Anyway, we must suppose that the pond is not deep.'

'No, it is not deep,' observed Sutchok, who spoke in a strange, far-away voice, as though he were in a dream, 'and there's sedge and mud at the bottom, and it's all overgrown with sedge. But there are deep holes too.'

'But if the sedge is so thick,' said Vladimir, 'it will be impossible to row.'

'Who thinks of rowing in a punt? One has to punt it. I will go with you; my pole is there—or else one can use a wooden spade.'

'With a spade it won't be easy; you won't touch the bottom perhaps in some places,' said Vladimir.

'It's true; it won't be easy.'

I sat down on a tomb-stone to wait for Yermolaï. Vladimir moved a little to one side out of respect to me, and also sat down. Sutchok remained standing in the same place, his head bent and his hands clasped behind his back, according to the old habit of house-serfs.

'Tell me, please,' I began, 'have you been the fisherman here long?'

'It is seven years now,' he replied, rousing himself with a start.

'And what was your occupation before?'

'I was coachman before.'

'Who dismissed you from being coachman?'

'The new mistress.'

'What mistress?'

'Oh, that bought us. Your honour does not know her; Alyona Timofyevna; she is so fat ... not young.'

'Why did she decide to make you a fisherman?'

'God knows. She came to us from her estate in Tamboff, gave orders for all the household to come together, and came out to us. We first kissed her hand, and she said nothing; she was not angry.... Then she began to question us in order; "How are you employed? what duties have you?" She came to me in my turn; so she asked: "What have you been?" I say, "Coachman." "Coachman? Well, a fine coachman you are; only look at you! You're not fit for a coachman, but be my fisherman, and shave your beard. On the occasions of my visits provide fish for the table; do you hear?" ... So since then I have been enrolled as a fisherman. "And mind you keep my pond in order." But how is one to keep it in order?'

'Whom did you belong to before?'

'To Sergaï Sergiitch Pehterev. We came to him by inheritance. But he did not own us long; only six years altogether. I was his coachman ... but not in town, he had others there—only in the country.'

'And were you always a coachman from your youth up?'

'Always a coachman? Oh, no! I became a coachman in Sergaï Sergiitch's time, but before that I was a cook—but not town-cook; only a cook in the country.'

'Whose cook were you, then?'

'Oh, my former master's, Afanasy Nefeditch, Sergaï Sergiitch's uncle. Lgov was bought by him, by Afanasy Nefeditch, but it came to Sergaï Sergiitch by inheritance from him.'

'Whom did he buy it from?'

'From Tatyana Vassilyevna.'

'What Tatyana Vassilyevna was that?'

'Why, that died last year in Bolhov ... that is, at Karatchev, an old maid.... She had never married. Don't you know her? We came to her from her father, Vassily Semenitch. She owned us a goodish while ... twenty years.'

'Then were you cook to her?'

'At first, to be sure, I was cook, and then I was coffee-bearer.'

'What were you?'

'Coffee-bearer.'

'What sort of duty is that?'

'I don't know, your honour. I stood at the sideboard, and was called Anton instead of Kuzma. The mistress ordered that I should be called so.'

'Your real name, then, is Kuzma?'

'Yes.'

'And were you coffee-bearer all the time?'

'No, not all the time; I was an actor too.'

'Really?'

'Yes, I was.... I played in the theatre. Our mistress set up a theatre of her own.'

'What kind of parts did you take?'

'What did you please to say?'

'What did you do in the theatre?'

'Don't you know? Why, they take me and dress me up; and I walk about dressed up, or stand or sit down there as it happens, and they say, "See, this is what you must say," and I say it. Once I represented a blind man.... They laid little peas under each eyelid.... Yes, indeed.'

'And what were you afterwards?'

'Afterwards I became a cook again.'

'Why did they degrade you to being a cook again?'

'My brother ran away.'

'Well, and what were you under the father of your first mistress?'

'I had different duties; at first I found myself a page; I have been a postilion, a gardener, and a whipper-in.'

'A whipper-in?... And did you ride out with the hounds?'

'Yes, I rode with the hounds, and was nearly killed; I fell off my horse, and the horse was injured. Our old master was very severe; he ordered them to flog me, and to send me to learn a trade to Moscow, to a shoemaker.'

'To learn a trade? But you weren't a child, I suppose, when you were a whipper-in?'

'I was twenty and over then.'

'But could you learn a trade at twenty?'

'I suppose one could, some way, since the master ordered it. But he luckily died soon after, and they sent me back to the country.'

'And when were you taught to cook?'

Sutchok lifted his thin yellowish little old face and grinned.

'Is that a thing to be taught?... Old women can cook.'

'Well,' I commented, 'you have seen many things, Kuzma, in your time! What do you do now as a fisherman, seeing there are no fish?'

'Oh, your honour, I don't complain. And, thank God, they made me a fisherman. Why another old man like me—Andrey Pupir—the mistress ordered to be put into the paper factory, as a ladler. "It's a sin," she said, "to eat bread in idleness." And Pupir had even hoped for favour; his cousin's son was clerk in the mistress's counting-house: he had promised to send his name up to the mistress, to remember him: a fine way he remembered him!... And Pupir fell at his cousin's knees before my eyes.'

'Have you a family? Have you married?'

'No, your honour, I have never been married. Tatyana Vassilyevna—God rest her soul!—did not allow anyone to marry. "God forbid!" she said sometimes, "here am I living single: what indulgence! What are they thinking of!"'

'What do you live on now? Do you get wages?'

'Wages, your honour!... Victuals are given me, and thanks be to Thee, Lord! I am very contented. May God give our lady long life!'

Yermolaï returned.

'The boat is repaired,' he announced churlishly. 'Go after your pole— you there!'

Sutchok ran to get his pole. During the whole time of my conversation with the poor old man, the sportsman Vladimir had been staring at him with a contemptuous smile.

'A stupid fellow,' was his comment, when the latter had gone off; 'an absolutely uneducated fellow; a peasant, nothing more. One cannot even call him a house-serf, and he was boasting all the time. How could he be an actor, be pleased to judge for yourself! You were pleased to trouble yourself for no good in talking to him.'

A quarter of an hour later we were sitting in Sutchok's punt. The dogs we left in a hut in charge of my coachman. We were not very comfortable, but sportsmen are not a fastidious race. At the rear end, which was flattened and straight, stood Sutchok, punting; I sat with Vladimir on the planks laid across the boat, and Yermolaï ensconced himself in front, in the very beak. In spite of the tow, the water soon made its appearance under our feet. Fortunately, the weather was calm and the pond seemed slumbering.

We floated along rather slowly. The old man had difficulty in drawing his long pole out of the sticky mud; it came up all tangled in green threads of water-sedge; the flat round leaves of the water-lily also hindered the progress of our boat last we got up to the reeds, and then the fun began. Ducks flew up noisily from the pond, scared by our unexpected appearance in their domains, shots sounded at once after them; it was a pleasant sight to see these short-tailed game turning somersaults in the air, splashing heavily into the water. We could not, of course, get at all the ducks that were shot; those who were slightly wounded swam away; some which had been quite killed fell into such thick reeds that even Yermolaï's little lynx eyes could not discover them, yet our boat was nevertheless filled to the brim with game for dinner.

Vladimir, to Yermolaï's great satisfaction, did not shoot at all well; he seemed surprised after each unsuccessful shot, looked at his gun and blew down it, seemed puzzled, and at last explained to us the reason why he had missed his aim. Yermolaï, as always, shot triumphantly; I— rather badly, after my custom. Sutchok looked on at us with the eyes of a man who has been the servant of others from his youth up; now and then he cried out: 'There, there, there's another little duck'; and he constantly rubbed his back, not with his hands, but by a peculiar movement of the shoulder-blades. The weather kept magnificent; curly white clouds moved calmly high above our heads, and were reflected clearly in the water; the reeds were whispering around us; here and there the pond sparkled in the sunshine like steel. We were preparing to return to the village, when suddenly a rather unpleasant adventure befel us.

For a long time we had been aware that the water was gradually filling our punt. Vladimir was entrusted with the task of baling it out by means of a ladle, which my thoughtful huntsman had stolen to be ready for any emergency from a peasant woman who was staring away in another direction. All went well so long as Vladimir did not neglect his duty. But just at the end the ducks, as if to take leave of us, rose in such flocks that we scarcely had time to load our guns. In the heat of the sport we did not pay attention to the state of our punt—when suddenly, Yermolaï, in trying to reach a wounded duck, leaned his whole weight on the boat's-edge; at his over-eager movement our old tub veered on one side, began to fill, and majestically sank to the bottom, fortunately not in a deep place. We cried out, but it was too late; in an instant we were standing in the water up to our necks, surrounded by the floating bodies of the slaughtered ducks. I cannot help laughing now when I recollect the scared white faces of my companions (probably my own face was not particularly rosy at that moment), but I must confess at the time it did not enter my head to feel amused. Each of us kept his gun above his head, and Sutchok, no doubt from the habit of imitating his masters, lifted his pole above him. The first to break the silence was Yermolaï.

'Tfoo! curse it!' he muttered, spitting into the water; 'here's a go. It's all you, you old devil!' he added, turning wrathfully to Sutchok; 'you've such a boat!'

'It's my fault,' stammered the old man.

'Yes; and you're a nice one,' continued my huntsman, turning his head in Vladimir's direction; 'what were you thinking of? Why weren't you baling out?—you, you?'

But Vladimir was not equal to a reply; he was shaking like a leaf, his teeth were chattering, and his smile was utterly meaningless. What had become of his fine language, his feeling of fine distinctions, and of his own dignity!

The cursed punt rocked feebly under our feet... At the instant of our ducking the water seemed terribly cold to us, but we soon got hardened to it, when the first shock had passed off. I looked round me; the reeds rose up in a circle ten paces from us; in the distance above their tops the bank could be seen. 'It looks bad,' I thought.

'What are we to do?' I asked Yermolaï.

'Well, we'll take a look round; we can't spend the night here,' he answered. 'Here, you, take my gun,' he said to Vladimir.

Vladimir obeyed submissively.

'I will go and find the ford,' continued Yermolaï, as though there must infallibly be a ford in every pond: he took the pole from Sutchok, and went off in the direction of the bank, warily sounding the depth as he walked.

'Can you swim?' I asked him.

'No, I can't,' his voice sounded from behind the reeds.

'Then he'll be drowned,' remarked Sutchok indifferently. He had been terrified at first, not by the danger, but through fear of our anger, and now, completely reassured, he drew a long breath from time to time, and seemed not to be aware of any necessity for moving from his present position.

'And he will perish without doing any good,' added Vladimir piteously.

Yermolaï did not return for more than an hour. That hour seemed an eternity to us. At first we kept calling to him very energetically; then his answering shouts grew less frequent; at last he was completely silent. The bells in the village began ringing for evening service. There was not much conversation between us; indeed, we tried not to look at one another. The ducks hovered over our heads; some seemed disposed to settle near us, but suddenly rose up into the air and flew away quacking. We began to grow numb. Sutchok shut his eyes as though he were disposing himself to sleep.

At last, to our indescribable delight, Yermolaï returned.

'Well?'

'I have been to the bank; I have found the ford.... Let us go.'

We wanted to set off at once; but he first brought some string out of his pocket out of the water, tied the slaughtered ducks together by their legs, took both ends in his teeth, and moved slowly forward; Vladimir came behind him, and I behind Vladimir, and Sutchok brought up the rear. It was about two hundred paces to the bank. Yermolaï walked boldly and without stopping (so well had he noted the track), only occasionally crying out: 'More to the left—there's a hole here to the right!' or 'Keep to the right—you'll sink in there to the left....' Sometimes the water was up to our necks, and twice poor Sutchok, who was shorter than all the rest of us, got a mouthful and spluttered. 'Come, come, come!' Yermolaï shouted roughly to him—and Sutchok, scrambling, hopping and skipping, managed to reach a shallower place, but even in his greatest extremity was never so bold as to clutch at the skirt of my coat. Worn out, muddy and wet, we at last reached the bank.

Two hours later we were all sitting, as dry as circumstances would allow, in a large hay barn, preparing for supper. The coachman Yehudiil, an exceedingly deliberate man, heavy in gait, cautious and sleepy, stood at the entrance, zealously plying Sutchok with snuff (I have noticed that coachmen in Russia very quickly make friends); Sutchok was taking snuff with frenzied energy, in quantities to make him ill; he was spitting, sneezing, and apparently enjoying himself greatly. Vladimir had assumed an air of languor; he leaned his head on one side, and spoke little. Yermolaï was cleaning our guns. The dogs were wagging their tails at a great rate in the expectation of porridge; the horses were stamping and neighing in the out-house.... The sun had set; its last rays were broken up into broad tracts of purple; golden clouds were drawn out over the heavens into finer and ever finer threads, like a fleece washed and combed out. ... There was the sound of singing in the village.

VIII

BYEZHIN PRAIRIE

It was a glorious July day, one of those days which only come after many days of fine weather. From earliest morning the sky is clear; the sunrise does not glow with fire; it is suffused with a soft roseate flush. The sun, not fiery, not red-hot as in time of stifling drought, not dull purple as before a storm, but with a bright and genial radiance, rises peacefully behind a long and narrow cloud, shines out freshly, and plunges again into its lilac mist. The delicate upper edge of the strip of cloud flashes in little gleaming snakes; their brilliance is like polished silver. But, lo! the dancing rays flash forth again, and in solemn joy, as though flying upward, rises the mighty orb. About mid-day there is wont to be, high up in the sky, a multitude of rounded clouds, golden-grey, with soft white edges. Like islands scattered over an overflowing river, that bathes them in its unbroken reaches of deep transparent blue, they scarcely stir; farther down the heavens they are in movement, packing closer; now there is no blue to be seen between them, but they are themselves almost as blue as the sky, filled full with light and heat. The colour of the horizon, a faint pale lilac, does not change all day, and is the same all round; nowhere is there storm gathering and darkening; only somewhere rays of bluish colour stretch down from the sky; it is a sprinkling of scarce- perceptible rain. In the evening these clouds disappear; the last of them, blackish and undefined as smoke, lie streaked with pink, facing the setting sun; in the place where it has gone down, as calmly as it rose, a crimson glow lingers long over the darkening earth, and, softly flashing like a candle carried carelessly, the evening star flickers in the sky. On such days all the colours are softened, bright but not glaring; everything is suffused with a kind of touching tenderness. On such days the heat is sometimes very great; often it is even 'steaming' on the slopes of the fields, but a wind dispels this growing sultriness, and whirling eddies of dust—sure sign of settled, fine weather—move along the roads and across the fields in high white columns. In the pure dry air there is a scent of wormwood, rye in blossom, and buckwheat; even an hour before nightfall there is no moisture in the air. It is for such weather that the farmer longs, for harvesting his wheat....

On just such a day I was once out grouse-shooting in the Tchern district of the province of Tula. I started and shot a fair amount of game; my full game-bag cut my shoulder mercilessly; but already the evening glow had faded, and the cool shades of twilight were beginning to grow thicker, and to spread across the sky, which was still bright, though no longer lighted up by the rays of the setting sun, when I at last decided to turn back homewards. With swift steps I passed through the long 'square' of underwoods, clambered up a hill, and instead of the familiar plain I expected to see, with the oakwood on the right and the little white church in the distance, I saw before me a scene completely different, and quite new to me. A narrow valley lay at my feet, and directly facing me a dense wood of aspen-trees rose up like a thick wall. I stood still in perplexity, looked round me.... 'Aha!' I thought, 'I have somehow come wrong; I kept too much to the right,' and surprised at my own mistake, I rapidly descended the hill. I was at once plunged into a disagreeable clinging mist, exactly as though I had gone down into a cellar; the thick high grass at the bottom of the valley, all drenched with dew, was white like a smooth tablecloth; one felt afraid somehow to walk on it. I made haste to get on the other side, and walked along beside the aspenwood, bearing to the left. Bats were already hovering over its slumbering tree-tops, mysteriously flitting and quivering across the clear obscure of the sky; a young belated hawk flew in swift, straight course upwards, hastening to its nest. 'Here, directly I get to this corner,' I thought to myself, 'I shall find the road at once; but I have come a mile out of my way!'

I did at last reach the end of the wood, but there was no road of any sort there; some kind of low bushes overgrown with long grass extended far and wide before me; behind them in the far, far distance could be discerned a tract of waste land. I stopped again. 'Well? Where am I?' I began ransacking my brain to recall how and where I had been walking during the day.... 'Ah! but these are the bushes at Parahin,' I cried at last; 'of course! then this must be Sindyev wood. But how did I get here? So far?... Strange! Now I must bear to the right again.'

I went to the right through the bushes. Meantime the night had crept close and grown up like a storm-cloud; it seemed as though, with the mists of evening, darkness was rising up on all sides and flowing down from overhead. I had come upon some sort of little, untrodden, overgrown path; I walked along it, gazing intently before me. Soon all was blackness and silence around—only the quail's cry was heard from time to time. Some small night-bird, flitting noiselessly near the ground on its soft wings, almost flapped against me and skurried away in alarm. I came out on the further side of the bushes, and made my way along a field by the hedge. By now I could hardly make out distant objects; the field showed dimly white around; beyond it rose up a sullen darkness, which seemed moving up closer in huge masses every instant. My steps gave a muffled sound in the air, that grew colder and colder. The pale sky began again to grow blue—but it was the blue of night. The tiny stars glimmered and twinkled in it.

What I had been taking for a wood turned out to be a dark round hillock. 'But where am I, then?' I repeated again aloud, standing still for the third time and looking inquiringly at my spot and tan English dog, Dianka by name, certainly the most intelligent of four-footed creatures. But the most intelligent of four-footed creatures only wagged her tail, blinked her weary eyes dejectedly, and gave me no sensible advice. I felt myself disgraced in her eyes and pushed desperately forward, as though I had suddenly guessed which way I ought to go; I scaled the hill, and found myself in a hollow of no great depth, ploughed round.

A strange sensation came over me at once. This hollow had the form of an almost perfect cauldron, with sloping sides; at the bottom of it were some great white stones standing upright—it seemed as though they had crept there for some secret council—and it was so still and dark in it, so dreary and weird seemed the sky, overhanging it, that my heart sank. Some little animal was whining feebly and piteously among the stones. I made haste to get out again on to the hillock. Till then I had not quite given up all hope of finding the way home; but at this point I finally decided that I was utterly lost, and without any further attempt to make out the surrounding objects, which were almost completely plunged in darkness, I walked straight forward, by the aid of the stars, at random.... For about half-an-hour I walked on in this way, though I could hardly move one leg before the other. It seemed as if I had never been in such a deserted country in my life; nowhere was there the glimmer of a fire, nowhere a sound to be heard. One sloping hillside followed another; fields stretched endlessly upon fields; bushes seemed to spring up out of the earth under my very nose. I kept walking and was just making up my mind to lie down somewhere till morning, when suddenly I found myself on the edge of a horrible precipice.

I quickly drew back my lifted foot, and through the almost opaque darkness I saw far below me a vast plain. A long river skirted it in a semi-circle, turned away from me; its course was marked by the steely reflection of the water still faintly glimmering here and there. The hill on which I found myself terminated abruptly in an almost overhanging precipice, whose gigantic profile stood out black against the dark-blue waste of sky, and directly below me, in the corner formed by this precipice and the plain near the river, which was there a dark, motionless mirror, under the lee of the hill, two fires side by side were smoking and throwing up red flames. People were stirring round them, shadows hovered, and sometimes the front of a little curly head was lighted up by the glow.

I found out at last where I had got to. This plain was well known in our parts under the name of Byezhin Prairie.... But there was no possibility of returning home, especially at night; my legs were sinking under me from weariness. I decided to get down to the fires and to wait for the dawn in the company of these men, whom I took for drovers. I got down successfully, but I had hardly let go of the last branch I had grasped, when suddenly two large shaggy white dogs rushed angrily barking upon me. The sound of ringing boyish voices came from round the fires; two or three boys quickly got up from the ground. I called back in response to their shouts of inquiry. They ran up to me, and at once called off the dogs, who were specially struck by the appearance of my Dianka. I came down to them.

51

I had been mistaken in taking the figures sitting round the fires for drovers. They were simply peasant boys from a neighbouring village, who were in charge of a drove of horses. In hot summer weather with us they drive the horses out at night to graze in the open country: the flies and gnats would give them no peace in the daytime; they drive out the drove towards evening, and drive them back in the early morning: it's a great treat for the peasant boys. Bare-headed, in old fur-capes, they bestride the most spirited nags, and scurry along with merry cries and hooting and ringing laughter, swinging their arms and legs, and leaping into the air. The fine dust is stirred up in yellow clouds and moves along the road; the tramp of hoofs in unison resounds afar; the horses race along, pricking up their ears; in front of all, with his tail in the air and thistles in his tangled mane, prances some shaggy chestnut, constantly shifting his paces as he goes.

I told the boys I had lost my way, and sat down with them. They asked me where I came from, and then were silent for a little and turned away. Then we talked a little again. I lay down under a bush, whose shoots had been nibbled off, and began to look round. It was a marvellous picture: about the fire a red ring of light quivered and seemed to swoon away in the embrace of a background of darkness; the flame flaring up from time to time cast swift flashes of light beyond the boundary of this circle; a fine tongue of light licked the dry twigs and died away at once; long thin shadows, in their turn breaking in for an instant, danced right up to the very fires; darkness was struggling with light. Sometimes, when the fire burnt low and the circle of light shrank together, suddenly out of the encroaching darkness a horse's head was thrust in, bay, with striped markings or all white, stared with intent blank eyes upon us, nipped hastily the long grass, and drawing back again, vanished instantly. One could only hear it still munching and snorting. From the circle of light it was hard to make out what was going on in the darkness; everything close at hand seemed shut off by an almost black curtain; but farther away hills and forests were dimly visible in long blurs upon the horizon.

The dark unclouded sky stood, inconceivably immense, triumphant, above us in all its mysterious majesty. One felt a sweet oppression at one's heart, breathing in that peculiar, overpowering, yet fresh fragrance— the fragrance of a summer night in Russia. Scarcely a sound was to be heard around.... Only at times, in the river near, the sudden splash of a big fish leaping, and the faint rustle of a reed on the bank, swaying lightly as the ripples reached it ... the fires alone kept up a subdued crackling.

The boys sat round them: there too sat the two dogs, who had been so eager to devour me. They could not for long after reconcile themselves to my presence, and, drowsily blinking and staring into the fire, they growled now and then with an unwonted sense of their own dignity; first they growled, and then whined a little, as though deploring the impossibility of carrying out their desires. There were altogether five boys: Fedya, Pavlusha, Ilyusha, Kostya and Vanya. (From their talk I learnt their names, and I intend now to introduce them to the reader.)

The first and eldest of all, Fedya, one would take to be about fourteen. He was a well-made boy, with good-looking, delicate, rather small features, curly fair hair, bright eyes, and a perpetual half- merry, half-careless smile. He belonged, by all appearances, to a well- to-do family, and had ridden out to the prairie, not through necessity, but for amusement. He wore a gay print shirt, with a yellow border; a short new overcoat slung round his neck was almost slipping off his narrow shoulders; a comb hung from his blue belt. His boots, coming a little way up the leg, were certainly his own—not his father's. The second boy, Pavlusha, had tangled black hair, grey eyes, broad cheek- bones, a pale face pitted with small-pox, a large but well-cut mouth; his head altogether was large—'a beer-barrel head,' as they say—and his figure was square and clumsy. He was not a good-looking boy— there's no denying it!—and yet I liked him; he looked very sensible and straightforward, and there was a vigorous ring in his voice. He had nothing to boast of in his attire; it consisted simply of a homespun shirt and patched trousers. The face of the third, Ilyusha, was rather uninteresting; it was a long face, with short-sighted eyes and a hook nose; it expressed a kind of dull, fretful uneasiness; his tightly- drawn lips seemed rigid; his contracted brow never relaxed; he seemed continually blinking from the firelight. His flaxen—almost white—hair hung out in thin wisps under his low felt hat, which he kept pulling down with both hands over his ears. He had on new bast-shoes and leggings; a thick string, wound three times round his figure, carefully held together his neat black smock. Neither he nor Pavlusha looked more than twelve years old. The fourth, Kostya, a boy of ten, aroused my curiosity by his thoughtful and sorrowful look. His whole face was small, thin, freckled, pointed at the chin like a squirrel's; his lips were barely perceptible; but his great black eyes, that shone with liquid brilliance, produced a strange impression; they seemed trying to express something for which the tongue—his tongue, at least—had no words. He was undersized and weakly, and dressed rather poorly. The remaining boy, Vanya, I had not noticed at first; he was lying on the ground, peacefully curled up under a square rug, and only occasionally thrust his curly brown head out from under it: this boy was seven years old at the most.

So I lay under the bush at one side and looked at the boys. A small pot was hanging over one of the fires; in it potatoes were cooking. Pavlusha was looking after them, and on his knees he was trying them by poking a splinter of wood into the boiling water. Fedya was lying leaning on his elbow, and smoothing out the skirts of his coat. Ilyusha was sitting beside Kostya, and still kept blinking constrainedly. Kostya's head drooped despondently, and he looked away into the distance. Vanya did not stir under his rug. I pretended to be asleep. Little by little, the boys began talking again.

At first they gossiped of one thing and another, the work of to-morrow, the horses; but suddenly Fedya turned to Ilyusha, and, as though taking up again an interrupted conversation, asked him:

'Come then, so you've seen the domovoy?'

'No, I didn't see him, and no one ever can see him,' answered Ilyusha, in a weak hoarse voice, the sound of which was wonderfully in keeping with the expression of his face; 'I heard him…. Yes, and not I alone.'

'Where does he live—in your place?' asked Pavlusha.

'In the old paper-mill.'

'Why, do you go to the factory?'

'Of course we do. My brother Avdushka and I, we are paper-glazers.'

'I say—factory-hands!'

'Well, how did you hear it, then?' asked Fedya.

'It was like this. It happened that I and my brother Avdushka, with Fyodor of Mihyevska, and Ivashka the Squint-eyed, and the other Ivashka who comes from the Red Hills, and Ivashka of Suhorukov too—and there were some other boys there as well— there were ten of us boys there altogether—the whole shift, that is—it happened that we spent the night at the paper-mill; that's to say, it didn't happen, but Nazarov, the overseer, kept us. 'Why,' said he, "should you waste time going home, boys; there's a lot of work to-morrow, so don't go home, boys." So we stopped, and were all lying down together, and Avdushka had just begun to say, "I say, boys, suppose the domovoy were to come?" And before he'd finished saying so, some one suddenly began walking over our heads; we were lying down below, and he began walking upstairs overhead, where the wheel is. We listened: he walked; the boards seemed to be bending under him, they creaked so; then he crossed over, above our heads; all of a sudden the water began to drip and drip over the wheel; the wheel rattled and rattled and again began to turn, though the sluices of the conduit above had been let down. We wondered who could have lifted them up so that the water could run; any way, the wheel turned and turned a little, and then stopped. Then he went to the door overhead and began coming down-stairs, and came down like this, not hurrying himself; the stairs seemed to groan under him too.... Well, he came right down to our door, and waited and waited ... and all of a sudden the door simply flew open. We were in a fright; we looked— there was nothing.... Suddenly what if the net on one of the vats didn't begin moving; it got up, and went rising and ducking and moving in the air as though some one were stirring with it, and then it was in its place again. Then, at another vat, a hook came off its nail, and then was on its nail again; and then it seemed as if some one came to the door, and suddenly coughed and choked like a sheep, but so loudly!... We all fell down in a heap and huddled against one another.... Just weren't we in a fright that night!'

'I say!' murmured Pavel, 'what did he cough for?'

'I don't know; perhaps it was the damp.'

All were silent for a little.

'Well,' inquired Fedya, 'are the potatoes done?'

Pavlusha tried them.

'No, they are raw.... My, what a splash!' he added, turning his face in the direction of the river; 'that must be a pike.... And there's a star falling.'

'I say, I can tell you something, brothers,' began Kostya, in a shrill little voice; 'listen what my dad told me the other day.'

'Well, we are listening,' said Fedya with a patronising air.

'You know Gavrila, I suppose, the carpenter up in the big village?'

'Yes, we know him.'

'And do you know why he is so sorrowful always, never speaks? do you know? I'll tell you why he's so sorrowful; he went one day, daddy said, he went, brothers, into the forest nutting. So he went nutting into the forest and lost his way; he went on—God only can tell where he got to. So he went on and on, brothers—but 'twas no good!—he could not find the way; and so night came on out of doors. So he sat down under a tree. "I'll wait till morning," thought he. He sat down and began to drop asleep. So as he was falling asleep, suddenly he heard some one call him. He looked up; there was no one. He fell asleep again; again he was called. He looked and looked again; and in front of him there sat a russalka on a branch, swinging herself and calling him to her, and simply dying with laughing; she laughed so.... And the moon was shining bright, so bright, the moon shone so clear—everything could be seen plain, brothers. So she called him, and she herself was as bright and as white sitting on the branch as some dace or a roach, or like some little carp so white and silvery.... Gavrila the carpenter almost fainted, brothers, but she laughed without stopping, and kept beckoning him to her like this. Then Gavrila was just getting up; he was just going to yield to the russalka, brothers, but—the Lord put it into his heart, doubtless—he crossed himself like this.... And it was so hard for him to make that cross, brothers; he said, "My hand was simply like a stone; it would not move." ... Ugh! the horrid witch.... So when he made the cross, brothers, the russalka, she left off laughing, and all at once how she did cry.... She cried, brothers, and wiped her eyes with her hair, and her hair was green as any hemp. So Gavrila looked and looked at her, and at last he fell to questioning her. "Why are you weeping, wild thing of the woods?" And the russalka began to speak to him like this: "If you had not crossed yourself, man," she says, "you should have lived with me in gladness of heart to the end of your days; and I weep, I am grieved at heart because you crossed yourself; but I will not grieve alone; you too shall grieve at heart to the end of your days." Then she vanished, brothers, and at once it was plain to Gavrila how to get out of the forest.... Only since then he goes always sorrowful, as you see.'

'Ugh!' said Fedya after a brief silence; 'but how can such an evil thing of the woods ruin a Christian soul—he did not listen to her?'

'And I say!' said Kostya. 'Gavrila said that her voice was as shrill and plaintive as a toad's.'

'Did your father tell you that himself?' Fedya went on.

'Yes. I was lying in the loft; I heard it all.'

'It's a strange thing. Why should he be sorrowful?... But I suppose she liked him, since she called him.'

'Ay, she liked him!' put in Ilyusha. 'Yes, indeed! she wanted to tickle him to death, that's what she wanted. That's what they do, those russalkas.'

'There ought to be russalkas here too, I suppose,' observed Fedya.

'No,' answered Kostya, 'this is a holy open place. There's one thing, though: the river's near.'

All were silent. Suddenly from out of the distance came a prolonged, resonant, almost wailing sound, one of those inexplicable sounds of the night, which break upon a profound stillness, rise upon the air, linger, and slowly die away at last. You listen: it is as though there were nothing, yet it echoes still. It is as though some one had uttered a long, long cry upon the very horizon, as though some other had answered him with shrill harsh laughter in the forest, and a faint, hoarse hissing hovers over the river. The boys looked round about shivering....

'Christ's aid be with us!' whispered Ilyusha.

'Ah, you craven crows!' cried Pavel, 'what are you frightened of? Look, the potatoes are done.' (They all came up to the pot and began to eat the smoking potatoes; only Vanya did not stir.) 'Well, aren't you coming?' said Pavel.

But he did not creep out from under his rug. The pot was soon completely emptied.

'Have you heard, boys,' began Ilyusha, 'what happened with us at Varnavitsi?'

'Near the dam?' asked Fedya.

'Yes, yes, near the dam, the broken-down dam. That is a haunted place, such a haunted place, and so lonely. All round there are pits and quarries, and there are always snakes in pits.'

'Well, what did happen? Tell us.'

'Well, this is what happened. You don't know, perhaps, Fedya, but there a drowned man was buried; he was drowned long, long ago, when the water was still deep; only his grave can still be seen, though it can only just be seen ... like this—a little mound.... So one day the bailiff called the huntsman Yermil, and says to him, "Go to the post, Yermil." Yermil always goes to the post for us; he has let all his dogs die; they never will live with him, for some reason, and they have never lived with him, though he's a good huntsman, and everyone liked him. So Yermil went to the post, and he stayed a bit in the town, and when he rode back, he was a little tipsy. It was night, a fine night; the moon was shining.... So Yermil rode across the dam; his way lay there. So, as he rode along, he saw, on the drowned man's grave, a little lamb, so white and curly and pretty, running about. So Yermil thought, "I will take him," and he got down and took him in his arms. But the little lamb didn't take any notice. So Yermil goes back to his horse, and the horse stares at him, and snorts and shakes his head; however, he said "wo" to him and sat on him with the lamb, and rode on again; he held the lamb in front of him. He looks at him, and the lamb looks him straight in the face, like this. Yermil the huntsman felt upset. "I don't remember," he said, "that lambs ever look at any one like that"; however, he began to stroke it like this on its wool, and to say, "Chucky! chucky!" And the lamb suddenly showed its teeth and said too, "Chucky! chucky!"'

The boy who was telling the story had hardly uttered this last word, when suddenly both dogs got up at once, and, barking convulsively, rushed away from the fire and disappeared in the darkness. All the boys were alarmed. Vanya jumped up from under his rug. Pavlusha ran shouting after the dogs. Their barking quickly grew fainter in the distance.... There was the noise of the uneasy tramp of the frightened drove of horses. Pavlusha shouted aloud: 'Hey Grey! Beetle!' ... In a few minutes the barking ceased; Pavel's voice sounded still in the distance.... A little time more passed; the boys kept looking about in perplexity, as though expecting something to happen.... Suddenly the tramp of a galloping horse was heard; it stopped short at the pile of wood, and, hanging on to the mane, Pavel sprang nimbly off it. Both the dogs also leaped into the circle of light and at once sat down, their red tongues hanging out.

'What was it? what was it?' asked the boys.

'Nothing,' answered Pavel, waving his hand to his horse; 'I suppose the dogs scented something. I thought it was a wolf,' he added, calmly drawing deep breaths into his chest.

I could not help admiring Pavel. He was very fine at that moment. His ugly face, animated by his swift ride, glowed with hardihood and determination. Without even a switch in his hand, he had, without the slightest hesitation, rushed out into the night alone to face a wolf.... 'What a splendid fellow!' I thought, looking at him.

'Have you seen any wolves, then?' asked the trembling Kostya.

'There are always a good many of them here,' answered Pavel; 'but they are only troublesome in the winter.'

He crouched down again before the fire. As he sat down on the ground, he laid his hand on the shaggy head of one of the dogs. For a long while the flattered brute did not turn his head, gazing sidewise with grateful pride at Pavlusha.

Vanya lay down under his rug again.

'What dreadful things you were telling us, Ilyusha!' began Fedya, whose part it was, as the son of a well-to-do peasant, to lead the conversation. (He spoke little himself, apparently afraid of lowering his dignity.) 'And then some evil spirit set the dogs barking.... Certainly I have heard that place was haunted.'

'Varnavitsi?... I should think it was haunted! More than once, they say, they have seen the old master there—the late master. He wears, they say, a long skirted coat, and keeps groaning like this, and looking for something on the ground. Once grandfather Trofimitch met him. "What," says he, "your honour, Ivan Ivanitch, are you pleased to look for on the ground?"'

'He asked him?' put in Fedya in amazement.

'Yes, he asked him.'

'Well, I call Trofimitch a brave fellow after that.... Well, what did he say?'

'"I am looking for the herb that cleaves all things," says he. But he speaks so thickly, so thickly. "And what, your honour, Ivan Ivanitch, do you want with the herb that cleaves all things?" "The tomb weighs on me; it weighs on me, Trofimitch: I want to get away— away."'

'My word!' observed Fedya, 'he didn't enjoy his life enough, I suppose.'

'What a marvel!' said Kosyta. 'I thought one could only see the departed on All Hallows' day.'

'One can see the departed any time,' Ilyusha interposed with conviction. From what I could observe, I judged he knew the village superstitions better than the others.... 'But on

All Hallows' day you can see the living too; those, that is, whose turn it is to die that year. You need only sit in the church porch, and keep looking at the road. They will come by you along the road; those, that is, who will die that year. Last year old Ulyana went to the porch.'

'Well, did she see anyone?' asked Kostya inquisitively.

'To be sure she did. At first she sat a long, long while, and saw no one and heard nothing ... only it seemed as if some dog kept whining and whining like this somewhere.... Suddenly she looks up: a boy comes along the road with only a shirt on. She looked at him. It was Ivashka Fedosyev.'

'He who died in the spring?' put in Fedya.

'Yes, he. He came along and never lifted up his head. But Ulyana knew him. And then she looks again: a woman came along. She stared and stared at her.... Ah, God Almighty! ... it was herself coming along the road; Ulyana herself.'

'Could it be herself?' asked Fedya.

'Yes, by God, herself.'

'Well, but she is not dead yet, you know?' 'But the year is not over yet. And only look at her; her life hangs on a thread.'

All were still again. Pavel threw a handful of dry twigs on to the fire. They were soon charred by the suddenly leaping flame; they cracked and smoked, and began to contract, curling up their burning ends. Gleams of light in broken flashes glanced in all directions, especially upwards. Suddenly a white dove flew straight into the bright light, fluttered round and round in terror, bathed in the red glow, and disappeared with a whirr of its wings.

'It's lost its home, I suppose,' remarked Pavel. 'Now it will fly till it gets somewhere, where it can rest till dawn.'

'Why, Pavlusha,' said Kostya, 'might it not be a just soul flying to heaven?'

Pavel threw another handful of twigs on to the fire.

'Perhaps,' he said at last.

'But tell us, please, Pavlusha,' began Fedya, 'what was seen in your parts at Shalamovy at the heavenly portent?'

[Footnote: This is what the peasants call an eclipse.—*Author's Note*.]

'When the sun could not be seen? Yes, indeed.'

'Were you frightened then?'

'Yes; and we weren't the only ones. Our master, though he talked to us beforehand, and said there would be a heavenly portent, yet when it got dark, they say he himself was frightened out of his wits. And in the house-serfs' cottage the old woman, directly it grew dark, broke all the dishes in the oven with the poker. 'Who will eat now?' she said; 'the last day has come.' So the soup was all running about the place. And in the village there were such tales about among us: that white wolves would run over the earth, and would eat men, that a bird of prey would pounce down on us, and that they would even see Trishka.'

[Footnote: The popular belief in Trishka is probably derived from some tradition of Antichrist.—*Author's Note*.]

'What is Trishka?' asked Kostya.

'Why, don't you know?' interrupted Ilyusha warmly. 'Why, brother, where have you been brought up, not to know Trishka? You're a stay-at-home, one-eyed lot in your village, really! Trishka will be a marvellous man, who will come one day, and he will be

57

such a marvellous man that they will never be able to catch him, and never be able to do anything with him; he will be such a marvellous man. The people will try to take him; for example, they will come after him with sticks, they will surround him, but he will blind their eyes so that they fall upon one another. They will put him in prison, for example; he will ask for a little water to drink in a bowl; they will bring him the bowl, and he will plunge into it and vanish from their sight. They will put chains on him, but he will only clap his hands—they will fall off him. So this Trishka will go through villages and towns; and this Trishka will be a wily man; he will lead astray Christ's people ... and they will be able to do nothing to him.... He will be such a marvellous, wily man.'

'Well, then,' continued Pavel, in his deliberate voice, 'that's what he 's like. And so they expected him in our parts. The old men declared that directly the heavenly portent began, Trishka would come. So the heavenly portent began. All the people were scattered over the street, in the fields, waiting to see what would happen. Our place, you know, is open country. They look; and suddenly down the mountain-side from the big village comes a man of some sort; such a strange man, with such a wonderful head ... that all scream: "Oy, Trishka is coming! Oy, Trishka is coming!" and all run in all directions! Our elder crawled into a ditch; his wife stumbled on the door-board and screamed with all her might; she terrified her yard-dog, so that he broke away from his chain and over the hedge and into the forest; and Kuzka's father, Dorofyitch, ran into the oats, lay down there, and began to cry like a quail. 'Perhaps' says he, 'the Enemy, the Destroyer of Souls, will spare the birds, at least.' So they were all in such a scare! But he that was coming was our cooper Vavila; he had bought himself a new pitcher, and had put the empty pitcher over his head.'

All the boys laughed; and again there was a silence for a while, as often happens when people are talking in the open air. I looked out into the solemn, majestic stillness of the night; the dewy freshness of late evening had been succeeded by the dry heat of midnight; the darkness still had long to lie in a soft curtain over the slumbering fields; there was still a long while left before the first whisperings, the first dewdrops of dawn. There was no moon in the heavens; it rose late at that time. Countless golden stars, twinkling in rivalry, seemed all running softly towards the Milky Way, and truly, looking at them, you were almost conscious of the whirling, never—resting motion of the earth.... A strange, harsh, painful cry, sounded twice together over the river, and a few moments later, was repeated farther down....

Kostya shuddered. 'What was that?'

'That was a heron's cry,' replied Pavel tranquilly.

'A heron,' repeated Kostya.... 'And what was it, Pavlusha, I heard yesterday evening,' he added, after a short pause; 'you perhaps will know.'

'What did you hear?'

'I will tell you what I heard. I was going from Stony Ridge to Shashkino; I went first through our walnut wood, and then passed by a little pool—you know where there's a sharp turn down to the ravine— there is a water-pit there, you know; it is quite overgrown with reeds; so I went near this pit, brothers, and suddenly from this came a sound of some one groaning, and piteously, so piteously; oo-oo, oo-oo! I was in such a fright, my brothers; it was late, and the voice was so miserable. I felt as if I should cry myself.... What could that have been, eh?'

'It was in that pit the thieves drowned Akim the forester, last summer,' observed Pavel; 'so perhaps it was his soul lamenting.'

'Oh, dear, really, brothers,' replied Kostya, opening wide his eyes, which were round enough before, 'I did not know they had drowned Akim in that pit. Shouldn't I have been frightened if I'd known!'

'But they say there are little, tiny frogs,' continued Pavel, 'who cry piteously like that.'

'Frogs? Oh, no, it was not frogs, certainly not. (A heron again uttered a cry above the river.) Ugh, there it is!' Kostya cried involuntarily; 'it is just like a wood-spirit shrieking.'

'The wood-spirit does not shriek; it is dumb,' put in Ilyusha; 'it only claps its hands and rattles.'

'And have you seen it then, the wood-spirit?' Fedya asked him ironically.

'No, I have not seen it, and God preserve me from seeing it; but others have seen it. Why, one day it misled a peasant in our parts, and led him through the woods and all in a circle in one field…. He scarcely got home till daylight.'

'Well, and did he see it?'

'Yes. He says it was a big, big creature, dark, wrapped up, just like a tree; you could not make it out well; it seemed to hide away from the moon, and kept staring and staring with its great eyes, and winking and winking with them….'

'Ugh!' exclaimed Fedya with a slight shiver, and a shrug of the shoulders; 'pfoo.'

'And how does such an unclean brood come to exist in the world?' said Pavel; 'it's a wonder.'

'Don't speak ill of it; take care, it will hear you,' said Ilyusha.

Again there was a silence.

'Look, look, brothers,' suddenly came Vanya's childish voice; 'look at God's little stars; they are swarming like bees!'

He put his fresh little face out from under his rug, leaned on his little fist, and slowly lifted up his large soft eyes. The eyes of all the boys were raised to the sky, and they were not lowered quickly.

'Well, Vanya,' began Fedya caressingly, 'is your sister Anyutka well?'

'Yes, she is very well,' replied Vanya with a slight lisp.

'You ask her, why doesn't she come to see us?'

'I don't know.'

'You tell her to come.'

'Very well.'

'Tell her I have a present for her.'

'And a present for me too?'

'Yes, you too.'

Vanya sighed.

'No; I don't want one. Better give it to her; she is so kind to us at home.'

And Vanya laid his head down again on the ground. Pavel got up and took the empty pot in his hand.

'Where are you going?' Fedya asked him.

'To the river, to get water; I want some water to drink.'

The dogs got up and followed him.

'Take care you don't fall into the river!' Ilyusha cried after him.

'Why should he fall in?' said Fedya. 'He will be careful.'

'Yes, he will be careful. But all kinds of things happen; he will stoop over, perhaps, to draw the water, and the water-spirit will clutch him by the hand, and drag him to him. Then they will say, "The boy fell into the water." … Fell in, indeed! … "There, he has crept in among the reeds," he added, listening.

The reeds certainly 'shished,' as they call it among us, as they were parted.

'But is it true,' asked Kostya, 'that crazy Akulina has been mad ever since she fell into the water?'

'Yes, ever since…. How dreadful she is now! But they say she was a beauty before then. The water-spirit bewitched her. I suppose he did not expect they would get her out so soon. So down there at the bottom he bewitched her.'

(I had met this Akulina more than once. Covered with rags, fearfully thin, with face as black as a coal, blear-eyed and for ever grinning, she would stay whole hours in one place in the road, stamping with her feet, pressing her fleshless hands to her breast, and slowly shifting from one leg to the other, like a wild beast in a cage. She understood nothing that was said to her, and only chuckled spasmodically from time to time.)

'But they say,' continued Kostya, 'that Akulina threw herself into the river because her lover had deceived her.'

'Yes, that was it.'

'And do you remember Vasya? added Kostya, mournfully.

'What Vasya?' asked Fedya.

'Why, the one who was drowned,' replied Kostya,' in this very river. Ah, what a boy he was! What a boy he was! His mother, Feklista, how she loved him, her Vasya! And she seemed to have a foreboding, Feklista did, that harm would come to him from the water. Sometimes, when Vasya went with us boys in the summer to bathe in the river, she used to be trembling all over. The other women did not mind; they passed by with the pails, and went on, but Feklista put her pail down on the ground, and set to calling him, 'Come back, come back, my little joy; come back, my darling!' And no one knows how he was drowned. He was playing on the bank, and his mother was there haymaking; suddenly she hears, as though some one was blowing bubbles through the water, and behold! there was only Vasya's little cap to be seen swimming on the water. You know since then Feklista has not been right in her mind: she goes and lies down at the place where he was drowned; she lies down, brothers, and sings a song—you remember Vasya was always singing a song like that—so she sings it too, and weeps and weeps, and bitterly rails against God.'

'Here is Pavlusha coming,' said Fedya.

Pavel came up to the fire with a full pot in his hand.

'Boys,' he began, after a short silence, 'something bad happened.'

'Oh, what?' asked Kostya hurriedly.

'I heard Vasya's voice.'

They all seemed to shudder.

'What do you mean? what do you mean?' stammered Kostya.

'I don't know. Only I went to stoop down to the water; suddenly I hear my name called in Vasya's voice, as though it came from below water: "Pavlusha, Pavlusha, come here." I came away. But I fetched the water, though.'

'Ah, God have mercy upon us!' said the boys, crossing themselves.

'It was the water-spirit calling you, Pavel,' said Fedya; 'we were just talking of Vasya.'

'Ah, it's a bad omen,' said Ilyusha, deliberately.

'Well, never mind, don't bother about it,' Pavel declared stoutly, and he sat down again; 'no one can escape his fate.'

The boys were still. It was clear that Pavel's words had produced a strong impression on them. They began to lie down before the fire as though preparing to go to sleep.

'What is that?' asked Kostya, suddenly lifting his head.

Pavel listened.

'It's the curlews flying and whistling.'

'Where are they flying to?'

'To a land where, they say, there is no winter.'

'But is there such a land?'

'Yes.'

'Is it far away?'

'Far, far away, beyond the warm seas.'

Kostya sighed and shut his eyes.

More than three hours had passed since I first came across the boys. The moon at last had risen; I did not notice it at first; it was such a tiny crescent. This moonless night was as solemn and hushed as it had been at first.... But already many stars, that not long before had been high up in the heavens, were setting over the earth's dark rim; everything around was perfectly still, as it is only still towards morning; all was sleeping the deep unbroken sleep that comes before daybreak. Already the fragrance in the air was fainter; once more a dew seemed falling.... How short are nights in summer!... The boys' talk died down when the fires did. The dogs even were dozing; the horses, so far as I could make out, in the hardly-perceptible, faintly shining light of the stars, were asleep with downcast heads.... I fell into a state of weary unconsciousness, which passed into sleep.

A fresh breeze passed over my face. I opened my eyes; the morning was beginning. The dawn had not yet flushed the sky, but already it was growing light in the east. Everything had become visible, though dimly visible, around. The pale grey sky was growing light and cold and bluish; the stars twinkled with a dimmer light, or disappeared; the earth was wet, the leaves covered with dew, and from the distance came sounds of life and voices, and a light morning breeze went fluttering over the earth. My body responded to it with a faint shudder of delight. I got up quickly and went to the boys. They were all sleeping as though they were tired out round the smouldering fire; only Pavel half rose and gazed intently at me.

I nodded to him, and walked homewards beside the misty river. Before I had walked two miles, already all around me, over the wide dew-drenched prairie, and in front from forest to forest, where the hills were growing green again, and behind, over the long dusty road and the sparkling bushes, flushed with the red glow, and the river faintly blue now under the lifting mist, flowed fresh streams of burning light, first pink, then red and golden.... All things began to stir, to awaken, to sing, to flutter, to speak. On all sides thick drops of dew sparkled in glittering diamonds; to welcome me, pure and clear as though bathed in the freshness of morning, came the notes of a bell, and suddenly there rushed by me, driven by the boys I had parted from, the drove of horses, refreshed and rested....

Sad to say, I must add that in that year Pavel met his end. He was not drowned; he was killed by a fall from his horse. Pity! he was a splendid fellow!

IX

KASSYAN OF FAIR SPRINGS

I was returning from hunting in a jolting little trap, and overcome by the stifling heat of a cloudy summer day (it is well known that the heat is often more insupportable on such days than in bright days, especially when there is no wind), I dozed and was shaken about, resigning myself with sullen fortitude to being persecuted by the fine white dust which was incessantly raised from the beaten road by the warped and creaking wheels, when suddenly my attention was aroused by the extraordinary uneasiness and agitated movements of my coachman, who had till that instant been more soundly dozing than I.

He began tugging at the reins, moved uneasily on the box, and started shouting to the horses, staring all the while in one direction. I looked round. We were driving through a wide ploughed plain; low hills, also ploughed over, ran in gently sloping, swelling waves over it; the eye took in some five miles of deserted country; in the distance the round-scolloped tree-tops of some small birch-copses were the only objects to break the almost straight line of the horizon. Narrow paths ran over the fields, disappeared into the hollows, and wound round the hillocks. On one of these paths, which happened to run into our road five hundred paces ahead of us, I made out a kind of procession. At this my coachman was looking.

It was a funeral. In front, in a little cart harnessed with one horse, and advancing at a walking pace, came the priest; beside him sat the deacon driving; behind the cart four peasants, bareheaded, carried the coffin, covered with a white cloth; two women followed the coffin. The shrill wailing voice of one of them suddenly reached my ears; I listened; she was intoning a dirge. Very dismal sounded this chanted, monotonous, hopelessly-sorrowful lament among the empty fields. The coachman whipped up the horses; he wanted to get in front of this procession. To meet a corpse on the road is a bad omen. And he did succeed in galloping ahead beyond this path before the funeral had had time to turn out of it into the high-road; but we had hardly got a hundred paces beyond this point, when suddenly our trap jolted violently, heeled on one side, and all but overturned. The coachman pulled up the galloping horses, and spat with a gesture of his hand.

'What is it?' I asked.

My coachman got down without speaking or hurrying himself.

'But what is it?'

'The axle is broken ... it caught fire,' he replied gloomily, and he suddenly arranged the collar on the off-side horse with such indignation that it was almost pushed over, but it stood its ground, snorted, shook itself, and tranquilly began to scratch its foreleg below the knee with its teeth.

I got out and stood for some time on the road, a prey to a vague and unpleasant feeling of helplessness. The right wheel was almost completely bent in under the trap, and it seemed to turn its centre- piece upwards in dumb despair.

'What are we to do now?' I said at last.

'That's what's the cause of it!' said my coachman, pointing with his whip to the funeral procession, which had just turned into the highroad and was approaching us. 'I have always noticed that,' he went on; 'it's a true saying—"Meet a corpse"—yes, indeed.'

And again he began worrying the off-side horse, who, seeing his ill- humour, resolved to remain perfectly quiet, and contented itself with discreetly switching its tail now and then. I walked up and down a little while, and then stopped again before the wheel.

Meanwhile the funeral had come up to us. Quietly turning off the road on to the grass, the mournful procession moved slowly past us. My coachman and I took off our caps, saluted the priest, and exchanged glances with the bearers. They moved with difficulty under their burden, their broad chests standing out under the strain. Of the two women who followed the coffin, one was very old and pale; her set face, terribly distorted as it was by grief, still kept an expression of grave and severe dignity. She walked in silence, from time to time lifting her wasted hand to her thin drawn lips. The other, a young woman of five-and-twenty, had her eyes red and moist and her whole face swollen with weeping; as she passed us she ceased wailing, and hid her face in her sleeve.... But when the funeral had got round us and turned again into the road, her piteous, heart-piercing lament began again. My coachman followed the measured swaying of the coffin with his eyes in silence. Then he turned to me.

'It's Martin, the carpenter, they're burying,' he said; 'Martin of Ryaby.'

'How do you know?'

'I know by the women. The old one is his mother, and the young one's his wife.'

'Has he been ill, then?'

'Yes ... fever. The day before yesterday the overseer sent for the doctor, but they did not find the doctor at home. He was a good carpenter; he drank a bit, but he was a good carpenter. See how upset his good woman is.... But, there; women's tears don't cost much, we know. Women's tears are only water ... yes, indeed.'

And he bent down, crept under the side-horse's trace, and seized the wooden yoke that passes over the horses' heads with both hands.

'Any way,' I observed, 'what are we going to do?'

My coachman just supported himself with his knees on the shaft-horse's shoulder, twice gave the back-strap a shake, and straightened the pad; then he crept out of the side-horse's trace again, and giving it a blow on the nose as he passed, went up to the wheel. He went up to it, and, never taking his eyes off it, slowly took out of the skirts of his coat a box, slowly pulled open its lid by a strap, slowly thrust into it his two fat fingers (which pretty well filled it up), rolled and rolled up some snuff, and creasing up his nose in anticipation, helped himself to it several times in succession, accompanying the snuff-taking every time by a prolonged sneezing. Then, his streaming eyes blinking faintly, he relapsed into profound meditation.

'Well?' I said at last.

My coachman thrust his box carefully into his pocket, brought his hat forward on to his brows without the aid of his hand by a movement of his head, and gloomily got up on the box.

'What are you doing?' I asked him, somewhat bewildered.

'Pray be seated,' he replied calmly, picking up the reins.

'But how can we go on?'

'We will go on now.'

'But the axle.'

'Pray be seated.'

'But the axle is broken.'

'It is broken; but we will get to the settlement ... at a walking pace, of course. Over here, beyond the copse, on the right, is a settlement; they call it Yudino.'

'And do you think we can get there?'

My coachman did not vouchsafe me a reply.

'I had better walk,' I said.

'As you like....' And he nourished his whip. The horses started.

We did succeed in getting to the settlement, though the right front wheel was almost off, and turned in a very strange way. On one hillock it almost flew off, but my coachman shouted in a voice of exasperation, and we descended it in safety.

Yudino settlement consisted of six little low-pitched huts, the walls of which had already begun to warp out of the perpendicular, though they had certainly not been long built; the back-yards of some of the huts were not even fenced in with a hedge. As we drove into this settlement we did not meet a single living soul; there were no hens even to be seen in the street, and no dogs, but one black crop-tailed cur, which at our approach leaped hurriedly out of a perfectly dry and empty trough, to which it must have been

63

driven by thirst, and at once, without barking, rushed headlong under a gate. I went up to the first hut, opened the door into the outer room, and called for the master of the house. No one answered me. I called once more; the hungry mewing of a cat sounded behind the other door. I pushed it open with my foot; a thin cat ran up and down near me, her green eyes glittering in the dark. I put my head into the room and looked round; it was empty, dark, and smoky. I returned to the yard, and there was no one there either.... A calf lowed behind the paling; a lame grey goose waddled a little away. I passed on to the second hut. Not a soul in the second hut either. I went into the yard....

In the very middle of the yard, in the glaring sunlight, there lay, with his face on the ground and a cloak thrown over his head, a boy, as it seemed to me. In a thatched shed a few paces from him a thin little nag with broken harness was standing near a wretched little cart. The sunshine falling in streaks through the narrow cracks in the dilapidated roof, striped his shaggy, reddish-brown coat in small bands of light. Above, in the high bird-house, starlings were chattering and looking down inquisitively from their airy home. I went up to the sleeping figure and began to awaken him.

He lifted his head, saw me, and at once jumped up on to his feet....
'What? what do you want? what is it?' he muttered, half asleep.

I did not answer him at once; I was so much impressed by his appearance.

Picture to yourself a little creature of fifty years old, with a little round wrinkled face, a sharp nose, little, scarcely visible, brown eyes, and thick curly black hair, which stood out on his tiny head like the cap on the top of a mushroom. His whole person was excessively thin and weakly, and it is absolutely impossible to translate into words the extraordinary strangeness of his expression.

'What do you want?' he asked me again. I explained to him what was the matter; he listened, slowly blinking, without taking his eyes off me.

'So cannot we get a new axle?' I said finally; 'I will gladly pay for it.'

'But who are you? Hunters, eh?' he asked, scanning me from head to foot.

'Hunters.'

'You shoot the fowls of heaven, I suppose?... the wild things of the woods?... And is it not a sin to kill God's birds, to shed the innocent blood?'

The strange old man spoke in a very drawling tone. The sound of his voice also astonished me. There was none of the weakness of age to be heard in it; it was marvellously sweet, young and almost feminine in its softness.

'I have no axle,' he added after a brief silence. 'That thing will not suit you.' He pointed to his cart. 'You have, I expect, a large trap.'

'But can I get one in the village?'

'Not much of a village here!... No one has an axle here.... And there is no one at home either; they are all at work. You must go on,' he announced suddenly; and he lay down again on the ground.

I had not at all expected this conclusion.

'Listen, old man,' I said, touching him on the shoulder; 'do me a kindness, help me.'

'Go on, in God's name! I am tired; I have driven into the town,' he said, and drew his cloak over his head.

'But pray do me a kindness,' I said. 'I ... I will pay for it.' 'I don't want your money.'

'But please, old man.'

He half raised himself and sat up, crossing his little legs.

'I could take you perhaps to the clearing. Some merchants have bought the forest here—God be their judge! They are cutting down the forest, and they have built a counting-house there—God be their judge! You might order an axle of them there, or buy one ready made.'

'Splendid!' I cried delighted; 'splendid! let us go.'

'An oak axle, a good one,' he continued, not getting up from his place.

'And is it far to this clearing?'

'Three miles.'

'Come, then! we can drive there in your trap.'

'Oh, no....'

'Come, let us go,' I said; 'let us go, old man! The coachman is waiting for us in the road.'

The old man rose unwillingly and followed me into the street. We found my coachman in an irritable frame of mind; he had tried to water his horses, but the water in the well, it appeared, was scanty in quantity and bad in taste, and water is the first consideration with coachmen.... However, he grinned at the sight of the old man, nodded his head and cried: 'Hallo! Kassyanushka! good health to you!'

'Good health to you, Erofay, upright man!' replied Kassyan in a dejected voice.

I at once made known his suggestion to the coachman; Erofay expressed his approval of it and drove into the yard. While he was busy deliberately unharnessing the horses, the old man stood leaning with his shoulders against the gate, and looking disconsolately first at him and then at me. He seemed in some uncertainty of mind; he was not very pleased, as it seemed to me, at our sudden visit.

'So they have transported you too?' Erofay asked him suddenly, lifting the wooden arch of the harness.

'Yes.'

'Ugh!' said my coachman between his teeth. 'You know Martin the carpenter.... Of course, you know Martin of Ryaby?'

'Yes.'

'Well, he is dead. We have just met his coffin.'

Kassyan shuddered.

'Dead?' he said, and his head sank dejectedly.

'Yes, he is dead. Why didn't you cure him, eh? You know they say you cure folks; you're a doctor.'

My coachman was apparently laughing and jeering at the old man.

'And is this your trap, pray?' he added, with a shrug of his shoulders in its direction.

'Yes.'

'Well, a trap ... a fine trap!' he repeated, and taking it by the shafts almost turned it completely upside down. 'A trap!... But what will you drive in it to the clearing?... You can't harness our horses in these shafts; our horses are all too big.'

'I don't know,' replied Kassyan, 'what you are going to drive; that beast perhaps,' he added with a sigh.

'That?' broke in Erofay, and going up to Kassyan's nag, he tapped it disparagingly on the back with the third finger of his right hand. 'See,' he added contemptuously, 'it's asleep, the scare-crow!'

I asked Erofay to harness it as quickly as he could. I wanted to drive myself with Kassyan to the clearing; grouse are fond of such places. When the little cart was quite ready, and I, together with my dog, had been installed in the warped wicker body of it, and Kassyan huddled up into a little ball, with still the same dejected expression on his

65

face, had taken his seat in front, Erofay came up to me and whispered with an air of mystery:

'You did well, your honour, to drive with him. He is such a queer fellow; he's cracked, you know, and his nickname is the Flea. I don't know how you managed to make him out....'

I tried to say to Erofay that so far Kassyan had seemed to me a very sensible man; but my coachman continued at once in the same voice:

'But you keep a look-out where he is driving you to. And, your honour, be pleased to choose the axle yourself; be pleased to choose a sound one.... Well, Flea,' he added aloud, 'could I get a bit of bread in your house?'

'Look about; you may find some,' answered Kassyan. He pulled the reins and we rolled away.

His little horse, to my genuine astonishment, did not go badly. Kassyan preserved an obstinate silence the whole way, and made abrupt and unwilling answers to my questions. We quickly reached the clearing, and then made our way to the counting-house, a lofty cottage, standing by itself over a small gully, which had been dammed up and converted into a pool. In this counting-house I found two young merchants' clerks, with snow-white teeth, sweet and soft eyes, sweet and subtle words, and sweet and wily smiles. I bought an axle of them and returned to the clearing. I thought that Kassyan would stay with the horse and await my return; but he suddenly came up to me.

'Are you going to shoot birds, eh?' he said.

'Yes, if I come across any.'

'I will come with you.... Can I?'

'Certainly, certainly.'

So we went together. The land cleared was about a mile in length. I must confess I watched Kassyan more than my dogs. He had been aptly called 'Flea.' His little black uncovered head (though his hair, indeed, was as good a covering as any cap) seemed to flash hither and thither among the bushes. He walked extraordinarily swiftly, and seemed always hopping up and down as he moved; he was for ever stooping down to pick herbs of some kind, thrusting them into his bosom, muttering to himself, and constantly looking at me and my dog with such a strange searching gaze. Among low bushes and in clearings there are often little grey birds which constantly flit from tree to tree, and which whistle as they dart away. Kassyan mimicked them, answered their calls; a young quail flew from between his feet, chirruping, and he chirruped in imitation of him; a lark began to fly down above him, moving his wings and singing melodiously: Kassyan joined in his song. He did not speak to me at all....

The weather was glorious, even more so than before; but the heat was no less. Over the clear sky the high thin clouds were hardly stirred, yellowish-white, like snow lying late in spring, flat and drawn out like rolled-up sails. Slowly but perceptibly their fringed edges, soft and fluffy as cotton-wool, changed at every moment; they were melting away, even these clouds, and no shadow fell from them. I strolled about the clearing for a long while with Kassyan. Young shoots, which had not yet had time to grow more than a yard high, surrounded the low blackened stumps with their smooth slender stems; and spongy funguses with grey edges—the same of which they make tinder—clung to these; strawberry plants flung their rosy tendrils over them; mushrooms squatted close in groups. The feet were constantly caught and entangled in the long grass, that was parched in the scorching sun; the eyes were dazzled on all sides by the glaring metallic glitter on the young reddish leaves of the trees; on all sides were the variegated blue clusters of vetch, the golden cups of bloodwort, and the half-lilac, half-yellow blossoms of the heart's-ease. In some places near the disused paths, on which the tracks of wheels were marked by streaks on the fine bright grass, rose piles of wood, blackened by wind and rain, laid in yard-lengths; there was a faint shadow cast from them in slanting oblongs; there was no other shade anywhere. A light breeze rose, then sank again; suddenly it would blow straight in the face and seem to be rising; everything would begin to rustle merrily, to nod, to shake around one; the supple tops of the ferns bow down gracefully, and one rejoices in it, but at once it dies away again, and all is at rest once more. Only the grasshoppers chirrup in chorus with frenzied energy, and wearisome is this unceasing, sharp dry sound. It is in keeping with the persistent heat of mid-day; it seems akin to it, as though evoked by it out of the glowing earth.

Without having started one single covey we at last reached another clearing. There the aspen-trees had only lately been felled, and lay stretched mournfully on the ground, crushing the grass and small undergrowth below them: on some the leaves were still green, though they were already dead, and hung limply from the motionless branches; on others they were crumpled and dried up. Fresh golden-white chips lay in heaps round the stumps that were covered with bright drops; a peculiar, very pleasant, pungent odour rose from them. Farther away, nearer the wood, sounded the dull blows of the axe, and from time to time, bowing and spreading wide its arms, a bushy tree fell slowly and majestically to the ground.

For a long time I did not come upon a single bird; at last a corncrake flew out of a thick clump of young oak across the wormwood springing up round it. I fired; it turned over in the air and fell. At the sound of the shot, Kassyan quickly covered his eyes with his hand, and he did not stir till I had reloaded the gun and picked up the bird. When I had moved farther on, he went up to the place where the wounded bird had fallen, bent down to the grass, on which some drops of blood were sprinkled, shook his head, and looked in dismay at me.... I heard him afterwards whispering: 'A sin!... Ah, yes, it's a sin!'

The heat forced us at last to go into the wood. I flung myself down under a high nut-bush, over which a slender young maple gracefully stretched its light branches. Kassyan sat down on the thick trunk of a felled birch-tree. I looked at him. The leaves faintly stirred overhead, and their thin greenish shadows crept softly to and fro over his feeble body, muffled in a dark coat, and over his little face. He did not lift his head. Bored by his silence, I lay on my back and began to admire the tranquil play of the tangled foliage on the background of the bright, far away sky. A marvellously sweet occupation it is to lie on one's back in a wood and gaze upwards! You may fancy you are looking into a bottomless sea; that it stretches wide below you; that the trees are not rising out of the earth, but, like the roots of gigantic weeds, are dropping—falling straight down into those glassy, limpid depths; the leaves on the trees are at one moment transparent as emeralds, the next, they condense into golden, almost black green. Somewhere, afar off, at the end of a slender twig, a single leaf hangs motionless against the blue patch of transparent sky, and beside it another trembles with the motion of a fish on the line, as though moving of its own will, not shaken by the wind. Round white clouds float calmly across, and calmly pass away like submarine islands; and suddenly, all this ocean, this shining ether, these branches and leaves steeped in sunlight—all is rippling, quivering in fleeting brilliance, and a fresh trembling whisper awakens like the tiny, incessant plash of suddenly stirred eddies. One does not move—one looks, and no word can tell what peace, what joy, what sweetness reigns in the heart. One looks: the deep, pure blue stirs on one's lips a smile, innocent as itself; like the clouds over the sky, and, as it were, with them, happy memories pass in slow procession over the soul, and still one fancies one's gaze goes deeper and deeper, and draws one with it up into that peaceful, shining immensity, and that one cannot be brought back from that height, that depth....

'Master, master!' cried Kassyan suddenly in his musical voice.

I raised myself in surprise: up till then he had scarcely replied to my questions, and now he suddenly addressed me of himself.

'What is it?' I asked.

'What did you kill the bird for?' he began, looking me straight in the face.

'What for? Corncrake is game; one can eat it.'

'That was not what you killed it for, master, as though you were going to eat it! You killed it for amusement.'

'Well, you yourself, I suppose, eat geese or chickens?'

'Those birds are provided by God for man, but the corncrake is a wild bird of the woods: and not he alone; many they are, the wild things of the woods and the fields, and the wild things of the rivers and marshes and moors, flying on high or creeping below; and a sin it is to slay them: let them live their allotted life upon the earth. But for man another food has been provided; his food is other, and other his sustenance: bread, the good gift of God, and the water of heaven, and the tame beasts that have come down to us from our fathers of old.'

I looked in astonishment at Kassyan. His words flowed freely; he did not hesitate for a word; he spoke with quiet inspiration and gentle dignity, sometimes closing his eyes.

'So is it sinful, then, to kill fish, according to you?' I asked.

'Fishes have cold blood,' he replied with conviction. 'The fish is a dumb creature; it knows neither fear nor rejoicing. The fish is a voiceless creature. The fish does not feel; the blood in it is not living.... Blood,' he continued, after a pause, 'blood is a holy thing! God's sun does not look upon blood; it is hidden away from the light ... it is a great sin to bring blood into the light of day; a great sin and horror.... Ah, a great sin!'

He sighed, and his head drooped forward. I looked, I confess, in absolute amazement at the strange old man. His language did not sound like the language of a peasant; the common people do not speak like that, nor those who aim at fine speaking. His speech was meditative, grave, and curious.... I had never heard anything like it.

'Tell me, please, Kassyan,' I began, without taking my eyes off his slightly flushed face, 'what is your occupation?'

He did not answer my question at once. His eyes strayed uneasily for an instant.

'I live as the Lord commands,' he brought out at last; 'and as for occupation—no, I have no occupation. I've never been very clever from a child: I work when I can: I'm not much of a workman—how should I be? I have no health; my hands are awkward. In the spring I catch nightingales.'

'You catch nightingales?... But didn't you tell me that we must not touch any of the wild things of the woods and the fields, and so on?'

'We must not kill them, of a certainty; death will take its own without that. Look at Martin the carpenter; Martin lived, and his life was not long, but he died; his wife now grieves for her husband, for her little children.... Neither for man nor beast is there any charm against death. Death does not hasten, nor is there any escaping it; but we must not aid death.... And I do not kill nightingales—God forbid! I do not catch them to harm them, to spoil their lives, but for the pleasure of men, for their comfort and delight.'

'Do you go to Kursk to catch them?'

'Yes, I go to Kursk, and farther too, at times. I pass nights in the marshes, or at the edge of the forests; I am alone at night in the fields, in the thickets; there the curlews call and the hares squeak and the wild ducks lift up their voices.... I note them at evening; at morning I give ear to them; at daybreak I cast my net over the bushes.... There are nightingales that sing so pitifully sweet ... yea, pitifully.'

'And do you sell them?'

'I give them to good people.'

'And what are you doing now?'

'What am I doing?'

'Yes, how are you employed?'

The old man was silent for a little.

'I am not employed at all.... I am a poor workman. But I can read and write.'

'You can read?'

'Yes, I can read and write. I learnt, by the help of God and good people.'

'Have you a family?'

'No, not a family.'

'How so?... Are they dead, then?'

'No, but ... I have never been lucky in life. But all that is in God's hands; we are all in God's hands; and a man should be righteous—that is all! Upright before God, that is it.'

'And you have no kindred?'

'Yes ... well....'

The old man was confused.

'Tell me, please,' I began: 'I heard my coachman ask you why you did not cure Martin? You cure disease?'

'Your coachman is a righteous man,' Kassyan answered thoughtfully. 'I too am not without sin. They call me a doctor.... Me a doctor, indeed! And who can heal the sick? That is all a gift from God. But there are ... yes, there are herbs, and there are flowers; they are of use, of a certainty. There is plantain, for instance, a herb good for man; there is bud-marigold too; it is not sinful to speak of them: they are holy herbs of God. Then there are others not so; and they may be of use, but it's a sin; and to speak of them is a sin. Still, with prayer, may be.... And doubtless there are such words.... But who has faith, shall be saved,' he added, dropping his voice.

'You did not give Martin anything?' I asked.

'I heard of it too late,' replied the old man. 'But what of it! Each man's destiny is written from his birth. The carpenter Martin was not to live; he was not to live upon the earth: that was what it was. No, when a man is not to live on the earth, him the sunshine does not warm like another, and him the bread does not nourish and make strong; it is as though something is drawing him away.... Yes: God rest his soul!'

'Have you been settled long amongst us?' I asked him after a short pause.

Kassyan started.

'No, not long; four years. In the old master's time we always lived in our old houses, but the trustees transported us. Our old master was a kind heart, a man of peace—the Kingdom of Heaven be his! The trustees doubtless judged righteously.'

'And where did you live before?'

'At Fair Springs.'

'Is it far from here?'

'A hundred miles.'

'Well, were you better off there?'

'Yes ... yes, there there was open country, with rivers; it was our home: here we are cramped and parched up.... Here we are strangers. There at home, at Fair Springs, you could get up on to a hill—and ah, my God, what a sight you could see! Streams and plains and forests, and there was a church, and then came plains beyond. You could see far, very far. Yes, how far you could look—you could look and look, ah, yes! Here, doubtless, the soil is better; it is clay—good fat clay, as the peasants say; for me the corn grows well enough everywhere.'

'Confess then, old man; you would like to visit your birth-place again?'

'Yes, I should like to see it. Still, all places are good. I am a man without kin, without neighbours. And, after all, do you gain much, pray, by staying at home? But, behold! as you walk, and as you walk,' he went on, raising his voice, 'the heart grows lighter, of a truth. And the sun shines upon you, and you are in the sight of God, and the singing comes more tunefully. Here, you look—what herb is growing; you look on it—you pick it. Here water runs, perhaps—spring water, a source of pure holy water; so you drink of it—you look on it too. The birds of heaven sing.... And beyond Kursk come the steppes, that steppes-country: ah, what a marvel, what a delight for man! what freedom, what a blessing of God! And they go on, folks tell, even to the warm seas where dwells the sweet-voiced bird, the Hamayune, and from the trees the leaves fall not, neither in autumn nor in winter, and apples grow of gold, on silver branches, and every man lives in uprightness and content. And I would go even there.... Have I journeyed so little already! I have been to Romyon and to Simbirsk the fair city, and even to Moscow of the golden domes; I have been to Oka the good nurse, and to Tsna the dove, and to our mother Volga, and many folks, good Christians have I seen, and noble cities I have visited.... Well, I would go thither ... yes ... and more too ... and I am not the only one, I a poor sinner ... many other Christians go in bast-shoes, roaming over the world, seeking truth, yea!... For what is there at home? No righteousness in man—it's that.'

These last words Kassyan uttered quickly, almost unintelligibly; then he said something more which I could not catch at all, and such a strange expression passed over his face that I involuntarily recalled the epithet 'cracked.' He looked down, cleared his throat, and seemed to come to himself again. 'What sunshine!' he murmured in a low voice. 'It is a blessing, oh, Lord! What warmth in the woods!'

He gave a movement of the shoulders and fell into silence. With a vague look round him he began softly to sing. I could not catch all the words of his slow chant; I heard the following:

'They call me Kassyan,
But my nickname's the Flea.'

'Oh!' I thought, 'so he improvises.' Suddenly he started and ceased singing, looking intently at a thick part of the wood. I turned and saw a little peasant girl, about seven years old, in a blue frock, with a checked handkerchief over her head, and a woven bark-basket in her little bare sunburnt hand. She had certainly not expected to meet us; she had, as they say, 'stumbled upon' us, and she stood motionless in a shady recess among the thick foliage of the nut-trees, looking dismayed at me with her black eyes. I had scarcely time to catch a glimpse of her; she dived behind a tree.

'Annushka! Annushka! come here, don't be afraid!' cried the old man caressingly.

'I'm afraid,' came her shrill voice.

'Don't be afraid, don't be afraid; come to me.'

Annushka left her hiding place in silence, walked softly round—her little childish feet scarcely sounded on the thick grass—and came out of the bushes near the old man. She was not a child of seven, as I had fancied at first, from her diminutive stature, but a girl of thirteen or fourteen. Her whole person was small and thin, but very neat and graceful, and her pretty little face was strikingly like Kassyan's own, though he was certainly not handsome. There were the same thin features, and the same strange expression, shy and confiding, melancholy and shrewd, and her gestures were the same.... Kassyan kept his eyes fixed on her; she took her stand at his side.

'Well, have you picked any mushrooms?' he asked.

'Yes,' she answered with a shy smile.

'Did you find many?'

'Yes.' (She stole a swift look at him and smiled again.)

'Are they white ones?'

'Yes.'

'Show me, show me.... (She slipped the basket off her arm and half-lifted the big burdock leaf which covered up the mushrooms.) 'Ah!' said Kassyan, bending down over the basket; 'what splendid ones! Well done, Annushka!'

'She's your daughter, Kassyan, isn't she?' I asked. (Annushka's face flushed faintly.)

'No, well, a relative,' replied Kassyan with affected indifference. 'Come, Annushka, run along,' he added at once, 'run along, and God be with you! And take care.'

'But why should she go on foot?' I interrupted. 'We could take her with us.'

Annushka blushed like a poppy, grasped the handle of her basket with both hands, and looked in trepidation at the old man.

'No, she will get there all right,' he answered in the same languid and indifferent voice. 'Why not?... She will get there.... Run along.'

Annushka went rapidly away into the forest. Kassyan looked after her, then looked down and smiled to himself. In this prolonged smile, in the few words he had spoken to Annushka, and in the very sound of his voice when he spoke to her, there was an intense, indescribable love and tenderness. He looked again in the direction she had gone, again smiled to himself, and, passing his hand across his face, he nodded his head several times.

'Why did you send her away so soon?' I asked him. 'I would have bought her mushrooms.'

'Well, you can buy them there at home just the same, sir, if you like,' he answered, for the first time using the formal 'sir' in addressing me.

'She's very pretty, your girl.'

'No ... only so-so,' he answered, with seeming reluctance, and from that instant he relapsed into the same uncommunicative mood as at first.

Seeing that all my efforts to make him talk again were fruitless, I went off into the clearing. Meantime the heat had somewhat abated; but my ill-success, or, as they say among us, my 'ill-luck,' continued, and I returned to the settlement with nothing but one corncrake and the new axle. Just as we were driving into the yard, Kassyan suddenly turned to me.

'Master, master,' he began, 'do you know I have done you a wrong; it was I cast a spell to keep all the game off.'

'How so?'

'Oh, I can do that. Here you have a well-trained dog and a good one, but he could do nothing. When you think of it, what are men? what are they? Here's a beast; what have they made of him?'

It would have been useless for me to try to convince Kassyan of the impossibility of 'casting a spell' on game, and so I made him no reply. Meantime we had turned into the yard.

Annushka was not in the hut: she had had time to get there before us, and to leave her basket of mushrooms. Erofay fitted in the new axle, first exposing it to a severe and most unjust criticism; and an hour later I set off, leaving a small sum of money with Kassyan, which at first he was unwilling to accept, but afterwards, after a moment's thought, holding it in his hand, he put it in his bosom. In the course of this hour he had scarcely uttered a single word; he stood as before, leaning against the gate. He made no reply to the reproaches of my coachman, and took leave very coldly of me.

Directly I turned round, I could see that my worthy Erofay was in a gloomy frame of mind.... To be sure, he had found nothing to eat in the country; the only water for his horses was bad. We drove off. With dissatisfaction expressed even in the back of his head, he sat on the box, burning to begin to talk to me. While waiting for me to begin by some question, he confined himself to a low muttering in an undertone, and some rather caustic instructions to the horses. 'A village,' he muttered; 'call that a village? You ask for a drop of kvas—not a drop of kvas even.... Ah, Lord!... And the water—simply filth!' (He spat loudly.) 'Not a cucumber, nor kvas, nor nothing.... Now, then!' he added aloud, turning to the right trace-horse; 'I know you, you humbug.' (And he gave him a cut with the whip.) 'That horse has learnt to shirk his work entirely, and yet he was a willing beast once. Now, then—look alive!'

'Tell me, please, Erofay,' I began, 'what sort of a man is Kassyan?'

Erofay did not answer me at once: he was, in general, a reflective and deliberate fellow; but I could see directly that my question was soothing and cheering to him.

'The Flea?' he said at last, gathering up the reins; 'he's a queer fellow; yes, a crazy chap; such a queer fellow, you wouldn't find another like him in a hurry. You know, for example, he's for all the world like our roan horse here; he gets out of everything—out of work, that's to say. But, then, what sort of workman could he be?... He's hardly body enough to keep his soul in ... but still, of course.... He's been like that from a child up, you know. At first he followed his uncle's business as a carrier   there were three of them in the business; but then he got tired of it, you know—he threw it up. He began to live at home, but he could not keep at home long; he's so restless—a regular flea, in fact. He happened, by good luck, to have a good master—he didn't worry him. Well, so ever since he has been wandering about like a lost sheep. And then, he's so strange; there's no understanding him. Sometimes he'll be as silent as a post, and then he'll begin talking, and God knows what he'll say! Is that good manners, pray? He's an absurd fellow, that he is. But he sings well, for all that.'

'And does he cure people, really?'

'Cure people!... Well, how should he? A fine sort of doctor! Though he did cure me of the king's evil, I must own.... But how can he? He's a stupid fellow, that's what he is,' he added, after a moment's pause.

'Have you known him long?'

'A long while. I was his neighbour at Sitchovka up at Fair Springs.'

'And what of that girl—who met us in the wood, Annushka—what relation is she to him?'

Erofay looked at me over his shoulder, and grinned all over his face.

'He, he!... yes, they are relations. She is an orphan; she has no mother, and it's not even known who her mother was. But she must be a relation; she's too much like him.... Anyway, she lives with him. She's a smart girl, there's no denying; a good girl; and as for the old man, she's simply the apple of his eye; she's a good girl. And, do you know, you wouldn't believe it, but do you know, he's managed to teach Annushka to read? Well, well! that's quite like him; he's such an extraordinary fellow, such a changeable fellow; there's no reckoning on him, really.... Eh! eh! eh!' My coachman suddenly interrupted himself, and stopping the horses, he bent over on one side and began sniffing. 'Isn't there a smell of burning? Yes! Why, that new axle, I do declare!... I thought I'd greased it.... We must get on to some water; why, here is a puddle, just right.'

And Erofay slowly got off his seat, untied the pail, went to the pool, and coming back, listened with a certain satisfaction to the hissing of the box of the wheel as the water suddenly touched it.... Six times during some eight miles he had to pour water on the smouldering axle, and it was quite evening when we got home at last.

X

THE AGENT

Twelve miles from my place lives an acquaintance of mine, a landowner and a retired officer in the Guards—Arkady Pavlitch Pyenotchkin. He has a great deal of game on his estate, a house built after the design of a French architect, and servants dressed after the English fashion; he gives capital dinners, and a cordial reception to visitors, and, with all that, one goes to see him reluctantly. He is a sensible and practical man, has received the excellent education now usual, has been in the service, mixed in the highest society, and is now devoting himself to his estate with great success. Arkady Pavlitch is, to judge by his own words, severe but just; he looks after the good of the peasants under his control and punishes them—for their good. 'One has to treat them like children,' he says on such occasions; 'their ignorance, *mon cher; il faut prendre cela en considération.*' When this so-called painful necessity arises, he eschews all sharp or violent gestures, and prefers not to raise his voice, but with a straight blow in the culprit's face, says calmly, 'I believe I asked you to do something, my friend?' or 'What is the matter, my boy? what are you thinking about?' while he sets his teeth a little, and the corners of his mouth are drawn. He is not tall, but has an elegant figure, and is very good-looking; his hands and nails are kept perfectly exquisite; his rosy cheeks and lips are simply the picture of health. He has a ringing, light-hearted laugh, and there is sometimes a very genial twinkle in his clear brown eyes. He dresses in excellent taste; he orders French books, prints, and papers, though he's no great lover of reading himself: he has hardly as much as waded through the *Wandering Jew*. He plays cards in masterly style. Altogether, Arkady Pavlitch is reckoned one of the most cultivated gentlemen and most eligible matches in our province; the ladies are perfectly wild over him, and especially admire his manners. He is wonderfully well conducted, wary as a cat, and has never from his cradle been mixed up in any scandal, though he is fond of making his power felt, intimidating or snubbing a nervous man, when he gets a chance. He has a positive distaste for doubtful society—he is afraid of compromising himself; in his lighter moments, however, he will avow himself a follower of Epicurus, though as a rule he speaks slightingly of philosophy, calling it the foggy food fit for German brains, or at times, simply, rot. He is fond of music too; at the card-table he is given to humming through his teeth, but with feeling; he knows by heart some snatches from *Lucia* and *Somnambula*, but he is always apt to sing everything a little sharp. The winters he spends in Petersburg. His house is kept in extraordinarily good order; the very grooms feel his influence, and every day not only rub the harness and brush their coats, but even wash their faces. Arkady Pavlitch's house-serfs have, it is true, something of a hang-dog look; but among us Russians there's no knowing what is sullenness and what is sleepiness. Arkady Pavlitch speaks in a soft, agreeable voice, with emphasis and, as it were, with satisfaction; he brings out each word through his handsome perfumed moustaches; he uses a good many French expressions too, such as: *Mais c'est impayable! Mais comment donc*? and so so. For all that, I, for one, am never over-eager to visit him, and if it were not for the grouse and the partridges, I should probably have dropped his acquaintance altogether. One is possessed by a strange sort of uneasiness in his house; the very comfort is distasteful to one, and every evening when a befrizzed valet makes his appearance in a blue livery with heraldic buttons, and begins, with cringing servility, drawing off one's boots, one feels that if his pale, lean figure could suddenly be replaced by the amazingly broad cheeks and incredibly thick nose of a stalwart young labourer fresh from the plough, who has yet had time in his ten months of service to tear his new nankin coat open at every seam, one would be unutterably overjoyed, and would gladly run the risk of having one's whole leg pulled off with the boot....

In spite of my aversion for Arkady Pavlitch, I once happened to pass a night in his house. The next day I ordered my carriage to be ready early in the morning, but he would not let me start without a regular breakfast in the English style, and conducted me into his study. With our tea they served us cutlets, boiled eggs, butter, honey, cheese, and so on. Two footmen in clean white gloves swiftly and silently anticipated our faintest desires. We sat on a Persian divan. Arkady Pavlitch was arrayed in loose silk trousers, a black velvet smoking jacket, a red fez with a blue tassel, and yellow Chinese slippers without heels. He drank his tea, laughed, scrutinised his finger-nails, propped himself up with cushions, and was altogether in an excellent humour. After making a hearty breakfast with obvious satisfaction, Arkady Pavlitch poured himself out a glass of red wine, lifted it to his lips, and suddenly frowned.

'Why was not the wine warmed?' he asked rather sharply of one of the footmen.

The footman stood stock-still in confusion, and turned white.

'Didn't I ask you a question, my friend?' Arkady Pavlitch resumed tranquilly, never taking his eyes off the man.

The luckless footman fidgeted in his place, twisted the napkin, and uttered not a word.

Arkady Pavlitch dropped his head and looked up at him thoughtfully from under his eyelids.

'*Pardon, mon cher*', he observed, patting my knee amicably, and again he stared at the footman. 'You can go,' he added, after a short silence, raising his eyebrows, and he rang the bell.

A stout, swarthy, black-haired man, with a low forehead, and eyes positively lost in fat, came into the room.

'About Fyodor ... make the necessary arrangements,' said Arkady Pavlitch in an undertone, and with complete composure.

'Yes, sir,' answered the fat man, and he went out.

'*Voilà, mon cher, les désagréments de la campagne*,' Arkady Pavlitch remarked gaily. 'But where are you off to? Stop, you must stay a little.'

'No,' I answered; 'it's time I was off.'

'Nothing but sport! Oh, you sportsmen! And where are you going to shoot just now?'

'Thirty-five miles from here, at Ryabovo.'

'Ryabovo? By Jove! now in that case I will come with you. Ryabovo's only four miles from my village Shipilovka, and it's a long while since I've been over to Shipilovka; I've never been able to get the time. Well, this is a piece of luck; you can spend the day shooting in Ryabovo and come on in the evening to me. We'll have supper together— we'll take the cook with us, and you'll stay the night with me. Capital! capital!' he added without waiting for my answer.

'*C'est arrangé*.... Hey, you there! Have the carriage brought out, and look sharp. You have never been in Shipilovka? I should be ashamed to suggest your putting up for the night in my agent's cottage, but you're not particular, I know, and at Ryabovo you'd have slept in some hayloft.... We will go, we will go!'

And Arkady Pavlitch hummed some French song.

'You don't know, I dare say,' he pursued, swaying from side to side; 'I've some peasants there who pay rent. It's the custom of the place— what was I to do? They pay their rent very punctually, though. I should, I'll own, have put them back to payment in labour, but there's so little land. I really wonder how they manage to make both ends meet. However, *c'est leur affaire*. My agent there's a fine fellow, *une forte tête*, a man of real administrative power! You shall see.... Really, how luckily things have turned out!'

There was no help for it. Instead of nine o'clock in the morning, we started at two in the afternoon. Sportsmen will sympathise with my impatience. Arkady Pavlitch liked, as he expressed it, to be comfortable when he had the chance, and he took with him such a supply of linen, dainties, wearing apparel, perfumes, pillows, and dressing- cases of all sorts, that a careful and self-denying German would have found enough to last him for a year. Every time we went down a steep hill, Arkady Pavlitch addressed some brief but powerful remarks to the coachman, from which I was able to deduce that my worthy friend was a thorough coward. The journey was, however, performed in safety, except that, in crossing a lately-repaired bridge, the trap with the cook in it broke down, and he got squeezed in the stomach against the hind- wheel.

Arkady Pavlitch was alarmed in earnest at the sight of the fall of Karem, his home-made professor of the culinary art, and he sent at once to inquire whether his hands were injured. On receiving a reassuring reply to this query, his mind was set at rest immediately. With all this, we were rather a long time on the road; I was in the same carriage as Arkady Pavlitch, and towards the end of the journey I was a prey to deadly boredom, especially as in a few hours my companion ran perfectly dry of subjects of conversation, and even fell to expressing his liberal views on politics. At last we did arrive—not at Ryabovo, but at Shipilovka; it happened so somehow. I could have got no shooting now that day in any case, and so, raging inwardly, I submitted to my fate.

The cook had arrived a few minutes before us, and apparently had had time to arrange things and prepare those whom it concerned, for on our very entrance within the village boundaries we were met by the village bailiff (the agent's son), a stalwart, red-haired peasant of seven feet; he was on horseback, bareheaded, and wearing a new overcoat, not buttoned up. 'And where's Sofron?' Arkady Pavlitch asked him. The bailiff first jumped nimbly off his horse, bowed to his master till he was bent double, and said: 'Good health to you, Arkady Pavlitch, sir!' then raised his head, shook himself, and announced that Sofron had gone to Perov, but they had sent after him.

'Well, come along after us,' said Arkady Pavlitch. The bailiff deferentially led his horse to one side, clambered on to it, and followed the carriage at a trot, his cap in his hand. We drove through the village. A few peasants in empty carts happened to meet us; they were driving from the threshing-floor and singing songs, swaying backwards and forwards, and swinging their legs in the air; but at the sight of our carriage and the bailiff they were suddenly silent, took off their winter caps (it was summer-time) and got up as though waiting for orders. Arkady Pavlitch nodded to them graciously. A flutter of excitement had obviously spread through the hamlet. Peasant women in check petticoats flung splinters of wood at indiscreet or over-zealous dogs; an old lame man with a beard that began just under his eyes pulled a horse away from the well before it had drunk, gave it, for some obscure reason, a blow on the side, and fell to bowing low. Boys in long smocks ran with a howl to the huts, flung themselves on their bellies on the high door-sills, with their heads down and legs in the air, rolled over with the utmost haste into the dark outer rooms, from which they did not reappear again. Even the hens sped in a hurried scuttle to the turning; one bold cock with a black throat like a satin waistcoat and a red tail, rumpled up to his very comb, stood his ground in the road, and even prepared for a crow, then suddenly took fright and scuttled off too. The agent's cottage stood apart from the rest in the middle of a thick green patch of hemp. We stopped at the gates. Mr.

Pyenotchkin got up, flung off his cloak with a picturesque motion, and got out of the carriage, looking affably about him. The agent's wife met us with low curtseys, and came up to kiss the master's hand. Arkady Pavlitch let her kiss it to her heart's content, and mounted the steps. In the outer room, in a dark corner, stood the bailiff's wife, and she too curtsied, but did not venture to approach his hand. In the cold hut, as it is called—to the right of the outer room—two other women were still busily at work; they were carrying out all the rubbish, empty tubs, sheepskins stiff as boards, greasy pots, a cradle with a heap of dish-clouts and a baby covered with spots, and sweeping out the dirt with bathbrooms. Arkady Pavlitch sent them away, and installed himself on a bench under the holy pictures. The coachmen began bringing in the trunks, bags, and other conveniences, trying each time to subdue the noise of their heavy boots.

Meantime Arkady Pavlitch began questioning the bailiff about the crops, the sowing, and other agricultural subjects. The bailiff gave satisfactory answers, but spoke with a sort of heavy awkwardness, as though he were buttoning up his coat with benumbed fingers. He stood at the door and kept looking round on the watch to make way for the nimble footman. Behind his powerful shoulders I managed to get a glimpse of the agent's wife in the outer room surreptitiously belabouring some other peasant woman. Suddenly a cart rumbled up and stopped at the steps; the agent came in.

This man, as Arkady Pavlitch said, of real administrative power, was short, broad-shouldered, grey, and thick-set, with a red nose, little blue eyes, and a beard of the shape of a fan. We may observe, by the way, that ever since Russia has existed, there has never yet been an instance of a man who has grown rich and prosperous without a big, bushy beard; sometimes a man may have had a thin, wedge-shape beard all his life; but then he begins to get one all at once, it is all round his face like a halo—one wonders where the hair has come from! The agent must have been making merry at Perov: his face was unmistakably flushed, and there was a smell of spirits about him.

'Ah, our father, our gracious benefactor!' he began in a sing-song voice, and with a face of such deep feeling that it seemed every minute as if he would burst into tears; 'at last you have graciously deigned to come to us ... your hand, your honour's hand,' he added, his lips protruded in anticipation. Arkady Pavlitch gratified his desire. 'Well, brother Sofron, how are things going with you?' he asked in a friendly voice.

'Ah, you, our father!' cried Sofron; 'how should they go ill? how should things go ill, now that you, our father, our benefactor, graciously deign to lighten our poor village with your presence, to make us happy till the day of our death? Thank the Lord for thee, Arkady Pavlitch! thank the Lord for thee! All is right by your gracious favour.'

At this point Sofron paused, gazed upon his master, and, as though carried away by a rush of feeling (tipsiness had its share in it too), begged once more for his hand, and whined more than before.

'Ah, you, our father, benefactor ... and ... There, God bless me! I'm a regular fool with delight.... God bless me! I look and can't believe my eyes! Ah, our father!'

Arkady Pavlitch glanced at me, smiled, and asked: '*N'est-ce pas que c'est touchant?*'

'But, Arkady Pavlitch, your honour,' resumed the indefatigable agent; 'what are you going to do? You'll break my heart, your honour; your honour didn't graciously let me know of your visit. Where are you to put up for the night? You see here it's dirty, nasty.'

'Nonsense, Sofron, nonsense!' Arkady Pavlitch responded, with a smile; 'it's all right here.'

'But, our father, all right—for whom? For peasants like us it's all right; but for you ... oh, our father, our gracious protector! oh, you ... our father!... Pardon an old fool like me; I'm off my head, bless me! I'm gone clean crazy.'

Meanwhile supper was served; Arkady Pavlitch began to eat. The old man packed his son off, saying he smelt too strong.

'Well, settled the division of land, old chap, hey?' enquired Mr. Pyenotchkin, obviously trying to imitate the peasant speech, with a wink to me.

'We've settled the land shares, your honour; all by your gracious favour. Day before yesterday the list was made out. The Hlinovsky folks made themselves disagreeable about it at first ... they were disagreeable about it, certainly. They wanted this ... and they wanted that ... and God knows what they didn't want! but they're a set of fools, your honour!—an ignorant lot. But we, your honour, graciously please you, gave an earnest of our gratitude, and satisfied Nikolai Nikolaitch, the mediator; we acted in everything according to your orders, your honour; as you graciously ordered, so we did, and nothing did we do unbeknown to Yegor Dmitritch.'

'Yegor reported to me,' Arkady Pavlitch remarked with dignity.

'To be sure, your honour, Yegor Dmitritch, to be sure.'

'Well, then, now I suppose you 're satisfied.'

Sofron had only been waiting for this.

'Ah, you are our father, our benefactor!' he began, in the same sing- song as before. 'Indeed, now, your honour ... why, for you, our father, we pray day and night to God Almighty.... There's too little land, of course....'

Pyenotchkin cut him short.

'There, that'll do, that'll do, Sofron; I know you're eager in my service.... Well, and how goes the threshing?'

Sofron sighed.

'Well, our father, the threshing's none too good. But there, your honour, Arkady Pavlitch, let me tell you about a little matter that came to pass.' (Here he came closer to Mr. Pyenotchkin, with his arms apart, bent down, and screwed up one eye.) 'There was a dead body found on our land.'

'How was that?'

'I can't think myself, your honour; it seems like the doing of the evil one. But, luckily, it was found near the boundary; on our side of it, to tell the truth. I ordered them to drag it on to the neighbour's strip of land at once, while it was still possible, and set a watch there, and sent word round to our folks. "Mum's the word," says I. But I explained how it was to the police officer in case of the worst. "You see how it was," says I; and of course I had to treat him and slip some notes into his hand.... Well, what do you say, your honour? We shifted the burden on to other shoulders; you see a dead body's a matter of two hundred roubles, as sure as ninepence.'

Mr. Pyenotchkin laughed heartily at his agent's cunning, and said several times to me, indicating him with a nod, '*Quel gaillard*, eh!'

Meantime it was quite dark out of doors; Arkady Pavlitch ordered the table to be cleared, and hay to be brought in. The valet spread out sheets for us, and arranged pillows; we lay down. Sofron retired after receiving his instructions for the next day. Arkady Pavlitch, before falling asleep, talked a little more about the first-rate qualities of the Russian peasant, and at that point made the observation that since Sofron had had the management of the place, the Shipilovka peasants had never been one farthing in arrears.... The watchman struck his board; a baby, who apparently had not yet had time to be imbued with a sentiment of dutiful self-abnegation, began crying somewhere in the cottage ... we fell asleep.

The next morning we got up rather early; I was getting ready to start for Ryabovo, but Arkady Pavlitch was anxious to show me his estate, and begged me to remain. I was not averse myself to seeing more of the first-rate qualities of that man of administrative power—Sofron—in their practical working. The agent made his appearance. He wore a blue loose coat, tied round the waist with a red handkerchief. He talked much less than on the previous evening, kept an alert, intent eye on his master's face, and gave connected and sensible answers. We set off with him to the threshing-floor. Sofron's son, the seven-foot bailiff, by every external sign a very slow-witted fellow, walked after us also, and we were joined farther on by the village constable, Fedosyitch, a retired soldier, with immense moustaches, and an extraordinary expression of face; he looked as though he had had some startling shock of astonishment a very long while ago, and had never quite got over it. We took a look at the threshing-floor, the barn, the corn-stacks, the outhouses, the windmill, the cattle-shed, the vegetables, and the hempfields; everything was, as a fact, in excellent order; only the dejected faces of the peasants rather puzzled me. Sofron had had an eye to the ornamental as well as the useful; he had planted all the ditches with willows, between the stacks he had made little paths to the threshing-floor and strewn them with fine sand; on the windmill he had constructed a weathercock of the shape of a bear with his jaws open and a red tongue sticking out; he had attached to the brick cattle-shed something of the nature of a Greek facade, and on it inscribed in white letters: 'Construt in the village Shipilovky 1 thousand eight Hunderd farthieth year. This cattle-shed.' Arkady Pavlitch was quite touched, and fell to expatiating in French to me upon the advantages of the system of rent-payment, adding, however, that labour-dues came more profitable to the owner—'but, after all, that wasn't everything.' He began giving the agent advice how to plant his potatoes, how to prepare cattle-food, and so on. Sofron heard his master's remarks out with attention, sometimes replied, but did not now address Arkady Pavlitch as his father, or his benefactor, and kept insisting that there was too little land; that it would be a good thing to buy more. 'Well, buy some then,' said Arkady Pavlitch; 'I've no objection; in my name, of course.' To this Sofron made no reply; he merely stroked his beard. 'And now it would be as well to ride down to the copse,' observed Mr. Pyenotchkin. Saddle-horses were led out to us at once; we went off to the copse, or, as they call it about us, the 'enclosure.' In this 'enclosure' we found thick undergrowth and abundance of wild game, for which Arkady Pavlitch applauded Sofron and clapped him on the shoulder. In regard to forestry, Arkady Pavlitch clung to the Russian ideas, and told me on that subject an amusing—in his words—anecdote, of how a jocose landowner had given his forester a good lesson by pulling out nearly half his beard, by way of a proof that growth is none the thicker for being cut back. In other matters, however, neither Sofron nor Arkady Pavlitch objected to innovations. On our return to the village, the agent took us to look at a winnowing machine he had recently ordered from Moscow. The winnowing machine did certainly work beautifully, but if Sofron had known what a disagreeable incident was in store for him and his master on this last excursion, he would doubtless have stopped at home with us.

This was what happened. As we came out of the barn the following spectacle confronted us. A few paces from the door, near a filthy pool, in which three ducks were splashing unconcernedly, there stood two peasants—one an old man of sixty, the other, a lad of twenty—both in patched homespun shirts, barefoot, and with cord tied round their waists for belts. The village constable Fedosyitch was busily engaged with them, and would probably have succeeded in inducing them to retire if we had lingered a little longer in the barn, but catching sight of us, he grew stiff all over, and seemed bereft of all sensation on the spot. Close by stood the bailiff gaping, his fists hanging irresolute. Arkady Pavlitch frowned, bit his lip, and went up to the suppliants. They both prostrated themselves at his feet in silence.

'What do you want? What are you asking about?' he inquired in a stern voice, a little through his nose. (The peasants glanced at one another, and did not utter a syllable, only blinked a little as if the sun were in their faces, and their breathing came quicker.)

'Well, what is it?' Arkady Pavlitch said again; and turning at once to Sofron, 'Of what family?'

'The Tobolyev family,' the agent answered slowly.

'Well, what do you want?' Mr. Pyenotchkin said again; 'have you lost your tongues, or what? Tell me, you, what is it you want?' he added, with a nod at the old man. 'And don't be afraid, stupid.'

The old man craned forward his dark brown, wrinkled neck, opened his bluish twitching lips, and in a hoarse voice uttered the words, 'Protect us, lord!' and again he bent his forehead to the earth. The young peasant prostrated himself too. Arkady Pavlitch looked at their bent necks with an air of dignity, threw back his head, and stood with his legs rather wide apart. 'What is it? Whom do you complain of?'

'Have mercy, lord! Let us breathe.... We are crushed, worried, tormented to death quite. (The old man spoke with difficulty.)

'Who worries you?'

'Sofron Yakovlitch, your honour.'

Arkady Pavlitch was silent a minute.

'What's your name?'

'Antip, your honour.'

'And who's this?'

'My boy, your honour.'

Arkady Pavlitch was silent again; he pulled his moustaches.

'Well! and how has he tormented you?' he began again, looking over his moustaches at the old man.

'Your honour, he has ruined us utterly. Two sons, your honour, he's sent for recruits out of turn, and now he is taking the third also. Yesterday, your honour, our last cow was taken from the yard, and my old wife was beaten by his worship here: that is all the pity he has for us!' (He pointed to the bailiff.)

'Hm!' commented Arkady Pavlitch.

'Let him not destroy us to the end, gracious protector!'

Mr. Pyenotchkin scowled, 'What's the meaning of this?' he asked the agent, in a low voice, with an air of displeasure.

'He's a drunken fellow, sir,' answered the agent, for the first time using this deferential address, 'and lazy too. He's never been out of arrears this five years back, sir.'

'Sofron Yakovlitch paid the arrears for me, your honour,' the old man went on; 'it's the fifth year's come that he's paid it, he's paid it— and he's brought me into slavery to him, your honour, and here—'

'And why did you get into arrears?' Mr. Pyenotchkin asked threateningly. (The old man's head sank.) 'You're fond of drinking, hanging about the taverns, I dare say.' (The old man opened his mouth to speak.) 'I know you,' Arkady Pavlitch went on emphatically; 'you think you've nothing to do but drink, and lie on the stove, and let steady peasants answer for you.'

'And he's an impudent fellow, too,' the agent threw in.

'That's sure to be so; it's always the way; I've noticed it more than once. The whole year round, he's drinking and abusive, and then he falls at one's feet.'

'Your honour, Arkady Pavlitch,' the old man began despairingly, 'have pity, protect us; when have I been impudent? Before God Almighty, I swear it was beyond my strength. Sofron Yakovlitch has taken a dislike to me; for some reason he dislikes me—God be his judge! He will ruin me utterly, your honour.... The last ... here ... the last boy ... and him he....' (A tear glistened in the old man's wrinkled yellow eyes). 'Have pity, gracious lord, defend us!'

'And it's not us only,' the young peasant began....

Arkady Pavlitch flew into a rage at once.

'And who asked your opinion, hey? Till you're spoken to, hold your tongue.... What's the meaning of it? Silence, I tell you, silence!... Why, upon my word, this is simply mutiny! No, my friend, I don't advise you to mutiny on my domain ... on my ... (Arkady Pavlitch stepped forward, but probably recollected my presence, turned round, and put his hands in his pockets ...) '*Je vous demande bien pardon, mon cher*,' he said, with a forced smile, dropping his voice significantly. '*C'est le mauvais côté de la médaille* ... There, that'll do, that'll do,' he went on, not looking at the peasants: 'I say ... that'll do, you can go.' (The peasants did not rise.) 'Well, haven't I told you ... that'll do. You can go, I tell you.'

Arkady Pavlitch turned his back on them. 'Nothing but vexation,' he muttered between his teeth, and strode with long steps homewards. Sofron followed him. The village constable opened his eyes wide, looking as if he were just about to take a tremendous leap into space. The bailiff drove a duck away from the puddle. The suppliants remained as they were a little, then looked at each other, and, without turning their heads, went on their way.

Two hours later I was at Ryabovo, and making ready to begin shooting, accompanied by Anpadist, a peasant I knew well. Pyenotchkin had been out of humour with Sofron up to the time I left. I began talking to Anpadist about the Shipilovka peasants, and Mr. Pyenotchkin, and asked him whether he knew the agent there.

'Sofron Yakovlitch? ... ugh!'

'What sort of man is he?'

'He's not a man; he's a dog; you couldn't find another brute like him between here and Kursk.'

'Really?'

'Why, Shipilovka's hardly reckoned as—what's his name?—Mr. Pyenotchkin's at all; he's not the master there; Sofron's the master.'

'You don't say so!'

'He's master, just as if it were his own. The peasants all about are in debt to him; they work for him like slaves; he'll send one off with the waggons; another, another way.... He harries them out of their lives.'

'They haven't much land, I suppose?'

'Not much land! He rents two hundred acres from the Hlinovsky peasants alone, and two hundred and eighty from our folks; there's more than three hundred and seventy-five acres he's got. And he doesn't only traffic in land; he does a trade in horses and stock, and pitch, and butter, and hemp, and one thing and the other.... He's sharp, awfully sharp, and rich too, the beast! But what's bad—he beats them. He's a brute, not a man; a dog, I tell you; a cur, a regular cur; that's what he is!'

'How is it they don't make complaints of him?'

'I dare say, the master'd be pleased! There's no arrears; so what does he care? Yes, you'd better,' he added, after a brief pause; 'I should advise you to complain! No, he'd let you know ... yes, you'd better try it on.... No, he'd let you know....'

I thought of Antip, and told him what I had seen.

'There,' commented Anpadist, 'he will eat him up now; he'll simply eat the man up. The bailiff will beat him now. Such a poor, unlucky chap, come to think of it! And what's his offence?... He had some wrangle in meeting with him, the agent, and he lost all patience, I suppose, and of course he wouldn't stand it.... A great matter, truly, to make so much of! So he began pecking at him, Antip. Now he'll eat him up altogether. You see, he's such a dog. Such a cur—God forgive my transgressions!—he knows whom to fall upon. The old men that are a bit richer, or've more children, he doesn't touch, the red-headed devil! but there's all the difference here! Why he's sent Antip's sons for recruits out of turn, the heartless ruffian, the cur! God forgive my transgressions!'

We went on our way.

XI

THE COUNTING-HOUSE

It was autumn. For some hours I had been strolling across country with my gun, and should probably not have returned till evening to the tavern on the Kursk high-road where my three-horse trap was awaiting me, had not an exceedingly fine and persistent rain, which had worried me all day with the obstinacy and ruthlessness of some old maiden lady, driven me at last to seek at least a temporary shelter somewhere in the neighbourhood. While I was still deliberating in which direction to go, my eye suddenly fell on a low shanty near a field sown with peas. I went up to the shanty, glanced under the thatched roof, and saw an old man so infirm that he reminded me at once of the dying goat Robinson Crusoe found in some cave on his island. The old man was squatting on his heels, his little dim eyes half-closed, while hurriedly, but carefully, like a hare (the poor fellow had not a single tooth), he munched a dry, hard pea, incessantly rolling it from side to side. He was so absorbed in this occupation that he did not notice my entrance.

'Grandfather! hey, grandfather!' said I. He ceased munching, lifted his eyebrows high, and with an effort opened his eyes.

'What?' he mumbled in a broken voice.

'Where is there a village near?' I asked.

The old man fell to munching again. He had not heard me. I repeated my question louder than before.

'A village?... But what do you want?'

'Why, shelter from the rain.'

'What?'

'Shelter from the rain.'

'Ah!' (He scratched his sunburnt neck.) 'Well, now, you go,' he said suddenly, waving his hands indefinitely, 'so ... as you go by the copse—see, as you go—there'll be a road; you pass it by, and keep right on to the right; keep right on, keep right on, keep right on.... Well, there will be Ananyevo. Or else you'd go to Sitovka.'

I followed the old man with difficulty. His moustaches muffled his voice, and his tongue too did not obey him readily.

'Where are you from?' I asked him.

'What?'

'Where are you from?'

'Ananyevo.'

'What are you doing here?'

'I'm watchman.'

'Why, what are you watching?'

'The peas.'

I could not help smiling.

'Really!—how old are you?'

'God knows.'

'Your sight's failing, I expect.'

'What?'

'Your sight's failing, I daresay?'

'Yes, it's failing. At times I can hear nothing.'

'Then how can you be a watchman, eh?'

'Oh, my elders know about that.'

'Elders!' I thought, and I gazed not without compassion at the poor old man. He fumbled about, pulled out of his bosom a bit of coarse bread, and began sucking it like a child, with difficulty moving his sunken cheeks.

I walked in the direction of the copse, turned to the right, kept on, kept right on as the old man had advised me, and at last got to a large village with a stone church in the new style, *i.e.* with columns, and a spacious manor-house, also with columns. While still some way off I noticed through the fine network of falling rain a cottage with a deal roof, and two chimneys, higher than the others, in all probability the dwelling of the village elder; and towards it I bent my steps in the hope of finding, in this cottage, a samovar, tea, sugar, and some not absolutely sour cream. Escorted by my half-frozen dog, I went up the steps into the outer room, opened the door, and instead of the usual appurtenances of a cottage, I saw several tables, heaped up with papers, two red cupboards, bespattered inkstands, pewter boxes of blotting sand weighing half a hundred-weight, long penholders, and so on. At one of the tables was sitting a young man of twenty with a swollen, sickly face, diminutive eyes, a greasy-looking forehead, and long straggling locks of hair. He was dressed, as one would expect, in a grey nankin coat, shiny with wear at the waist and the collar.

'What do you want?' he asked me, flinging his head up like a horse taken unexpectedly by the nose.

'Does the bailiff live here... or—'

'This is the principal office of the manor,' he interrupted. 'I'm the clerk on duty.... Didn't you see the sign-board? That's what it was put up for.'

'Where could I dry my clothes here? Is there a samovar anywhere in the village?'

'Samovars, of course,' replied the young man in the grey coat with dignity; 'go to Father Timofey's, or to the servants' cottage, or else to Nazar Tarasitch, or to Agrafena, the poultry-woman.'

'Who are you talking to, you blockhead? Can't you let me sleep, dummy!' shouted a voice from the next room.

'Here's a gentleman's come in to ask where he can dry himself.'

'What sort of a gentleman?'

'I don't know. With a dog and a gun.'

A bedstead creaked in the next room. The door opened, and there came in a stout, short man of fifty, with a bull neck, goggle-eyes, extraordinarily round cheeks, and his whole face positively shining with sleekness.

'What is it you wish?' he asked me.

'To dry my things.'

'There's no place here.'

'I didn't know this was the counting-house; I am willing, though, to pay...'

'Well, perhaps it could be managed here,' rejoined the fat man; 'won't you come inside here?' (He led me into another room, but not the one he had come from.) 'Would this do for you?'

'Very well.... And could I have tea and milk?'

'Certainly, at once. If you'll meantime take off your things and rest, the tea shall be got ready this minute.'

'Whose property is this?'

'Madame Losnyakov's, Elena Nikolaevna.'

He went out I looked round: against the partition separating my room from the office stood a huge leather sofa; two high-backed chairs, also covered in leather, were placed on both sides of the solitary window which looked out on the village street. On the walls, covered with a green paper with pink patterns on it, hung three immense oil paintings. One depicted a setter-dog with a blue collar, bearing the inscription: 'This is my consolation'; at the dog's feet flowed a river; on the opposite bank of the river a hare of quite disproportionate size with ears cocked up was sitting under a pine tree. In another picture two old men were eating a melon; behind the melon was visible in the distance a Greek temple with the inscription: 'The Temple of Satisfaction.' The third picture represented the half-nude figure of a woman in a recumbent position, much fore-shortened, with red knees and very big heels. My dog had, with superhuman efforts, crouched under the sofa, and apparently found a great deal of dust there, as he kept sneezing violently. I went to the window. Boards had been laid across the street in a slanting direction from the manor-house to the counting-house—a very useful precaution, as, thanks to our rich black soil and the persistent rain, the mud was terrible. In the grounds of the manor-house, which stood with its back to the street, there was the constant going and coming there always is about manor-houses: maids in faded chintz gowns flitted to and fro; house-serfs sauntered through the mud, stood still and scratched their spines meditatively; the constable's horse, tied up to a post, lashed his tail lazily, and with his nose high up, gnawed at the hedge; hens were clucking; sickly turkeys kept up an incessant gobble-gobble. On the steps of a dark crumbling out-house, probably the bath-house, sat a stalwart lad with a guitar, singing with some spirit the well-known ballad:

> 'I'm leaving this enchanting spot
> To go into the desert.'

The fat man came into the room.

'They're bringing you in your tea,' he told me, with an affable smile.

The young man in the grey coat, the clerk on duty, laid on the old card-table a samovar, a teapot, a tumbler on a broken saucer, a jug of cream, and a bunch of Bolhovo biscuit rings. The fat man went out.

'What is he?' I asked the clerk; 'the steward?'

'No, sir; he was the chief cashier, but now he has been promoted to be head-clerk.'

'Haven't you got a steward, then?'

'No, sir. There's an agent, Mihal Vikulov, but no steward.'

'Is there a manager, then?'

'Yes; a German, Lindamandol, Karlo Karlitch; only he does not manage the estate.'

'Who does manage it, then?'

'Our mistress herself.'

'You don't say so. And are there many of you in the office?'

The young man reflected.

'There are six of us.'

'Who are they?' I inquired.

'Well, first there's Vassily Nikolaevitch, the head cashier; then Piotr, one clerk; Piotr's brother, Ivan, another clerk; the other Ivan, a clerk; Konstantin Narkizer, another clerk; and me here—there's a lot of us, you can't count all of them.'

'I suppose your mistress has a great many serfs in her house?'

'No, not to say a great many.'

'How many, then?'

'I dare say it runs up to about a hundred and fifty.'

We were both silent for a little.

'I suppose you write a good hand, eh?' I began again.

The young man grinned from ear to ear, went into the office and brought in a sheet covered with writing.

'This is my writing,' he announced, still with the same smile on his face.

I looked at it; on the square sheet of greyish paper there was written, in a good bold hand, the following document:—

ORDER

> From the Chief Office of the Manor of Ananyevo to the Agent,
> Mihal Vikulov.

No. 209.

'Whereas some person unknown entered the garden at Ananyevo last night in an intoxicated condition, and with unseemly songs waked the French governess, Madame Engêne, and disturbed her; and whether the watchmen saw anything, and who were on watch in the garden and permitted such disorderliness: as regards all the above-written matters, your orders are to investigate in detail, and report immediately to the Office.'

'*Head-Clerk*, NIKOLAI HVOSTOV.'

A huge heraldic seal was attached to the order, with the inscription: 'Seal of the chief office of the manor of Ananyevo'; and below stood the signature: 'To be executed exactly, Elena Losnyakov.'

'Your lady signed it herself, eh?' I queried.

'To be sure; she always signs herself. Without that the order would be of no effect.'

'Well, and now shall you send this order to the agent?'

'No, sir. He'll come himself and read it. That's to say, it'll be read to him; you see, he's no scholar.' (The clerk on duty was silent again for a while.) 'But what do you say?' he added, simpering; 'is it well written?'

'Very well written.'

'It wasn't composed, I must confess, by me. Konstantin is the great one for that.'

'What?... Do you mean the orders have first to be composed among you?'

'Why, how else could we do? Couldn't write them off straight without making a fair copy.'

'And what salary do you get?' I inquired.

'Thirty-five roubles, and five roubles for boots.'

'And are you satisfied?'

'Of course I am satisfied. It's not everyone can get into an office like ours. It was God's will, in my case, to be sure; I'd an uncle who was in service as a butler.'

'And you're well-off?'

'Yes, sir. Though, to tell the truth,' he went on, with a sigh, 'a place at a merchant's, for instance, is better for the likes of us. At a merchant's they're very well off. Yesterday evening a merchant came to us from Venev, and his man got talking to me…. Yes, that's a good place, no doubt about it; a very good place.'

'Why? Do the merchants pay more wages?'

'Lord preserve us! Why, a merchant would soon give you the sack if you asked him for wages. No, at a merchant's you must live on trust and on fear. He'll give you food, and drink, and clothes, and all. If you give him satisfaction, he'll do more…. Talk of wages, indeed! You don't need them…. And a merchant, too, lives in plain Russian style, like ourselves; you go with him on a journey—he has tea, and you have it; what he eats, you eat. A merchant … one can put up with; a merchant's a very different thing from what a gentleman is; a merchant's not whimsical; if he's out of temper, he'll give you a blow, and there it ends. He doesn't nag nor sneer…. But with a gentleman it's a woeful business! Nothing's as he likes it—this is not right, and that he can't fancy. You hand him a glass of water or something to eat: "Ugh, the water stinks! positively stinks!" You take it out, stay a minute outside the door, and bring it back: "Come, now, that's good; this doesn't stink now." And as for the ladies, I tell you, the ladies are something beyond everything!… and the young ladies above all!…'

'Fedyushka!' came the fat man's voice from the office.

The clerk went out quickly. I drank a glass of tea, lay down on the sofa, and fell asleep. I slept for two hours.

When I woke, I meant to get up, but I was overcome by laziness; I closed my eyes, but did not fall asleep again. On the other side of the partition, in the office, they were talking in subdued voices. Unconsciously I began to listen.

'Quite so, quite so, Nikolai Eremyitch,' one voice was saying; 'quite so. One can't but take that into account; yes, certainly!… Hm!' (The speaker coughed.)

'You may believe me, Gavrila Antonitch,' replied the fat man's voice: 'don't I know how things are done here? Judge for yourself.'

'Who does, if you don't, Nikolai Eremyitch? you're, one may say, the first person here. Well, then, how's it to be?' pursued the voice I did not recognise; 'what decision are we to come to, Nikolai Eremyitch? Allow me to put the question.'

'What decision, Gavrila Antonitch? The thing depends, so to say, on you; you don't seem over anxious.'

'Upon my word, Nikolai Eremyitch, what do you mean? Our business is trading, buying; it's our business to buy. That's what we live by, Nikolai Eremyitch, one may say.'

'Eight roubles a measure,' said the fat man emphatically.

A sigh was audible.

'Nikolai Eremyitch, sir, you ask a heavy price.' 'Impossible, Gavrila Antonitch, to do otherwise; I speak as before God Almighty; impossible.'

Silence followed.

I got up softly and looked through a crack in the partition. The fat man was sitting with his back to me. Facing him sat a merchant, a man about forty, lean and pale, who looked as if he had been rubbed with oil. He was incessantly fingering his beard, and very rapidly blinking and twitching his lips.

'Wonderful the young green crops this year, one may say,' he began again; 'I've been going about everywhere admiring them. All the way from Voronezh they've come up wonderfully, first-class, one may say.'

'The crops are pretty fair, certainly,' answered the head-clerk; 'but you know the saying, Gavrila Antonitch, autumn bids fair, but spring may be foul.'

'That's so, indeed, Nikolai Eremyitch; all is in God's hands; it's the absolute truth what you've just remarked, sir.... But perhaps your visitor's awake now.'

The fat man turned round ... listened....

'No, he's asleep. He may, though....'

He went to the door.

'No, he's asleep,' he repeated and went back to his place.

'Well, so what are we to say, Nikolai Eremyitch?' the merchant began again; 'we must bring our little business to a conclusion.... Let it be so, Nikolai Eremyitch, let it be so,' he went on, blinking incessantly; 'two grey notes and a white for your favour, and there' (he nodded in the direction of the house), 'six and a half. Done, eh?'

'Four grey notes,' answered the clerk.

'Come, three, then.'

'Four greys, and no white.'

'Three, Nikolai Eremyitch.'

'Three and a half, and not a farthing less.'

'Three, Nikolai Eremyitch.'

'You're not talking sense, Gavrila Antonitch.'

'My, what a pig-headed fellow!' muttered the merchant. 'Then I'd better arrange it with the lady herself.'

'That's as you like,' answered the fat man; 'far better, I should say.
Why should you worry yourself, after all?... Much better, indeed!'

'Well, well! Nikolai Eremyitch. I lost my temper for a minute! That was nothing but talk.'

'No, really, why?...'

'Nonsense, I tell you.... I tell you I was joking. Well, take your three and a half; there's no doing anything with you.'

'I ought to have got four, but I was in too great a hurry—like an ass!' muttered the fat man.

'Then up there at the house, six and a half, Nikolai Eremyitch; the corn will be sold for six and a half?'

'Six and a half, as we said already.'

'Well, your hand on that then, Nikolai Eremyitch' (the merchant clapped his outstretched fingers into the clerk's palm). 'And good-bye, in God's name!' (The merchant got up.) 'So then, Nikolai Eremyitch, sir, I'll go now to your lady, and bid them send up my name, and so I'll say to her, "Nikolai Eremyitch," I'll say, "has made a bargain with me for six and a half."'

'That's what you must say, Gavrila Antonitch.'

'And now, allow me.'

The merchant handed the manager a small roll of notes, bowed, shook his head, picked up his hat with two fingers, shrugged his shoulders, and, with a sort of undulating motion, went out, his boots creaking after the approved fashion. Nikolai Eremyitch went to the wall, and, as far as I could make out, began sorting the notes handed him by the merchant. A red head, adorned with thick whiskers, was thrust in at the door.

'Well?' asked the head; 'all as it should be?'

'Yes.'

'How much?'

The fat man made an angry gesture with his hand, and pointed to my room.

'Ah, all right!' responded the head, and vanished.

The fat man went up to the table, sat down, opened a book, took out a reckoning frame, and began shifting the beads to and fro as he counted, using not the forefinger but the third finger of his right hand, which has a much more showy effect.

The clerk on duty came in.

'What is it?'

'Sidor is here from Goloplek.'

'Oh! ask him in. Wait a bit, wait a bit.... First go and look whether the strange gentleman's still asleep, or whether he has waked up.'

The clerk on duty came cautiously into my room. I laid my head on my game-bag, which served me as a pillow, and closed my eyes.

'He's asleep,' whispered the clerk on duty, returning to the counting-house.

The fat man muttered something.

'Well, send Sidor in,' he said at last.

I got up again. A peasant of about thirty, of huge stature, came in—a red-cheeked, vigorous-looking fellow, with brown hair, and a short curly beard. He crossed himself, praying to the holy image, bowed to the head-clerk, held his hat before him in both hands, and stood erect.

'Good day, Sidor,' said the fat man, tapping with the reckoning beads.

'Good-day to you, Nikolai Eremyitch.'

'Well, what are the roads like?'

'Pretty fair, Nikolai Eremyitch. A bit muddy.' (The peasant spoke slowly and not loud.)

'Wife quite well?'

'She's all right!'

The peasant gave a sigh and shifted one leg forward. Nikolai Eremyitch put his pen behind his ear, and blew his nose.

'Well, what have you come about?' he proceeded to inquire, putting his check handkerchief into his pocket.

'Why, they do say, Nikolai Eremyitch, they're asking for carpenters from us.'

'Well, aren't there any among you, hey?'

'To be sure there are, Nikolai Eremyitch; our place is right in the woods; our earnings are all from the wood, to be sure. But it's the busy time, Nikolai Eremyitch. Where's the time to come from?'

'The time to come from! Busy time! I dare say, you're so eager to work for outsiders, and don't care to work for your mistress.... It's all the same!'

'The work's all the same, certainly, Nikolai Eremyitch ... but....'

'Well?'

'The pay's ... very....'

'What next! You've been spoiled; that's what it is. Get along with you!'

'And what's more, Nikolai Eremyitch, there'll be only a week's work, but they'll keep us hanging on a month. One time there's not material enough, and another time they'll send us into the garden to weed the path.'

'What of it? Our lady herself is pleased to give the order, so it's useless you and me talking about it.'

Sidor was silent; he began shifting from one leg to the other.

Nikolai Eremyitch put his head on one side, and began busily playing with the reckoning beads.

'Our ... peasants ... Nikolai Eremyitch....' Sidor began at last, hesitating over each word; 'sent word to your honour ... there is ... see here....' (He thrust his big hand into the bosom of his coat, and began to pull out a folded linen kerchief with a red border.)

'What are you thinking of? Goodness, idiot, are you out of your senses?' the fat man interposed hurriedly. 'Go on; go to my cottage,' he continued, almost shoving the bewildered peasant out; 'ask for my wife there ... she'll give you some tea; I'll be round directly; go on. For goodness' sake, I tell you, go on.'

Sidor went away.

'Ugh!... what a bear!' the head clerk muttered after him, shaking his head, and set to work again on his reckoning frame.

Suddenly shouts of 'Kuprya! Kuprya! there's no knocking down Kuprya!' were heard in the street and on the steps, and a little later there came into the counting-house a small man of sickly appearance, with an extraordinarily long nose and large staring eyes, who carried himself with a great air of superiority. He was dressed in a ragged little old surtout, with a plush collar and diminutive buttons. He carried a bundle of firewood on his shoulder. Five house-serfs were crowding round him, all shouting, 'Kuprya! there's no suppressing Kuprya! Kuprya's been turned stoker; Kuprya's turned a stoker!' But the man in the coat with the plush collar did not pay the slightest attention to the uproar made by his companions, and was not in the least out of countenance. With measured steps he went up to the stove, flung down his load, straightened himself, took out of his tail-pocket a snuff- box, and with round eyes began helping himself to a pinch of dry trefoil mixed with ashes. At the entrance of this noisy party the fat man had at first knitted his brows and risen from his seat, but, seeing what it was, he smiled, and only told them not to shout. 'There's a sportsman,' said he, 'asleep in the next room.' 'What sort of sportsman?' two of them asked with one voice.

'A gentleman.'

'Ah!'

'Let them make a row,' said the man with the plush collar, waving his arms; 'what do I care, so long as they don't touch me? They've turned me into a stoker....'

'A stoker! a stoker!' the others put in gleefully.

'It's the mistress's orders,' he went on, with a shrug of his shoulders; 'but just you wait a bit ... they'll turn you into swineherds yet. But I've been a tailor, and a good tailor too, learnt my trade in the best house in Moscow, and worked for generals ... and nobody can take that from me. And what have you to boast of?... What? you're a pack of idlers, not worth your salt; that's what you are! Turn me off! I shan't die of hunger; I shall be all right; give me a passport. I'd send a good rent home, and satisfy the masters. But what would you do? You'd die off like flies, that's what you'd do!'

'That's a nice lie!' interposed a pock-marked lad with white eyelashes, a red cravat, and ragged elbows. 'You went off with a passport sharp enough, but never a halfpenny of rent did the masters see from you, and you never earned a farthing for yourself, you just managed to crawl home again and you've never had a new rag on you since.'

'Ah, well, what could one do! Konstantin Narkizitch,' responded Kuprya; 'a man falls in love—a man's ruined and done for! You go through what I have, Konstantin Narkizitch, before you blame me!'

'And you picked out a nice one to fall in love with!—a regular fright.'

'No, you must not say that, Konstantin Narkizitch.'

'Who's going to believe that? I've seen her, you know; I saw her with my own eyes last year in Moscow.'

'Last year she had gone off a little certainly,' observed Kuprya.

'No, gentlemen, I tell you what,' a tall, thin man, with a face spotted with pimples, a valet probably, from his frizzed and pomatumed head, remarked in a careless and disdainful voice; 'let Kuprya Afanasyitch sing us his song. Come on, now; begin, Kuprya Afanasyitch.'

'Yes! yes!' put in the others. 'Hoorah for Alexandra! That's one for Kuprya; 'pon my soul ... Sing away, Kuprya!... You're a regular brick, Alexandra!' (Serfs often use feminine terminations in referring to a man as an expression of endearment.) 'Sing away!'

'This is not the place to sing,' Kuprya replied firmly; 'this is the manor counting-house.'

'And what's that to do with you? you've got your eye on a place as clerk, eh?' answered Konstantin with a coarse laugh. 'That's what it is!'

'Everything rests with the mistress,' observed the poor wretch.

'There, that's what he's got his eye on! a fellow like him! oo! oo! a!'

And they all roared; some rolled about with merriment. Louder than all laughed a lad of fifteen, probably the son of an aristocrat among the house-serfs; he wore a waistcoat with bronze buttons, and a cravat of lilac colour, and had already had time to fill out his waistcoat.

'Come tell us, confess now, Kuprya,' Nikolai Eremyitch began complacently, obviously tickled and diverted himself; 'is it bad being stoker? Is it an easy job, eh?'

'Nikolai Eremyitch,' began Kuprya, 'you're head-clerk among us now, certainly; there's no disputing that, no; but you know you have been in disgrace yourself, and you too have lived in a peasant's hut.'

'You'd better look out and not forget yourself in my place,' the fat man interrupted emphatically; 'people joke with a fool like you; you ought, you fool, to have sense, and be grateful to them for taking notice of a fool like you.'

'It was a slip of the tongue, Nikolai Eremyitch; I beg your pardon....'

'Yes, indeed, a slip of the tongue.'

The door opened and a little page ran in.

'Nikolai Eremyitch, mistress wants you.'

'Who's with the mistress?' he asked the page.

'Aksinya Nikitishna, and a merchant from Venev.'

'I'll be there this minute. And you, mates,' he continued in a persuasive voice, 'better move off out of here with the newly-appointed stoker; if the German pops in, he'll make a complaint for certain.'

The fat man smoothed his hair, coughed into his hand, which was almost completely hidden in his coat-sleeve, buttoned himself, and set off with rapid strides to see the lady of the manor. In a little while the whole party trailed out after him, together with Kuprya. My old friend, the clerk-on duty, was left alone. He set to work mending the pens, and dropped asleep in his chair. A few flies promptly seized the opportunity and settled on his mouth. A mosquito alighted on his forehead, and, stretching its legs out with a regular motion, slowly buried its sting into his flabby flesh. The same red head with whiskers showed itself again at the door, looked in, looked again, and then came into the office, together with the rather ugly body belonging to it.

'Fedyushka! eh, Fedyushka! always asleep,' said the head.

The clerk on duty opened his eyes and got up from his seat.

'Nikolai Eremyitch has gone to the mistress?'

'Yes, Vassily Nikolaevitch.'

'Ah! ah!' thought I; 'this is he, the head cashier.'

The head cashier began walking about the room. He really slunk rather than walked, and altogether resembled a cat. An old black frock-coat with very narrow skirts hung about his shoulders; he kept one hand in his bosom, while the other was for ever fumbling about his high, narrow horse-hair collar, and he turned his head with a certain effort. He wore noiseless kid boots, and trod very softly.

'The landowner, Yagushkin, was asking for you to-day,' added the clerk on duty.

'Hm, asking for me? What did he say?'

'Said he'd go to Tyutyurov this evening and would wait for you. "I want to discuss some business with Vassily Nikolaevitch," said he, but what the business was he didn't say; "Vassily Nikolaevitch will know," says he.'

'Hm!' replied the head cashier, and he went up to the window.

'Is Nikolai Eremyitch in the counting-house?' a loud voice was heard asking in the outer room, and a tall man, apparently angry, with an irregular but bold and expressive face, and rather clean in his dress, stepped over the threshold.

'Isn't he here?' he inquired, looking rapidly round.

'Nikolai Eremyitch is with the mistress,' responded the cashier. 'Tell me what you want, Pavel Andreitch; you can tell me…. What is it you want?'

'What do I want? You want to know what I want?' (The cashier gave a sickly nod.) 'I want to give him a lesson, the fat, greasy villain, the scoundrelly tell-tale!… I'll give him a tale to tell!'

Pavel flung himself into a chair.

'What are you saying, Pavel Andreitch! Calm yourself…. Aren't you ashamed? Don't forget whom you're talking about, Pavel Andreitch!' lisped the cashier.

'Forget whom I'm talking about? What do I care for his being made head- clerk? A fine person they've found to promote, there's no denying that! They've let the goat loose in the kitchen garden, you may say!'

'Hush, hush, Pavel Andreitch, hush! drop that … what rubbish are you talking?'

'So Master Fox is beginning to fawn? I will wait for him,' Pavel said with passion, and he struck a blow on the table. 'Ah, here he's coming!' he added with a look at the window; 'speak of the devil. With your kind permission!' (He, got up.)

Nikolai Eremyitch came into the counting-house. His face was shining with satisfaction, but he was rather taken aback at seeing Pavel Andreitch.

'Good day to you, Nikolai Eremyitch,' said Pavel in a significant tone, advancing deliberately to meet him.

The head-clerk made no reply. The face of the merchant showed itself in the doorway.

'What, won't you deign to answer me?' pursued Pavel. 'But no … no,' he added; 'that's not it; there's no getting anything by shouting and abuse. No, you'd better tell me in a friendly way, Nikolai Eremyitch; what do you persecute me for? what do you want to ruin me for? Come, speak, speak.'

'This is no fit place to come to an understanding with you,' the head- clerk answered in some agitation, 'and no fit time. But I must say I wonder at one thing: what makes you suppose I want to ruin you, or that I'm persecuting you? And if you come to that, how can I persecute you? You're not in my counting-house.'

'I should hope not,' answered Pavel; 'that would be the last straw! But why are you hum-bugging, Nikolai Eremyitch?... You understand me, you know.'

'No, I don't understand.'

'No, you do understand.'

'No, by God, I don't understand!'

'Swearing too! Well, tell us, since it's come to that: have you no fear of God? Why can't you let the poor girl live in peace? What do you want of her?'

'Whom are you talking of?' the fat man asked with feigned amazement.

'Ugh! doesn't know; what next? I'm talking of Tatyana. Have some fear of God—what do you want to revenge yourself for? You ought to be ashamed: a married man like you, with children as big as I am; it's a very different thing with me.... I mean marriage: I'm acting straight- forwardly.'

'How am I to blame in that, Pavel Andreitch? The mistress won't permit you to marry; it's her seignorial will! What have I to do with it?'

'Why, haven't you been plotting with that old hag, the housekeeper, eh? Haven't you been telling tales, eh? Tell me, aren't you bringing all sorts of stories up against the defenceless girl? I suppose it's not your doing that she's been degraded from laundrymaid to washing dishes in the scullery? And it's not your doing that she's beaten and dressed in sackcloth?... You ought to be ashamed, you ought to be ashamed—an old man like you! You know there's a paralytic stroke always hanging over you.... You will have to answer to God.'

'You're abusive, Pavel Andreitch, you're abusive.... You shan't have a chance to be insolent much longer.'

Pavel fired up.

'What? You dare to threaten me?' he said passionately. 'You think I'm afraid of you. No, my man, I'm not come to that! What have I to be afraid of?... I can make my bread everywhere. For you, now, it's another thing! It's only here you can live and tell tales, and filch....'

'Fancy the conceit of the fellow!' interrupted the clerk, who was also beginning to lose patience; 'an apothecary's assistant, simply an apothecary's assistant, a wretched leech; and listen to him—fie upon you! you're a high and mighty personage!'

'Yes, an apothecary's assistant, and except for this apothecary's assistant you'd have been rotting in the graveyard by now.... It was some devil drove me to cure him,' he added between his teeth.

'You cured me?... No, you tried to poison me; you dosed me with aloes,' the clerk put in.

'What was I to do if nothing but aloes had any effect on you?'

'The use of aloes is forbidden by the Board of Health,' pursued Nikolai. 'I'll lodge a complaint against you yet.... You tried to compass my death—that was what you did! But the Lord suffered it not.'

'Hush, now, that's enough, gentlemen,' the cashier was beginning....

'Stand off!' bawled the clerk. 'He tried to poison me! Do you understand that?'

'That's very likely.... Listen, Nikolai Eremyitch,' Pavel began in despairing accents. 'For the last time, I beg you.... You force me to it—can't stand it any longer. Let us alone, do you hear? or else, by God, it'll go ill with one or other of us—I mean with you!'

The fat man flew into a rage.

'I'm not afraid of you!' he shouted; 'do you hear, milksop? I got the better of your father; I broke his horns—a warning to you; take care!'

'Don't talk of my father, Nikolai Eremyitch.'

'Get away! who are you to give me orders?'

'I tell you, don't talk of him!'

'And I tell you, don't forget yourself.... However necessary you think yourself, if our lady has a choice between us, it's not you'll be kept, my dear! None's allowed to mutiny, mind!' (Pavel was shaking with fury.) 'As for the wench, Tatyana, she deserves ... wait a bit, she'll get something worse!'

Pavel dashed forward with uplifted fists, and the clerk rolled heavily on the floor.

'Handcuff him, handcuff him,' groaned Nikolai Eremyitch....

I won't take upon myself to describe the end of this scene; I fear I have wounded the reader's delicate susceptibilities as it is.

The same day I returned home. A week later I heard that Madame Losnyakov had kept both Pavel and Nikolai in her service, but had sent away the girl Tatyana; it appeared she was not wanted.

XII

BIRYUK

I was coming back from hunting one evening alone in a racing droshky. I was six miles from home; my good trotting mare galloped bravely along the dusty road, pricking up her ears with an occasional snort; my weary dog stuck close to the hind-wheels, as though he were fastened there. A tempest was coming on. In front, a huge, purplish storm-cloud slowly rose from behind the forest; long grey rain-clouds flew over my head and to meet me; the willows stirred and whispered restlessly. The suffocating heat changed suddenly to a damp chilliness; the darkness rapidly thickened. I gave the horse a lash with the reins, descended a steep slope, pushed across a dry water-course overgrown with brushwood, mounted the hill, and drove into the forest. The road ran before me, bending between thick hazel bushes, now enveloped in darkness; I advanced with difficulty. The droshky jumped up and down over the hard roots of the ancient oaks and limes, which were continually intersected by deep ruts—the tracks of cart wheels; my horse began to stumble. A violent wind suddenly began to roar overhead; the trees blustered; big drops of rain fell with slow tap and splash on the leaves; there came a flash of lightning and a clap of thunder. The rain fell in torrents. I went on a step or so, and soon was forced to stop; my horse foundered; I could not see an inch before me. I managed to take refuge somehow in a spreading bush. Crouching down and covering my face, I waited patiently for the storm to blow over, when suddenly, in a flash of lightning, I saw a tall figure on the road. I began to stare intently in that direction—the figure seemed to have sprung out of the ground near my droshky.

'Who's that?' inquired a ringing voice.

'Why, who are you?'

'I'm the forester here.'

I mentioned my name.

'Oh, I know! Are you on your way home?'

'Yes. But, you see, in such a storm....'

'Yes, there is a storm,' replied the voice.

A pale flash of lightning lit up the forester from head to foot; a brief crashing clap of thunder followed at once upon it. The rain lashed with redoubled force.

'It won't be over just directly,' the forester went on.

'What's to be done?'

'I'll take you to my hut, if you like,' he said abruptly.

'That would be a service.'

'Please to take your seat'

He went up to the mare's head, took her by the bit, and pulled her up. We set off. I held on to the cushion of the droshky, which rocked 'like a boat on the sea,' and called my dog. My poor mare splashed with difficulty through the mud, slipped and stumbled; the forester hovered before the shafts to right and to left like a ghost. We drove rather a long while; at last my guide stopped. 'Here we are home, sir,' he observed in a quiet voice. The gate creaked; some puppies barked a welcome. I raised my head, and in a flash of lightning I made out a small hut in the middle of a large yard, fenced in with hurdles. From the one little window there was a dim light. The forester led his horse up to the steps and knocked at the door. 'Coming, coming!' we heard in a little shrill voice; there was the patter of bare feet, the bolt creaked, and a girl of twelve, in a little old smock tied round the waist with list, appeared in the doorway with a lantern in her hand.

'Show the gentleman a light,' he said to her 'and I will put your droshky in the shed.'

The little girl glanced at me, and went into the hut. I followed her.

The forester's hut consisted of one room, smoky, low-pitched, and empty, without curtains or partition. A tattered sheepskin hung on the wall. On the bench lay a single-barrelled gun; in the corner lay a heap of rags; two great pots stood near the oven. A pine splinter was burning on the table flickering up and dying down mournfully. In the very middle of the hut hung a cradle, suspended from the end of a long horizontal pole. The little girl put out the lantern, sat down on a tiny stool, and with her right hand began swinging the cradle, while with her left she attended to the smouldering pine splinter. I looked round—my heart sank within me: it's not cheering to go into a peasant's hut at night. The baby in the cradle breathed hard and fast.

'Are you all alone here?' I asked the little girl.

'Yes,' she uttered, hardly audibly.

'You're the forester's daughter?'

'Yes,' she whispered.

The door creaked, and the forester, bending his head, stepped across the threshold. He lifted the lantern from the floor, went up to the table, and lighted a candle.

'I dare say you're not used to the splinter light?' said he, and he shook back his curls.

I looked at him. Rarely has it been my fortune to behold such a comely creature. He was tall, broad-shouldered, and in marvellous proportion. His powerful muscles stood out in strong relief under his wet homespun shirt. A curly, black beard hid half of his stern and manly face; small brown eyes looked out boldly from under broad eyebrows which met in the middle. He stood before me, his arms held lightly akimbo.

I thanked him, and asked his name.

'My name's Foma,' he answered, 'and my nickname's Biryuk' (*i.e.* wolf). [Footnote: The name Biryuk is used in the Orel province to denote a solitary, misanthropic man.— *Author's Note*.]

'Oh, you're Biryuk.'

I looked with redoubled curiosity at him. From my Yermolaï and others I had often heard stories about the forester Biryuk, whom all the peasants of the surrounding districts feared as they feared fire. According to them there had never been such a master of his business in the world before. 'He won't let you carry off a handful of brushwood; he'll drop upon you like a fall of snow, whatever time it may be, even in the middle of the night, and you needn't think of resisting him— he's strong, and cunning as the devil.... And there's no getting at him anyhow; neither by brandy nor by money; there's no snare he'll walk into. More than once good folks have planned to put him out of the world, but no—it's never come off.'

That was how the neighbouring peasants spoke of Biryuk.

'So you're Biryuk,' I repeated; 'I've heard talk of you, brother. They say you show no mercy to anyone.'

'I do my duty,' he answered grimly; 'it's not right to eat the master's bread for nothing.'

He took an axe from his girdle and began splitting splinters.

'Have you no wife?' I asked him.

'No,' he answered, with a vigorous sweep of the axe.

'She's dead, I suppose?'

'No ... yes ... she's dead,' he added, and turned away. I was silent; he raised his eyes and looked at me.

'She ran away with a travelling pedlar,' he brought out with a bitter smile. The little girl hung her head; the baby waked up and began crying; the little girl went to the cradle. 'There, give it him,' said Biryuk, thrusting a dirty feeding-bottle into her hand. 'Him, too, she abandoned,' he went on in an undertone, pointing to the baby. He went up to the door, stopped, and turned round.

'A gentleman like you,' he began, 'wouldn't care for our bread, I dare say, and except bread, I've—'

'I'm not hungry.'

'Well, that's for you to say. I would have heated the samovar, but I've no tea.... I'll go and see how your horse is getting on.'

He went out and slammed the door. I looked round again, the hut struck me as more melancholy than ever. The bitter smell of stale smoke choked my breathing unpleasantly. The little girl did not stir from her place, and did not raise her eyes; from time to time she jogged the cradle, and timidly pulled her slipping smock up on to shoulder; her bare legs hung motionless.

'What's your name?' I asked her.

'Ulita,' she said, her mournful little face drooping more than ever.

The forester came in and sat down on the bench.

'The storm 's passing over,' he observed, after a brief silence; 'if you wish it, I will guide you out of the forest.'

I got up; Biryuk took his gun and examined the firepan.

'What's that for?' I inquired.

'There's mischief in the forest.... They're cutting a tree down on Mares' Ravine,' he added, in reply to my look of inquiry.

'Could you hear it from here?'

'I can hear it outside.'

We went out together. The rain had ceased. Heavy masses of storm-cloud were still huddled in the distance; from time to time there were long flashes of lightning; but here and there overhead the dark blue sky was already visible; stars twinkled through the swiftly flying clouds. The outline of the trees, drenched with rain, and stirred by the wind, began to stand out in the darkness. We listened. The forester took off his cap and bent his head.... 'Th ... there!' he said suddenly, and he stretched out his hand: 'see what a night he's pitched on.' I had heard nothing but the rustle of the leaves. Biryuk led the mare out of the shed. 'But, perhaps,' he added aloud, 'this way I shall miss him.' 'I'll go with you ... if you like?' 'Certainly,' he answered, and he backed the horse in again; 'we'll catch him in a trice, and then I'll take you. Let's be off.' We started, Biryuk in front, I following him. Heaven only knows how he found out his way, but he only stopped once or twice, and then merely to listen to the strokes of the axe. 'There,' he muttered, 'do you hear? do you hear?' 'Why, where?' Biryuk shrugged his shoulders. We went down into the ravine; the wind was still for an instant; the rhythmical strokes reached my hearing distinctly. Biryuk glanced at me and shook his head. We went farther through the wet bracken and nettles. A slow muffled crash was heard....

'He's felled it,' muttered Biryuk. Meantime the sky had grown clearer and clearer; there was a faint light in the forest. We clambered at last out of the ravine.

'Wait here a little,' the forester whispered to me. He bent down, and raising his gun above his head, vanished among the bushes. I began listening with strained attention. Across the continual roar of the wind faint sounds from close by reached me; there was a cautious blow of an axe on the brushwood, the crash of wheels, the snort of a horse....

'Where are you off to? Stop!' the iron voice of Biryuk thundered suddenly. Another voice was heard in a pitiful shriek, like a trapped hare.... *A struggle was beginning.*

'No, no, you've made a mistake,' Biryuk declared panting; 'you're not going to get off....' I rushed in the direction of the noise, and ran up to the scene of the conflict, stumbling at every step. A felled tree lay on the ground, and near it Biryuk was busily engaged holding the thief down and binding his hands behind his back with a kerchief. I came closer. Biryuk got up and set him on his feet. I saw a peasant drenched with rain, in tatters, and with a long dishevelled beard. A sorry little nag, half covered with a stiff mat, was standing by, together with a rough cart. The forester did not utter a word; the peasant too was silent; his head was shaking.

'Let him go,' I whispered in Biryuk's ears; 'I'll pay for the tree.'

Without a word Biryuk took the horse by the mane with his left hand; in his right he held the thief by the belt. 'Now turn round, you rat!' he said grimly.

'The bit of an axe there, take it,' muttered the peasant.

'No reason to lose it, certainly,' said the forester, and he picked up the axe. We started. I walked behind.... The rain began sprinkling again, and soon fell in torrents. With difficulty we made our way to the hut. Biryuk pushed the captured horse into the middle of the yard, led the peasant into the room, loosened the knot in the kerchief, and made him sit down in a corner. The little girl, who had fallen asleep near the oven, jumped up and began staring at us in silent terror. I sat down on the locker.

'Ugh, what a downpour!' remarked the forester; 'you will have to wait till it's over. Won't you lie down?'

'Thanks.'

'I would have shut him in the store loft, on your honour's account,' he went on, indicating the peasant; 'but you see the bolt—'

'Leave him here; don't touch him,' I interrupted.

The peasant stole a glance at me from under his brows. I vowed inwardly to set the poor wretch free, come what might. He sat without stirring on the locker. By the light of the lantern I could make out his worn, wrinkled face, his overhanging yellow eyebrows, his restless eyes, his thin limbs.... The little girl lay down on the floor, just at his feet, and again dropped asleep. Biryuk sat at the table, his head in his hands. A cricket chirped in the corner ... the rain pattered on the roof and streamed down the windows; we were all silent.

'Foma Kuzmitch,' said the peasant suddenly in a thick, broken voice;
'Foma Kuzmitch!'

'What is it?'

'Let me go.'

Biryuk made no answer.

'Let me go ... hunger drove me to it; let me go.'

'I know you,' retorted the forester severely; 'your set's all alike— all thieves.'

'Let me go,' repeated the peasant. 'Our manager ... we 're ruined, that's what it is—let me go!'

'Ruined, indeed!... Nobody need steal.'

'Let me go, Foma Kuzmitch.... Don't destroy me. Your manager, you know yourself, will have no mercy on me; that's what it is.'

Biryuk turned away. The peasant was shivering as though he were in the throes of fever. His head was shaking, and his breathing came in broken gasps.

'Let me go,' he repeated with mournful desperation. 'Let me go; by God, let me go! I'll pay; see, by God, I will! By God, it was through hunger!... the little ones are crying, you know yourself. It's hard for us, see.'

'You needn't go stealing, for all that.'

'My little horse,' the peasant went on, 'my poor little horse, at least ... our only beast ... let it go.'

'I tell you I can't. I'm not a free man; I'm made responsible. You oughtn't to be spoilt, either.'

'Let me go! It's through want, Foma Kuzmitch, want—and nothing else— let me go!'

'I know you!'

'Oh, let me go!'

'Ugh, what's the use of talking to you! sit quiet, or else you'll catch it. Don't you see the gentleman, hey?'

The poor wretch hung his head.... Biryuk yawned and laid his head on the table. The rain still persisted. I was waiting to see what would happen.

Suddenly the peasant stood erect. His eyes were glittering, and his face flushed dark red. 'Come, then, here; strike yourself, here,' he began, his eyes puckering up and the corners of his mouth dropping; 'come, cursed destroyer of men's souls! drink Christian blood, drink.'

The forester turned round.

'I'm speaking to you, Asiatic, blood-sucker, you!'

'Are you drunk or what, to set to being abusive?' began the forester, puzzled. 'Are you out of your senses, hey?'

'Drunk! not at your expense, cursed destroyer of souls—brute, brute, brute!'

'Ah, you——I'll show you!'

'What's that to me? It's all one; I'm done for; what can I do without a home? Kill me— it's the same in the end; whether it's through hunger or like this—it's all one. Ruin us all—wife, children ... kill us all at once. But, wait a bit, we'll get at you!'

Biryuk got up.

'Kill me, kill me,' the peasant went on in savage tones; 'kill me; come, come, kill me....' (The little girl jumped up hastily from the ground and stared at him.) 'Kill me, kill me!'

'Silence!' thundered the forester, and he took two steps forward.

'Stop, Foma, stop,' I shouted; 'let him go.... Peace be with him.'

'I won't be silent,' the luckless wretch went on. 'It's all the same— ruin anyway—you destroyer of souls, you brute; you've not come to ruin yet.... But wait a bit; you won't have long to boast of; they'll wring your neck; wait a bit!'

Biryuk clutched him by the shoulder. I rushed to help the peasant....

'Don't touch him, master!' the forester shouted to me.

I should not have feared his threats, and already had my fist in the air; but to my intense amazement, with one pull he tugged the kerchief off the peasant's elbows, took him by the scruff of the neck, thrust his cap over his eyes, opened the door, and shoved him out.

'Go to the devil with your horse!' he shouted after him; 'but mind, next time....'

He came back into the hut and began rummaging in the corner.

'Well, Biryuk,' I said at last, 'you've astonished me; I see you're a splendid fellow.'

'Oh, stop that, master,' he cut me short with an air of vexation; 'please don't speak of it. But I'd better see you on your way now,' he added; 'I suppose you won't wait for this little rain....'

In the yard there was the rattle of the wheels of the peasant's cart.

'He's off, then!' he muttered; 'but next time!'

Half-an-hour later he parted from me at the edge of the wood.

XIII

TWO COUNTRY GENTLEMEN

I have already had the honour, kind readers, of introducing to you several of my neighbours; let me now seize a favourable opportunity (it is always a favourable opportunity with us writers) to make known to you two more gentlemen, on whose lands I often used to go shooting— very worthy, well-intentioned persons, who enjoy universal esteem in several districts.

First I will describe to you the retired General-major Vyatcheslav Ilarionovitch Hvalinsky. Picture to yourselves a tall and once slender man, now inclined to corpulence, but not in the least decrepit or even elderly, a man of ripe age; in his very prime, as they say. It is true the once regular and even now rather pleasing features of his face have undergone some change; his cheeks are flabby; there are close wrinkles like rays about his eyes; a few teeth are not, as Saadi, according to Pushkin, used to say; his light brown hair—at least, all that is left of it—has assumed a purplish hue, thanks to a composition bought at the Romyon horse-fair of a Jew who gave himself out as an Armenian; but Vyatcheslav Ilarionovitch has a smart walk and a ringing laugh, jingles his spurs and curls his moustaches, and finally speaks of himself as an old cavalry man, whereas we all know that really old men never talk of being old. He usually wears a frock-coat buttoned up to the top, a high cravat, starched collars, and grey sprigged trousers of a military cut; he wears his hat tilted over his forehead, leaving all the back of his head exposed. He is a good-natured man, but of rather curious notions and principles. For instance, he can never treat noblemen of no wealth or standing as equals. When he talks to them, he usually looks sideways at them, his cheek pressed hard against his stiff white collar, and suddenly he turns and silently fixes them with a clear stony stare, while he moves the whole skin of his head under his hair; he even has a way of his own in pronouncing many words; he never says, for instance: 'Thank you, Pavel Vasilyitch,' or 'This way, if you please,

Mihalo Ivanitch,' but always 'Fanks, Pa'l 'Asilitch,' or "Is wy, please, Mil' 'Vanitch.' With persons of the lower grades of society, his behaviour is still more quaint; he never looks at them at all, and before making known his desires to them, or giving an order, he repeats several times in succession, with a puzzled, far-away air: 'What's your name?... what, what's your name?' with extraordinary sharp emphasis on the first word, which gives the phrase a rather close resemblance to the call of a quail. He is very fussy and terribly close-fisted, but manages his land badly; he had chosen as overseer on his estate a retired quartermaster, a Little Russian, and a man of really exceptional stupidity. None of us, though, in the management of land, has ever surpassed a certain great Petersburg dignitary, who, having perceived from the reports of his steward that the cornkilns in which the corn was dried on his estate were often liable to catch fire, whereby he lost a great deal of grain, gave the strictest orders that for the future they should not put the sheaves in till the fire had been completely put out! This same great personage conceived the brilliant idea of sowing his fields with poppies, as the result of an apparently simple calculation; poppy being dearer than rye, he argued, it is consequently more profitable to sow poppy. He it was, too, who ordered his women serfs to wear tiaras after a pattern bespoken from Moscow; and to this day the peasant women on his lands do actually wear the tiaras, only they wear them over their skull-caps.... But let us return to Vyatcheslav Ilarionovitch. Vyatcheslav Ilarionovitch is a devoted admirer of the fair sex, and directly he catches sight of a pretty woman in the promenade of his district town, he is promptly off in pursuit, but falls at once into a sort of limping gait—that is the remarkable feature of the case. He is fond of playing cards, but only with people of a lower standing; they toady him with 'Your Excellency' in every sentence, while he can scold them and find fault to his heart's content. When he chances to play with the governor or any official personage, a marvellous change comes over him; he is all nods and smiles; he looks them in the face; he seems positively flowing with honey.... He even loses without grumbling. Vyatcheslav Ilarionovitch does not read much; when he is reading he incessantly works his moustaches and eyebrows up and down, as if a wave were passing from below upwards over his face. This undulatory motion in Vyatcheslav Ilarionovitch's face is especially marked when (before company, of course) he happens to be reading the columns of the *Journal des Débats*. In the assemblies of nobility he plays a rather important part, but on grounds of economy he declines the honourable dignity of marshal. 'Gentlemen,' he usually says to the noblemen who press that office upon him, and he speaks in a voice filled with condescension and self-sufficiency: 'much indebted for the honour; but I have made up my mind to consecrate my leisure to solitude.' And, as he utters these words, he turns his head several times to right and to left, and then, with a dignified air, adjusts his chin and his cheek over his cravat. In his young days he served as adjutant to some very important person, whom he never speaks of except by his Christian name and patronymic; they do say he fulfilled other functions than those of an adjutant; that, for instance, in full parade get-up, buttoned up to the chin, he had to lather his chief in his bath—but one can't believe everything one hears. General Hvalinsky is not, however, fond of talking himself about his career in the army, which is certainly rather curious; it seems that he had never seen active service. General Hvalinsky lives in a small house alone; he has never known the joys of married life, and consequently he still regards himself as a possible match, and indeed a very eligible one. But he has a house-keeper, a dark-eyed, dark-browed, plump, fresh-looking woman of five-and-thirty with a moustache; she wears starched dresses even on week-days, and on Sundays puts on muslin sleeves as well. Vyatcheslav Ilarionovitch is at his best at the large invitation dinners given by gentlemen of the neighbourhood in honour of the governor and other dignitaries: then he is, one may say, in his natural element. On these occasions he usually sits, if not on the governor's right hand, at least at no great distance from him; at the beginning of dinner he is more disposed to nurse his sense of personal dignity, and, sitting back in his chair, he loftily scans the necks and stand-up collars of the guests, without turning his head, but towards the end of the meal he unbends, begins smiling in all directions (he had been all smiles for the governor from the first), and sometimes even proposes the toast in honour of the fair sex, the ornament of our planet, as he says. General Hvalinsky shows to advantage too at all solemn public functions, inspections, assemblies, and exhibitions; no one in church goes up for the benediction with such style. Vyatcheslav Ilarionovitch's servants are never noisy and clamorous on the breaking up of assemblies or in crowded thoroughfares; as they make a way for him through the crowd or call his carriage, they say in an agreeable guttural baritone: 'By your leave, by your leave allow General Hvalinsky to pass,' or 'Call for General Hvalinsky's carriage.' ... Hvalinsky's carriage is, it must be admitted, of a rather queer design, and the footmen's liveries are rather threadbare (that they are grey, with red facings, it is hardly necessary to remark); his horses too have seen a good deal of hard service in their time; but Vyatcheslav Ilarionovitch has no pretensions to splendour, and goes so far as to think it beneath his rank to make an ostentation of wealth. Hvalinsky has no special gift of eloquence, or possibly has no opportunity of displaying his rhetorical powers, as he has a particular aversion, not only for disputing, but for discussion in general, and assiduously avoids long conversation of all sorts, especially with young people. This was certainly judicious on his part; the worst of having to do with the younger generation is that they are so ready to forget the proper respect and submission due to their superiors. In the presence of persons of high rank Hvalinsky is for the most part silent, while with persons of a lower rank, whom to judge by appearances he despises, though he constantly associates with them, his remarks are sharp and abrupt, expressions such as the following occurring incessantly: 'That's a piece of folly, what you're saying now,' or 'I feel myself compelled, sir, to remind you,' or 'You ought to realise with whom you are dealing,' and so on. He is peculiarly dreaded by post-masters, officers of the local boards, and superintendents of posting stations. He never entertains any one in his house, and lives, as the rumour goes, like a screw. For all that, he's an excellent country gentleman, 'An old soldier, a disinterested fellow, a man of principle, *vieux grognard,*' his neighbours say of him. The provincial prosecutor alone permits himself to smile when General Hvalinsky's excellent and solid qualities are referred to before him—but what will not envy drive men to!...

However, we will pass now to another landed proprietor.

Mardary Apollonitch Stegunov has no sort of resemblance to Hvalinsky; I hardly think he has ever served under government in any capacity, and he has never been reckoned handsome. Mardary Apollonitch is a little, fattish, bald old man of a respectable corpulence, with a double chin and little soft hands. He is very hospitable and jovial; lives, as the saying is, for his comfort; summer and winter alike, he wears a striped wadded dressing-gown. There's only one thing in which he is like General Hvalinsky; he too is a bachelor. He owns five hundred souls. Mardary Apollonitch's interest in his estate is of a rather superficial description; not to be behind the age, he ordered a threshing-machine from Butenop's in Moscow, locked it up in a barn, and then felt his mind at rest on the subject. Sometimes on a fine summer day he would have out his racing droshky, and drive off to his fields, to look at the crops and gather corn-flowers. Mardary Apollonitch's existence is carried on in quite the old style. His house is of an old-fashioned construction; in the hall there is, of course, a smell of kvas, tallow candles, and leather; close at hand, on the right, there is a sideboard with pipes and towels; in the dining-room, family portraits, flies, a great pot of geraniums, and a squeaky piano; in the drawing-room, three sofas, three tables, two looking-glasses, and a wheezy clock of tarnished enamel with engraved bronze hands; in the study, a table piled up with papers, and a bluish-coloured screen covered with pictures cut out of various works of last century; a bookcase full of musty books, spiders, and black dust; a puffy armchair; an Italian window; a sealed-up door into the garden.... Everything, in short, just as it always is. Mardary Apollonitch has a multitude of servants, all dressed in the old-fashioned style; in long blue full coats, with high collars, shortish pantaloons of a muddy hue, and yellow waistcoats. They address visitors as 'father.' His estate is under the superintendence of an agent, a peasant with a beard that covers the whole of his sheepskin; his household is managed by a stingy, wrinkled old woman, whose face is always tied up in a cinnamon-coloured handkerchief. In Mardary Apollonitch's stable there are thirty horses of various kinds; he drives out in a coach built on the estate, that weighs four tons. He receives visitors very cordially, and entertains them sumptuously; in other words, thanks to the stupefying powers of our national cookery, he deprives them of all capacity for doing anything but playing preference. For his part, he never does anything, and has even given up reading the *Dream-book*. But there are a good many of our landed gentry in Russia exactly like this. It will be asked: 'What is my object in talking about him?...' Well, by way of answering that question, let me describe to you one of my visits at Mardary Apollonitch's.

I arrived one summer evening at seven o'clock. An evening service was only just over; the priest, a young man, apparently very timid, and only lately come from the seminary, was sitting in the drawing-room near the door, on the extreme edge of a chair. Mardary Apollonitch received me as usual, very cordially; he was genuinely delighted to see any visitor, and indeed he was the most good-natured of men altogether. The priest got up and took his hat.

'Wait a bit, wait a bit, father,' said Mardary Apollonitch, not yet leaving go of my hand; 'don't go ... I have sent for some vodka for you.'

'I never drink it, sir,' the priest muttered in confusion, blushing up to his ears.

'What nonsense!' answered Mardary Apollonitch; 'Mishka! Yushka! vodka for the father!'

Yushka, a tall, thin old man of eighty, came in with a glass of vodka on a dark-coloured tray, with a few patches of flesh-colour on it, all that was left of the original enamel.

The priest began to decline.

'Come, drink it up, father, no ceremony; it's too bad of you,' observed the landowner reproachfully.

The poor young man had to obey.

'There, now, father, you may go.'

The priest took leave.

'There, there, that'll do, get along with you....'

'A capital fellow,' pursued Mardary Apollonitch, looking after him, 'I like him very much; there's only one thing—he's young yet. But how are you, my dear sir?... What have you been doing? How are you? Let's come out on to the balcony—such a lovely evening.'

We went out on the balcony, sat down, and began to talk. Mardary Apollonitch glanced below, and suddenly fell into a state of tremendous excitement.

'Whose hens are those? whose hens are those?' he shouted: 'Whose are those hens roaming about in the garden?... Whose are those hens? How many times I've forbidden it! How many times I've spoken about it!'

Yushka ran out.

'What disorder!' protested Mardary Apollonitch; 'it's horrible!'

The unlucky hens, two speckled and one white with a topknot, as I still remember, went on stalking tranquilly about under the apple-trees, occasionally giving vent to their feelings in a prolonged clucking, when suddenly Yushka, bareheaded and stick in hand, with three other house-serfs of mature years, flew at them simultaneously. Then the fun began. The hens clucked, flapped their wings, hopped, raised a deafening cackle; the house-serfs ran, tripping up and tumbling over; their master shouted from the balcony like one possessed: 'Catch 'em, catch 'em, catch 'em, catch 'em, catch 'em, catch 'em, catch 'em!'

At last one servant succeeded in catching the hen with the topknot, tumbling upon her, and at the very same moment a little girl of eleven, with dishevelled hair, and a dry branch in her hand, jumped over the garden-fence from the village street.

'Ah, we see now whose hens!' cried the landowner in triumph. 'They're Yermil, the coachman's, hens! he's sent his Natalka to chase them out…. He didn't send his Parasha, no fear!' the landowner added in a low voice with a significant snigger. 'Hey, Yushka! let the hens alone; catch Natalka for me.'

But before the panting Yushka had time to reach the terrified little girl the house-keeper suddenly appeared, snatched her by the arm, and slapped her several times on the back….

'That's it! that's it!' cried the master, 'tut-tut-tut!… And carry off the hens, Avdotya,' he added in a loud voice, and he turned with a beaming face to me; 'that was a fine chase, my dear sir, hey?—I'm in a regular perspiration: look.'

And Mardary Apollonitch went off into a series of chuckles.

We remained on the balcony. The evening was really exceptionally fine.

Tea was served us.

'Tell me,' I began, 'Mardary Apollonitch: are those your peasants' huts, out there on the highroad, above the ravine?'

'Yes … why do you ask?'

'I wonder at you, Mardary Apollonitch? It's really sinful. The huts allotted to the peasants there are wretched cramped little hovels; there isn't a tree to be seen near them; there's not a pond even; there's only one well, and that's no good. Could you really find no other place to settle them?… And they say you're taking away the old hemp-grounds, too?'

'And what is one to do with this new division of the lands?' Mardary Apollonitch made answer. 'Do you know I've this re-division quite on my mind, and I foresee no sort of good from it. And as for my having taken away the hemp-ground, and their not having dug any ponds, or what not— as to that, my dear sir, I know my own business. I'm a plain man—I go on the old system. To my ideas, when a man's master—he's master; and when he's peasant—he's peasant. … That's what I think about it.'

To an argument so clear and convincing there was of course no answer.

'And besides,' he went on, 'those peasants are a wretched lot; they're in disgrace. Particularly two families there; why, my late father—God rest his soul—couldn't bear them; positively couldn't bear them. And you know my precept is: where the father's a thief, the son's a thief; say what you like…. Blood, blood—oh, that's the great thing!'

Meanwhile there was a perfect stillness in the air. Only rarely there came a gust of wind, which, as it sank for the last time near the house, brought to our ears the sound of rhythmically repeated blows, seeming to come from the stable. Mardary Apollonitch was in the act of lifting a saucer full of tea to his lips, and was just inflating his nostrils to sniff its fragrance—no true-born Russian, as we all know, can drink his tea without this preliminary—but he stopped short, listened, nodded his head, sipped his tea, and laying the saucer on the table, with the most good-natured smile imaginable, he murmured as though involuntarily accompanying the blows: 'Tchuki-tchuki-tchuk! Tchuki-tchuk!'

'What is it?' I asked puzzled. 'Oh, by my order, they're punishing a scamp of a fellow.... Do you happen to remember Vasya, who waits at the sideboard?'

'Which Vasya?'

'Why, that waited on us at dinner just now. He with the long whiskers.'

The fiercest indignation could not have stood against the clear mild gaze of Mardary Apollonitch.

'What are you after, young man? what is it?' he said, shaking his head. 'Am I a criminal or something, that you stare at me like that? "Whom he loveth he chasteneth"; you know that.'

A quarter of an hour later I had taken leave of Mardary Apollonitch. As I was driving through the village I caught sight of Vasya. He was walking down the village street, cracking nuts. I told the coachman to stop the horses and called him up.

'Well, my boy, so they've been punishing you to-day?' I said to him.

'How did you know?' answered Vasya.

'Your master told me.'

'The master himself?'

'What did he order you to be punished for?'

'Oh, I deserved it, father; I deserved it. They don't punish for trifles among us; that's not the way with us—no, no. Our master's not like that; our master ... you won't find another master like him in all the province.'

'Drive on!' I said to the coachman.' There you have it, old Russia!' I mused on my homeward way.

XIV

LEBEDYAN

One of the principal advantages of hunting, my dear readers, consists in its forcing you to be constantly moving from place to place, which is highly agreeable for a man of no occupation. It is true that sometimes, especially in wet weather, it's not over pleasant to roam over by-roads, to cut 'across country,' to stop every peasant you meet with the question, 'Hey! my good man! how are we to get to Mordovka?' and at Mordovka to try to extract from a half-witted peasant woman (the working population are all in the fields) whether it is far to an inn on the high-road, and how to get to it—and then when you have gone on eight miles farther, instead of an inn, to come upon the deserted village of Hudobubnova, to the great amazement of a whole herd of pigs, who have been wallowing up to their ears in the black mud in the middle of the village street, without the slightest anticipation of ever being disturbed. There is no great joy either in having to cross planks that dance under your feet; to drop down into ravines; to wade across boggy streams: it is not over-pleasant to tramp twenty-four hours on end through the sea of green that covers the highroads or (which God forbid!) stay for hours stuck in the mud before a striped milestone with the figures 22 on one side and 23 on the other; it is not wholly pleasant to live for weeks together on eggs, milk, and the rye-bread patriots affect to be so fond of.... But there is ample compensation for all these inconveniences and discomforts in pleasures and advantages of another sort. Let us come, though, to our story.

After all I have said above, there is no need to explain to the reader how I happened five years ago to be at Lebedyan just in the very thick of the horse-fair. We sportsmen may often set off on a fine morning from our more or less ancestral roof, in the full intention of returning there the following evening, and little by little, still in pursuit of snipe, may get at last to the blessed banks of Petchora. Besides, every lover of the gun and the dog is a passionate admirer of the noblest animal in the world, the horse. And so I turned up at Lebedyan, stopped at the hotel, changed my clothes, and went out to the fair. (The waiter, a thin lanky youth of twenty, had already informed me in a sweet nasal tenor that his Excellency Prince N——, who purchases the chargers of the—regiment, was staying at their house; that many other gentlemen had arrived; that some gypsies were to sing in the evenings, and there was to be a performance of *Pan Tvardovsky* at the theatre; that the horses were fetching good prices; and that there was a fine show of them.)

In the market square there were endless rows of carts drawn up, and behind the carts, horses of every possible kind: racers, stud-horses, dray horses, cart-horses, posting-hacks, and simple peasants' nags. Some fat and sleek, assorted by colours, covered with striped horse- cloths, and tied up short to high racks, turned furtive glances backward at the too familiar whips of their owners, the horse-dealers; private owners' horses, sent by noblemen of the steppes a hundred or two hundred miles away, in charge of some decrepit old coachman and two or three headstrong stable-boys, shook their long necks, stamped with ennui, and gnawed at the fences; roan horses, from Vyatka, huddled close to one another; race-horses, dapple-grey, raven, and sorrel, with large hindquarters, flowing tails, and shaggy legs, stood in majestic immobility like lions. Connoisseurs stopped respectfully before them. The avenues formed by the rows of carts were thronged with people of every class, age, and appearance; horse-dealers in long blue coats and high caps, with sly faces, were on the look-out for purchasers; gypsies, with staring eyes and curly heads, strolled up and down, like uneasy spirits, looking into the horses' mouths, lifting up a hoof or a tail, shouting, swearing, acting as go-betweens, casting lots, or hanging about some army horse-contractor in a foraging-cap and military cloak, with beaver collar. A stalwart Cossack rode up and down on a lanky gelding with the neck of a stag, offering it for sale 'in one lot,' that is, saddle, bridle, and all. Peasants, in sheepskins torn at the arm-pits, were forcing their way despairingly through the crowd, or packing themselves by dozens into a cart harnessed to a horse, which was to be 'put to the test,' or somewhere on one side, with the aid of a wily gypsy, they were bargaining till they were exhausted, clasping each other's hands a hundred times over, each still sticking to his price, while the subject of their dispute, a wretched little jade covered with a shrunken mat, was blinking quite unmoved, as though it was no concern of hers.... And, after all, what difference did it make to her who was to have the beating of her? Broad-browed landowners, with dyed moustaches and an expression of dignity on their faces, in Polish hats and cotton overcoats pulled half-on, were talking condescendingly with fat merchants in felt hats and green gloves. Officers of different regiments were crowding everywhere; an extraordinarily lanky cuirassier of German extraction was languidly inquiring of a lame horse-dealer 'what he expected to get for that chestnut.' A fair-haired young hussar, a boy of nineteen, was choosing a trace-horse to match a lean carriage-horse; a post-boy in a low- crowned hat, with a peacock's feather twisted round it, in a brown coat and long leather gloves tied round the arm with narrow, greenish bands, was looking for a shaft-horse. Coachmen were plaiting the horses' tails, wetting their manes, and giving respectful advice to their masters. Those who had completed a stroke of business were hurrying to hotel or to tavern, according to their class.... And all the crowd were moving, shouting, bustling, quarrelling and making it up again, swearing and laughing, all up to their knees in the mud. I wanted to buy a set of three horses for my covered trap; mine had begun to show signs of breaking down. I had found two, but had not yet succeeded in picking up a third. After a hotel dinner, which I cannot bring myself to describe (even Aeneas had discovered how painful it is to dwell on sorrows past), I repaired to a *café* so-called, which was the evening resort of the purchasers of cavalry mounts, horse-breeders, and other persons. In the billiard-room, which was plunged in grey floods of tobacco smoke, there were about twenty men. Here were free-and-easy young landowners in embroidered jackets and grey trousers, with long curling hair and little waxed moustaches, staring about them with gentlemanly insolence; other noblemen in Cossack dress, with extraordinarily short necks, and eyes lost in layers of fat, were snorting with distressing distinctness; merchants sat a little apart on the *qui-vive*, as it is called; officers were chatting freely among themselves. At the billiard-table was Prince N——a young man of two- and-twenty, with a lively and rather contemptuous face, in a coat hanging open, a red silk shirt, and loose velvet pantaloons; he was playing with the ex-lieutenant, Viktor Hlopakov.

The ex-lieutenant, Viktor Hlopakov, a little, thinnish, dark man of thirty, with black hair, brown eyes, and a thick snub nose, is a diligent frequenter of elections and horse-fairs. He walks with a skip and a hop, waves his fat hands with a jovial swagger, cocks his cap on one side, and tucks up the sleeves of his military coat, showing the blue-black cotton lining. Mr. Hlopakov knows how to gain the favour of rich scapegraces from Petersburg; smokes, drinks, and plays cards with them; calls them by their Christian names. What they find to like in him it is rather hard to comprehend. He is not clever; he is not amusing; he is not even a buffoon. It is true they treat him with friendly casualness, as a good-natured fellow, but rather a fool; they chum with him for two or three weeks, and then all of a sudden do not recognise him in the street, and he on his side, too, does not recognise them. The chief peculiarity of Lieutenant Hlopakov consists in his continually for a year, sometimes two at a time, using in season and out of season one expression, which, though not in the least humorous, for some reason or other makes everyone laugh. Eight years ago he used on every occasion to say, "'Umble respecks and duty," and his patrons of that date used always to fall into fits of laughter and make him repeat "Umble respecks and duty'; then he began to adopt a more complicated expression: 'No, that's too, too k'essk'say,' and with the same brilliant success; two years later he had invented a fresh saying: '*Ne voo* excite _voo_self *pa*, man of sin, sewn in a sheepskin,' and so on. And strange to say! these, as you see, not overwhelmingly witty phrases, keep him in food and drink and clothes. (He has run through his property ages ago, and lives solely upon his friends.) There is, observe, absolutely no other attraction about him; he can, it is true, smoke a hundred pipes of Zhukov tobacco in a day, and when he plays billiards, throws his right leg higher than his head, and while taking aim shakes his cue affectedly; but, after all, not everyone has a fancy for these accomplishments. He can drink, too … but in Russia it is hard to gain distinction as a drinker. In short, his success is a complete riddle to me…. There is one thing, perhaps; he is discreet; he has no taste for washing dirty linen away from home, never speaks a word against anyone.

'Well,' I thought, on seeing Hlopakov, 'I wonder what his catchword is now?'

The prince hit the white.

'Thirty love,' whined a consumptive marker, with a dark face and blue rings under his eyes.

The prince sent the yellow with a crash into the farthest pocket.

'Ah!' a stoutish merchant, sitting in the corner at a tottering little one-legged table, boomed approvingly from the depths of his chest, and immediately was overcome by confusion at his own presumption. But luckily no one noticed him. He drew a long breath, and stroked his beard.

'Thirty-six love!' the marker shouted in a nasal voice.

'Well, what do you say to that, old man?' the prince asked Hlopakov.

'What! rrrakaliooon, of course, simply rrrrakaliooooon!'

The prince roared with laughter.

'What? what? Say it again.'

'Rrrrrakaliooon!' repeated the ex-lieutenant complacently.

'So that's the catchword!' thought I.

The prince sent the red into the pocket.

'Oh! that's not the way, prince, that's not the way,' lisped a fair-haired young officer with red eyes, a tiny nose, and a babyish, sleepy face. 'You shouldn't play like that ... you ought ... not that way!'

'Eh?' the prince queried over his shoulder.

'You ought to have done it ... in a triplet.'

'Oh, really?' muttered the prince.

'What do you say, prince? Shall we go this evening to hear the gypsies?' the young man hurriedly went on in confusion. 'Styoshka will sing ... Ilyushka....'

The prince vouchsafed no reply.

'Rrrrrakaliooon, old boy,' said Hlopakov, with a sly wink of his left eye.

And the prince exploded.

'Thirty-nine to love,' sang out the marker.

'Love ... just look, I'll do the trick with that yellow.' ... Hlopakov, fidgeting his cue in his hand, took aim, and missed.

'Eh, rrrakalioon,' he cried with vexation.

The prince laughed again.

'What, what, what?'

'Your honour made a miss,' observed the marker. 'Allow me to chalk the cue.... Forty love.'

'Yes, gentlemen,' said the prince, addressing the whole company, and not looking at any one in particular; 'you know, Verzhembitskaya must be called before the curtain to-night.'

'To be sure, to be sure, of course,' several voices cried in rivalry, amazingly flattered at the chance of answering the prince's speech; 'Verzhembitskaya, to be sure....'

'Verzhembitskaya's an excellent actress, far superior to Sopnyakova,' whined an ugly little man in the corner with moustaches and spectacles. Luckless wretch! he was secretly sighing at Sopnyakova's feet, and the prince did not even vouchsafe him a look.

'Wai-ter, hey, a pipe!' a tall gentleman, with regular features and a most majestic manner—in fact, with all the external symptoms of a card-sharper—muttered into his cravat.

A waiter ran for a pipe, and when he came back, announced to his excellency that the groom Baklaga was asking for him.

'Ah! tell him to wait a minute and take him some vodka.'

'Yes, sir.'

Baklaga, as I was told afterwards, was the name of a youthful, handsome, and excessively depraved groom; the prince loved him, made him presents of horses, went out hunting with him, spent whole nights with him.... Now you would not know this same prince, who was once a rake and a scapegrace.... In what good odour he is now; how straight-laced, how supercilious! How devoted to the government—and, above all, so prudent and judicious!

However, the tobacco smoke had begun to make my eyes smart. After hearing Hlopakov's exclamation and the prince's chuckle one last time more, I went off to my room, where, on a narrow, hair-stuffed sofa pressed into hollows, with a high, curved back, my man had already made me up a bed.

The next day I went out to look at the horses in the stables, and began with the famous horsedealer Sitnikov's. I went through a gate into a yard strewn with sand. Before a wide open stable-door stood the horsedealer himself—a tall, stout man no longer young, in a hareskin coat, with a raised turnover collar. Catching sight of me, he moved slowly to meet me, held his cap in both hands above his head, and in a sing-song voice brought out:

'Ah, our respects to you. You'd like to have a look at the horses, may be?'

'Yes; I've come to look at the horses.'

'And what sort of horses, precisely, I make bold to ask?'

'Show me what you have.'

'With pleasure.'

We went into the stable. Some white pug-dogs got up from the hay and ran up to us, wagging their tails, and a long-bearded old goat walked away with an air of dissatisfaction; three stable-boys, in strong but greasy sheepskins, bowed to us without speaking. To right and to left, in horse-boxes raised above the ground, stood nearly thirty horses, groomed to perfection. Pigeons fluttered cooing about the rafters.

'What, now, do you want a horse for? for driving or for breeding?' Sitnikov inquired of me.

'Oh, I'll see both sorts.'

'To be sure, to be sure,' the horsedealer commented, dwelling on each syllable. 'Petya, show the gentleman Ermine.'

We came out into the yard.

'But won't you let them bring you a bench out of the hut?... You don't want to sit down.... As you please.'

There was the thud of hoofs on the boards, the crack of a whip, and Petya, a swarthy fellow of forty, marked by small-pox, popped out of the stable with a rather well-shaped grey stallion, made it rear, ran twice round the yard with it, and adroitly pulled it up at the right place. Ermine stretched himself, snorted, raised his tail, shook his head, and looked sideways at me.

'A clever beast,' I thought.

'Give him his head, give him his head,' said Sitniker, and he stared at me.

'What may you think of him?' he inquired at last.

'The horse's not bad—the hind legs aren't quite sound.'

'His legs are first-rate!' Sitnikov rejoined, with an air of conviction;' and his hind-quarters ... just look, sir ... broad as an oven—you could sleep up there.' 'His pasterns are long.'

'Long! mercy on us! Start him, Petya, start him, but at a trot, a trot ... don't let him gallop.'

Again Petya ran round the yard with Ermine. None of us spoke for a little.

'There, lead him back,' said Sitnikov,' and show us Falcon.'

Falcon, a gaunt beast of Dutch extraction with sloping hind-quarters, as black as a beetle, turned out to be little better than Ermine. He was one of those beasts of whom fanciers will tell you that 'they go chopping and mincing and dancing about,' meaning thereby that they prance and throw out their fore-legs to right and to left without making much headway. Middle-aged merchants have a great fancy for such horses; their action recalls the swaggering gait of a smart waiter; they do well in single harness for an after-dinner drive; with mincing paces and curved neck they zealously draw a clumsy droshky laden with an overfed coachman, a depressed, dyspeptic merchant, and his lymphatic wife, in a blue silk mantle, with a lilac handkerchief over her head. Falcon too I declined.

Sitnikov showed me several horses.... One at last, a dapple-grey beast of Voyakov breed, took my fancy. I could not restrain my satisfaction, and patted him on the withers. Sitnikov at once feigned absolute indifference.

"Well, does he go well in harness?" I inquired. (They never speak of a trotting horse as "being driven.")

"Oh, yes," answered the horsedealer carelessly.

"Can I see him?"

"If you like, certainly. Hi, Kuzya, put Pursuer into the droshky!"

Kuzya, the jockey, a real master of horsemanship, drove three times past us up and down the street. The horse went well, without changing its pace, nor shambling; it had a free action, held its tail high, and covered the ground well.

"And what are you asking for him?"

Sitnikov asked an impossible price. We began bargaining on the spot in the street, when suddenly a splendidly-matched team of three posting- horses flew noisily round the corner and drew up sharply at the gates before Sitnikov's house. In the smart little sportsman's trap sat Prince N——; beside him Hlopakov. Baklaga was driving ... and how he drove! He could have driven them through an earring, the rascal! The bay trace-horses, little, keen, black-eyed, black-legged beasts, were all impatience; they kept rearing—a whistle, and off they would have bolted! The dark-bay shaft-horse stood firmly, its neck arched like a swan's, its breast forward, its legs like arrows, shaking its head and proudly blinking.... They were splendid! No one could desire a finer turn out for an Easter procession!

'Your excellency, please to come in!' cried Sitnikov.

The prince leaped out of the trap. Hlopakov slowly descended on the other side.

'Good morning, friend ... any horses.'

'You may be sure we've horses for your excellency! Pray walk in.... Petya, bring out Peacock! and let them get Favourite ready too. And with you, sir,' he went on, turning to me, 'we'll settle matters another time.... Fomka, a bench for his excellency.'

From a special stable which I had not at first observed they led out Peacock. A powerful dark sorrel horse seemed to fly across the yard with all its legs in the air. Sitnikov even turned away his head and winked.

'Oh, rrakalion!' piped Hlopakov; 'Zhaymsah (*j'aime ça.*)'

The prince laughed.

Peacock was stopped with difficulty; he dragged the stable-boy about the yard; at last he was pushed against the wall. He snorted, started and reared, while Sitnikov still teased him, brandishing a whip at him.

'What are you looking at? there! oo!' said the horsedealer with caressing menace, unable to refrain from admiring his horse himself.

'How much?' asked the prince.

'For your excellency, five thousand.'

'Three.'

'Impossible, your excellency, upon my word.'

'I tell you three, rrakalion,' put in Hlopakov.

I went away without staying to see the end of the bargaining. At the farthest corner of the street I noticed a large sheet of paper fixed on the gate of a little grey house. At the top there was a pen-and-ink sketch of a horse with a tail of the shape of a pipe and an endless neck, and below his hoofs were the following words, written in an old- fashioned hand:

'Here are for sale horses of various colours, brought to the Lebedyan fair from the celebrated steppes stud of Anastasei Ivanitch Tchornobai, landowner of Tambov. These horses are of excellent sort; broken in to perfection, and free from vice. Purchasers will kindly ask for Anastasei Ivanitch himself: should Anastasei Ivanitch be absent, then ask for Nazar Kubishkin, the coachman. Gentlemen about to purchase, kindly honour an old man.'

I stopped. 'Come,' I thought, 'let's have a look at the horses of the celebrated steppes breeder, Mr. Tchornobai.'

I was about to go in at the gate, but found that, contrary to the common usage, it was locked. I knocked.

'Who's there?... A customer?' whined a woman's voice.

'Yes.'

'Coming, sir, coming.'

The gate was opened. I beheld a peasant-woman of fifty, bareheaded, in boots, and a sheepskin worn open.

'Please to come in, kind sir, and I'll go at once, and tell Anastasei Ivanitch ... Nazar, hey, Nazar!'

'What?' mumbled an old man's voice from the stable.

'Get a horse ready; here's a customer.'

The old woman ran into the house.

'A customer, a customer,' Nazar grumbled in response; 'I've not washed all their tails yet.'

'Oh, Arcadia!' thought I.

'Good day, sir, pleased to see you,' I heard a rich, pleasant voice saying behind my back. I looked round; before me, in a long-skirted blue coat, stood an old man of medium height, with white hair, a friendly smile, and fine blue eyes.

'You want a little horse? By all means, my dear sir, by all means.... But won't you step in and drink just a cup of tea with me first?'

I declined and thanked him.

'Well, well, as you please. You must excuse me, my dear sir; you see I'm old- fashioned.' (Mr. Tchornobai spoke with deliberation, and in a broad Doric.) 'Everything with me is done in a plain way, you know.... Nazar, hey, Nazar!' he added, not raising his voice, but prolonging each syllable. Nazar, a wrinkled old man with a little hawk nose and a wedge-shaped beard, showed himself at the stable door.

'What sort of horses is it you're wanting, my dear sir?' resumed Mr. Tchornobai.

'Not too expensive; for driving in my covered gig.'

'To be sure ... we have got them to suit you, to be sure.... Nazar, Nazar, show the gentleman the grey gelding, you know, that stands at the farthest corner, and the sorrel with the star, or else the other sorrel—foal of Beauty, you know.'

Nazar went back to the stable.

'And bring them out by their halters just as they are,' Mr. Tchornobai shouted after him. 'You won't find things with me, my good sir,' he went on, with a clear mild gaze into my face, 'as they are with the horse-dealers; confound their tricks! There are drugs of all sorts go in there, salt and malted grains; God forgive them! But with me, you will see, sir, everything's above-board; no underhandedness.'

The horses were led in; I did not care for them.

'Well, well, take them back, in God's name,' said Anastasei Ivanitch. 'Show us the others.'

Others were shown. At last I picked out one, rather a cheap one. We began to haggle over the price. Mr. Tchornobai did not get excited; he spoke so reasonably, with such dignity, that I could not help 'honouring' the old man; I gave him the earnest-money.

'Well, now,' observed Anastasei Ivanitch, 'allow me to give over the horse to you from hand to hand, after the old fashion.... You will thank me for him … as sound as a nut, see … fresh … a true child of the steppes! Goes well in any harness.'

He crossed himself, laid the skirt of his coat over his hand, took the halter, and handed me the horse.

'You're his master now, with God's blessing.... And you still won't take a cup of tea?'

'No, I thank you heartily; it's time I was going home.'

'That's as you think best.... And shall my coachman lead the horse after you?'

'Yes, now, if you please.'

'By all means, my dear sir, by all means.... Vassily, hey, Vassily! step along with the gentleman, lead the horse, and take the money for him. Well, good-bye, my good sir; God bless you.'

'Good-bye, Anastasei Ivanitch.'

They led the horse home for me. The next day he turned out to be broken-winded and lame. I tried having him put in harness; the horse backed, and if one gave him a flick with the whip he jibbed, kicked, and positively lay down. I set off at once to Mr. Tchornobai's. I inquired: 'At home?'

'Yes.'

'What's the meaning of this?' said I; 'here you've sold me a broken- winded horse.'

'Broken-winded?… God forbid!'

'Yes, and he's lame too, and vicious besides.'

'Lame! I know nothing about it: your coachman must have ill-treated him somehow.... But before God, I—'

'Look here, Anastasei Ivanitch, as things stand, you ought to take him back.'

'No, my good sir, don't put yourself in a passion; once gone out of the yard, is done with. You should have looked before, sir.'

I understood what that meant, accepted my fate, laughed, and walked off. Luckily, I had not paid very dear for the lesson.

Two days later I left, and in a week I was again at Lebedyan on my way home again. In the *café* I found almost the same persons, and again I came upon Prince N——at billiards. But the usual change in the fortunes of Mr. Hlopakov had taken place in this interval: the fair- haired young officer had supplanted him in the prince's favours. The poor ex-lieutenant once more tried letting off his catchword in my presence, on the chance it might succeed as before; but, far from smiling, the prince positively scowled and shrugged his shoulders. Mr. Hlopakov looked downcast, shrank into a corner, and began furtively filling himself a pipe....

END OF VOL. I.